The Final Word

Frank Infusino

The Final Word

ISBN 978-1506-900-68-1 PRINT
ISBN 978-1506-900-69-8 EBOOK

LCCN 2015956277

November 2015

Published and Distributed by
First Edition Design Publishing, Inc.
P.O. Box 20217, Sarasota, FL 34276-3217
www.firsteditiondesignpublishing.com

Death and evil will not have the last word…

Samuel Aguila
Denver Archbishop

For the believer, death does not have the final word.

R. C. Sproul
Ligonier Ministries

Prologue

Republic of Vietnam, 1970

Shadows!

Shadows, dancing in the moonlight or in the grey glare of flares under the jungle canopy, tricked the mind. Every tree, vine or piece of scrub could morph into the enemy at any time. Take chances with shadows and you might die.

On some nights the shadows became Vietcong guerrillas emerging from the undergrowth to kill, maim and harass the Marines defending the local village. Casualties mounted. Fear engulfed the defenders like a fog choking, blinding. But one Marine, a seventeen-year old lance corporal, frustrated, angry, overcame his fear and resolved to act. Marines were trained to attack. He would attack and use the shadows to his advantage.

After dark each night, with the knowledge of the sentries, but not his platoon commander, he slipped out of his platoon's perimeter and crawled under the razor wire into the darkness to blend with the shadows. Concealed in the dense foliage, he waited; his face blackened, a sharpened K-bar and 45-caliber pistol strapped to his belt. The first night a four-man sapper squad crept toward his position intent on breaching the Marine line and detonating their explosives. He slit the throat of each man from behind, last man first, as they slithered by single file. They never saw him, never heard him.

Every night for over a month, he hid himself until daylight springing on the enemy without warning if they showed up, lying still when they didn't. He killed twenty-five men before the attacks stopped. Mere mortals couldn't fight such a being, a phantom lurking in the shadows. The Vietcong called him MA—Ghost.

The lance corporal was decorated for his daring forays, but the experience changed him. He became reclusive, seldom ate. His uniform hung on his slender frame like a sack. His eyes betrayed his inner turmoil, dark, penetrating, wild like those of an animal prepared to strike.

His appearance and demeanor shocked his lieutenant who worried the Ghost had become a stone cold killer. On the lieutenant's recommendation, the young marine received a battlefield promotion to sergeant and was sent home to rest.

Scuttlebutt, of course, followed him. Stories of his exploits swept through the Corps. Veterans of the war regarded him with awe, as did eager recruits undergoing the rigors of boot camp, his bravery and daring the epitome of Esprit de Corps.

Yet the newly promoted sergeant did not revel in his acclaim. He realized how close he had come to crossing a line from which there was no return. The killing came easy after a while. He vowed never again to let rage consume him and believed nothing would provoke him to revisit that line or those shadows.

He was wrong.

Chapter 1

Pacific City, California
November 2002

She was every boy's dream, every man's fantasy; a bronzed California girl, angelic face, sun bleached blond hair cascading to her shoulders. Only her pale blue eyes revealed sadness born of experience that neither her looks nor youthful bravado could hide.

She sat on the couch, legs splayed, skirt hiked to mid-thigh, the top two buttons of her blouse unfastened. She smiled and patted the seat cushions beside her. "Come sit next to me, Jeffrey," she coaxed.

Her therapist, forty-one year old Jeffrey Palmer, PhD, forced a smile. Advances from attractive patients were common. Addicts would do anything to avoid facing their demons, even a seventeen year-old high school cheerleader. He accepted her as a patient because of the nature of her addiction, rare in one so young. He hoped successfully treating her might lead to a journal article to enhance his professional standing.

"Sitting next to you won't help us resolve your problem," he said in a calm, dispassionate tone.

"I don't have a problem," the girl said, crossing her arms and twisting her mouth into her best effort at a scowl.

"Your parents don't agree."

"My parents are out of it. To them smoking a joint makes me a hard core doper."

"They didn't bring you here for smoking a joint," Palmer said, his voice composed, clinical.

She scooted to the edge of the couch, her dress sliding over her hips exposing her panties. "What did they tell you?"

Palmer's gaze fell to the patch of white before he caught himself. She was not being seductive now. Her attitude had changed, her swagger gone.

"They told me everything," he lied, his eyes locked on hers. "They love you and want to help you."

The color drained from the girl's face. She brushed a dangling strand of hair from her forehead, wrapped her tanned arms around herself, remained like that for a minute or two, then recovered, thrusting her chin toward Palmer, challenging, arrogant. Her parents would never reveal the truth.

"They didn't tell you everything," she said. "Not everything."

Chapter 2

He was a fugitive on the run, deep-set brown eyes darting from side to side, jaw clenched, right leg shaking. Rivulets of sweat rolled down his back, each droplet a reminder of his fear and a warning of danger. One misstep would send him back behind bars—might even get him killed although he wasn't armed. *You couldn't predict what trigger-happy cops might do to a pervert like him.*

Four hours earlier, he escaped from Atascadero, a California maximum-security facility for violent sex offenders. Now, he slouched down in the backseat of a white Honda Civic inching south on a gridlocked interstate 405. The traffic ebbed and flowed, drivers jockeying for the slightest advantage. Horns blared, hand gestures flashed as men and women vented the frustrations of the day. Noxious fumes filled the air from a huge cement truck belching black smoke from an elevated exhaust pipe. An American Airlines Boeing 757 swept low over the highway on its approach to Los Angeles Airport, the whine of its powerful Rolls-Royce engines adding to the cacophony of sound and the dismal air quality.

The jammed roadway was both a haven and a trap. The man doubted anyone could spot him in this mess, but if they did, he was trapped. His altered appearance, he'd cut his long black hair, shaved his mustache, donned glasses, wouldn't fool his pursuers like it had the lax guards at Atascadero.

Those morons.

He used a forged identification badge and stolen lab coat to walk out of the main administration building with a group of visitors.

No time to gloat though. He was at the mercy of the traffic and fate. He scrunched further below the side window, eyes riveted on the back of the driver's head.

The driver gripped the wheel, one hand at ten o'clock, the other at two, his knuckles white, palms moist. He avoided the interplay between cars and drivers keeping a safe distance from other vehicles, no need to risk a fender bender and a visit from the highway patrol.

The driver was twenty-five years old, had been for all of two days, a gang-banger like his passenger. And like his passenger, he disguised himself. A black wig covered his shaved, bullet-shaped head, the gold crucifix that had dangled from his left ear, gone. He wore an open necked white dress shirt and a tan sport jacket; a banger since the age of thirteen; no stranger to the law. Yet, his offenses had been minor. He faced hard time if caught now.

His mouth dry, he swallowed often. No amount of shifting in his seat relieved the numbness in his butt. He kept jerking his head around to eye his homeboy. The man smiled each time but the driver saw fear in his eyes. He anticipated this and reached into his jacket pocket and flipped a baggy of white powder, along with a small mirror, over his shoulder into the backseat.

Knock yourself out, hombre, he thought but did not say.

His passenger flinched when the objects struck him on the chest and landed on the seat beside him. He looked around with a sheepish grin, as if someone might catch him breaking the law.

He took the baggy, sprinkled some of the powder on the mirror and snorted. The meth rush hit him within minutes. His face flushed, his nerves tingled, the power, the sexual excitement denied him for so long returned. He smiled at his reflection in the window.

I'm coming home, chicas.

Chapter 3

Reaper compiled the death list.

He sat alone in his room hunched over his desk, arm around the sheet of paper like a schoolboy protecting test answers from prying eyes. People would soon know him; he felt euphoric, ready.

He smiled and pulled from a drawer the files downloaded from the Internet long ago. He examined them often; newspaper and magazine accounts of the April 20, 1999, Columbine High School massacre; the photos of the shooters, Eric Harris 18, and Dylon Klebold 17, grainy and yellowed, but reassuring.

Reaper kept smiling as he read about the havoc wrecked by Harris and Klebold, twelve students and one teacher killed, twenty-three wounded. The drama played over and over on television screens, stories in newspapers and magazines for months. Images of kids running from school, once smug faces filled with terror, everyone trying to figure out why?

Reaper knew why. The pain of being humiliated tormented every day because you dared to be different. The jocks and cheerleaders who ran things, and the teachers who thought them so cool, treated him like dirt or ignored him, as if he had no feelings. They mistook appearance for worth.

High school sucked.

He tugged on the ring piercing his lower lip, eyes riveted on the inverted black cross tattooed on the back of his left hand. He had a plan and friends to help him. Columbine would be a footnote compared to the chaos they would create.

Reaper believed he was smarter than Harris and Klebold. Their plan to kill hundreds failed, many of their homemade bombs didn't work. They killed themselves when trapped in the school library, no escape route. Reaper was prepared to die but doubted it would come to that. He was smarter than Harris and Klebold.

He studied the finished list, twenty-five kids and teachers, the worst offenders, the most conceited, most arrogant, most hated; the last one, number twenty-five, the cheerleader bitch who wouldn't give him the time of day.

He'd take her out first if he got the chance.

Chapter 4

Mike Walker yearned for excitement.

A rookie cop, he had been with the Pacific City Police Department less than a year. Like all rookies he craved action and expected to find it on his new shift. When night fell, so did inhibitions, human behavior sank to its lowest levels.

It was Friday night, Saturday morning actually, and he thought about that as he maneuvered his blue and white Crown Victoria into the south parking lot of Wellington Park, a two and a half square mile recreation area in the heart of downtown. Alfred Wellington, an oil and railroad tycoon, helped found the city after the turn of the nineteenth century. His name graced more than one building including police headquarters.

Wellington's picture hung in the police department lobby along with a brief biography listing his contributions to the development of Pacific City, but Walker never stopped to read the stuff. History was for eggheads. He lived in the here and now.

The ten o'clock nightly curfew did little to discourage the denizens who found the wooded areas of Wellington Park enticing, the homeless, druggies, young and old partygoers. Walker enforced the curfew like any other law, police academy doctrine still fresh in his mind. His instructors emphasized the "broken windows" theory made popular by LA Police Chief Bratton. Stay on top of things like broken windows, graffiti, traffic violations and you cut down on major crime. The concept worked for Bratton in New York and got him the job in LA. Walker put the notion to the test his first week on patrol by citing the mayor for rolling through a stop sign, not a career enhancing move for a rookie but one laughed off by the mayor.

As the young officer scanned the area, he observed a late model Ford Taurus parked at the far end of the lot; the usual hang out for lovers and teenage beer drinkers. He pulled his cruiser behind the Taurus, blocking its exit and shined a spotlight into the vehicle expecting some worried, frightened kids or an embarrassed older couple to peer out a window. He detected no movement after several minutes so he ran the license plate with his on-board computer. The car came up registered to a John Lyon, age fifty-five, a local resident.

Kind of old to be playing games in the park, Walker thought.

But then he remembered the naked elderly couple doing the horizontal mambo in the park a while back. Somehow they rolled down a small embankment and become wedged between a large rock and a tree; took Paramedics to dislodge them. Walker told the story often to cheers, jeers and jokes from his buddies in the locker room. The tale got better with each rendition.

Walker, irritated, shook his head, dismissing those thoughts. He planned to catch a coffee break after cruising the park. Regular caffeine jolts kept him alert during these long hours. Instead, he notified dispatch he intended to investigate a vehicle parked in violation of the city curfew. He opened his door and pushed himself out, grabbed his baton and slipped it through the loop on his belt.

Walker was a poster boy for police recruitment. His blue uniform clung to his frame as if painted on, the result of pumping iron daily at a local gym. Popeye forearms stretched the fabric of his shirt, one tailored to ensure the look. His wide shoulders tapered to a narrow waist, brown hair cut high and tight, Jarhead style. He walked with a swagger, arms held wide, challenging, threatening.

Walker approached the Taurus cautiously still expecting to find scared teenagers or adults scrambling to gather clothes or trying to conceal alcohol or drugs. But a visual inspection with his flashlight revealed the vehicle empty, except for a small purse on the floor on the passenger side. He tried the doors, found them locked, but did not try to force his way in.

Walker knew from experience a few yards from the Taurus was a path leading to several clearings, which kids and adults used for late night trysts. He was not happy. He didn't want to scuff his spit-shined work boots, or further delay his break; nevertheless, he chose to explore the path at least to the first clearing. If he found no one, he'd have the vehicle towed since parking here after ten was prohibited. *Let the son-of-a-bitch pay to get the car out of impound.*

Walker, still not in good humor, entered the woods. His mood did not improve when several tree branches lashed his face as he staggered along a narrow path. The night air was stagnant and warm for this time of the year. Beads of sweat dotted his forehead. He paused in an attempt to hear either the sounds of merriment or the more personal sounds of sexual coupling. But all was quiet, even the usual jabbering of crows. He started down the path again keeping his left arm up to shield his face, entered the first clearing and stopped when his light illuminated a pair of bare legs on the ground several feet in front of him. He transferred the flashlight from his right hand to his left and released the holster safety strap securing his pistol.

Walker scanned the area then moved forward. Once beside the prone figure, he realized it was a young girl clad in a cheerleaders' uniform. She lay face down with one arm outstretched, both knees bent, as if sleeping, skirt bunched above her waist, naked below except for white socks and tennis shoes. Walker knelt to determine if the girl was breathing but her tongue protruded between her teeth, a sign of suffocation. To be sure, he placed two fingers on her neck to feel for a pulse, there was none. He used the mobile radio he carried to notify dispatch, unaware a dark figure watched his every move.

Chapter 5

His eyes never left the officer.

He crouched like a baseball catcher in the brush a few feet from the girl's body; face flushed, heart pounding, legs aching from trying to remain still. He felt lucky the cop hadn't seen him when he flashed the light in his direction. The black sweat suit helped but he couldn't stay hidden much longer. The area would soon be swarming with cops.

His right arm shook, perhaps out of fear, perhaps because of his cramped position. Perspiration dripped into his eyes, dampness congealed at the small of his back, courage seeped from his pores along with his sweat. He poised to run when the cop turned and walked back down the path towards his patrol car.

When the officer was gone, the dark figure pushed back through the underbrush. He had parked in a residential area to avoid detection and emerged from the woods fifty yards from the girl's body. He had to cross the access road into the park to get to his car. He crouched in the grass then sprinted across the road when no cars were in sight.

Once inside his car, he placed both hands on the wheel to steady himself and catch his breath. As he regained control, he realized what he had done. Fear enveloped him like a straightjacket sucking air from his lungs. At the same time, he felt exhilarated. He had been a flashlight beam away from being caught.

He reached into the pocket of his sweat pants for the girl's panties, didn't know why he took them, maybe as a trophy, maybe as a symbol of something else. At any rate, her perfumed smell was still strong. A vision of her lying naked on the ground flashed before him and he could once again feel her soft, cool flesh. He rubbed the panties against his cheek before putting them back in his pocket.

Still shaking, he started the engine and drove off with his lights out. In his rearview mirror, he caught a glimpse of the police cars speeding into the park, lights flashing but sirens silent.

Chapter 6

The ringing phone jolted him from sleep.

Lieutenant James Francis Deluca sat up and squinted to read the digital clock on the bedside table. Disoriented, he reached for the phone, which rested beside the clock. He had been in this condo for eighteen months, ever since the death of his wife, but he sometimes still awoke unsure of his surroundings. He'd knocked the damn phone to the floor more than once.

Clearing his head, he balanced on one elbow and put the phone to his ear. "Deluca," he snapped into the receiver as if trying to convince the caller he had been awake and alert. He listened for several minutes to the message delivered in clipped, professional tones by the headquarters dispatcher.

"OK," he said, when the dispatcher completed her report. "Have the uniforms secure the area, notify the coroner and the Crime Scene Unit. The coroner may need to get to the body right away but I want the CSU to wait for first light. We don't need people stumbling around in the dark destroying evidence. And call Big Tony! Have him meet me at the Park ASAP."

The dispatcher acknowledged the instructions. Deluca placed the phone back in its cradle, turned on a light and swung his feet to the floor. Sitting up, he rubbed the sleep from his eyes and massaged the indentation in his right shoulder just below his clavicle where a piece of shrapnel had pierced his skin and knocked him on his ass in a long ago war most people wanted to forget and some never could.

After a few moments, he pushed himself up and padded toward the bathroom to brush his teeth and splash water on his face. He glanced at his reflection in the mirror but didn't examine it as most people would. He gave that up some time ago when the face looking back at him had become his father's. He'd laughed when it first happened remembering the warning by ancient baseball pitcher Satchel Page: "Never look over your shoulder, someone might be gaining on you." Deluca thought that someone might be father time.

But the veteran cop was too hard on himself. His body was still lean, his stomach flat, the skin on his tanned, weathered face tight. The laugh lines around his mouth and eyes, though deeply etched, gave him a rugged appearance that women found sexy. His steel grey eyes danced when he joked or bore into you when he was angry. "The Lieutenant can turn you inside out with the stare," a patrolman once complained.

Deluca came to Pacific City from the LAPD famous for his daring exploits. As a SWAT commander, he defied death more than once in vicious confrontations with gangs and heavily armed thugs. The video of his single-handed counter attack of brazen bank robbers using automatic weapons was shown to recruits at the police academy. He won the Medal of Valor, LAPD's highest award for bravery, three times.

Deluca reveled in the danger but his wife worried and begged him to leave law enforcement. Instead, he resigned from the LAPD and came to Pacific City, where shootouts and homicides were rare. There hadn't been a killing in the city in many years. The report of an apparent murder and rape in Wellington Park surprised him.

He thought about that as he finished in the bathroom, walked back into the bedroom and pushed the sliding closet doors apart. His starched, pressed shirts hung on the left, jackets and pants on the right. Several pairs of spit shined shoes rested on the floor. He selected a white shirt, gray slacks, black blazer with the department emblem on the left breast pocket and a maroon tie.

Dressed, he retrieved his Smith and Wesson 9 mm semiautomatic along with his handcuffs from the top drawer of the dresser, snapped them to his belt, turned off the light and strode out the door.

Thirty minutes later, he pulled into the south lot at Wellington Park and drove to where several marked and unmarked police vehicles parked at angles to each other, lights flashing, signaling to everyone something serious was going down.

Deluca uncoiled his six foot three inch frame from his vintage Mustang and walked toward the one unofficial truck sandwiched among the police vehicles, a battered, Ford F150. He grinned as he read the faded rear bumper sticker: "Keep honking…I'm reloading."

The truck belonged to Anthony "Big Tony" Segal, one of two sergeants in the homicide unit. Late forties, a neck sprouting from massive shoulders like a tree trunk, Segal had a moon face, a perpetual smile and the constant look of a man hungry to devour his next Big Mac. Dressed in a flowered Hawaiian shirt, jeans and Nike running shoes, he resembled a giant hibiscus bush with a head. A former high school football player, he had been a detective for the past ten years, three of those as Deluca's partner.

Segal stood next to his truck talking with a uniformed officer Deluca recognized as Mike Walker. The trio exchanged greetings. "Fill me in Mike," Deluca said, as he pulled his notepad from the inside pocket of his jacket.

"Don't know who she is yet, Lieutenant, no ID on the body," Walker began. "I noticed a purse on the passenger side of the Taurus but didn't want to force the door before CSU got here. The car is registered to a John Lyon, age fifty-five. Possibly the kid's father."

Walker ran through the events leading to the discovery of the dead girl and informed Deluca the County coroner would be delayed for several hours.

Deluca's left hand moved to his right shoulder. "Ok then. We can be sure evidence is not destroyed in the dark. No one has been down that trail, I hope, since you got here."

"Affirmative, sir," Walker said, bracing his back. Even in the dim light cast by the assembled police cars, Deluca could see the officer's face tighten. His expression conveyed the message, "I may be a rook, but I'm not a dumb rook."

Deluca dipped his head and suppressed a smile. "Good, keep the area buttoned up until the coroner and the CSU gets here."

He motioned Segal to follow as he walked back to his car to await the coroner.

Chapter 7

The county Coroner arrived with the gray morning light. Patches of ground fog gave the cluttered parking lot a surreal appearance, like the set of a B-movie featuring vampires and werewolves. The coroner greeted the detectives with a slight nod but did not stop to talk. He went to the trail leading to the clearing and slipped under the yellow crime scene tape all but tiptoeing down the path to avoid contact with the overhanging tree branches and waist high brush. Deluca and Segal followed doing their best to mimic the evasive actions of the county official. The two detectives looked like oversized high wire performers balancing on a tightrope.

The coroner on duty today was diminutive, slight of build with tufts of gray hair surrounding a baldpate. He wore a tweed jacket, open-necked white dress shirt and dark slacks; carried the tools of his trade in a small black bag.

In California, the Government and Health and Safety Codes stipulate a coroner must investigate any sudden death, all twenty-seven types. Homicide tops the list, which includes accidental poisoning, suicide, drug overdoses and fatal fires as well as suspected Sudden Infant Death Syndrome (SIDS). The code prompted Deluca to wait for the coroner before allowing his detectives and CSU team to move into the area. County bureaucrats could jerk you around if you pissed them off.

The coroner, when he got to the girl, mimicked officer Walker and placed two fingers along her neck, as if to validate she was, in fact, dead. He then began the meticulous task of gathering evidence. With a Polaroid camera, he took pictures from different angles. Later, he scraped beneath her fingernails and bagged the samples. Next, he swabbed each of her orifices and placed the swabs in bags also. Using a small magnifying glass, he collected hair and cloth fibers and anything else he thought significant. More intrusive tests would be performed at the morgue.

Deluca stood several feet away and witnessed the macabre scenario, preoccupied with his thoughts. The procedure, though necessary and required, seemed disrespectful. His daughter was still a teenager, nineteen, a college freshman. He did not want to think of her lying exposed, to be poked and prodded, examined like a laboratory specimen.

He was no stranger to death. Vietnam had been a meat grinder. Kids felled every day by snipers or booby traps. More than once he had been splattered by parts of what moments before had been a buddy. The carnage changed him, turned him into someone to be feared, a Marine Corps legend—a Ghost.

There had also been deaths during his almost three decades on the force, less gruesome and personal than in combat but no less troubling to the spirit. A knot formed in the pit of his stomach. Soon, the remains of the girl would be placed in a black body bag and shipped to the morgue. The same type of bag used to ship Marines home from Vietnam. Kids not much older than the victim, kids whose lives were cut short long before their time. Kids who thought, and were told, they fought for a righteous cause. Their deaths could at least be explained if not understood.

But nothing changes. A new war raged, different enemy, same result, kids dying. They were hailed as heroes now, given respect the fighting men of Deluca's generation did not receive. The equation didn't change, though, death still the bottom-line for many. *Hell, there was dignity, even honor, in dying for your country.*

Deluca believed that. But the loss of a child, a teenager, was seldom expected and not the normal process of life and death, at least not in peacetime. He empathized with the parents who would soon live their worst nightmare. Two good people, no doubt, asked to identify this decaying corpse as their cherished daughter who hours before had been enjoying life as only teenagers can. Maybe it wasn't father time gaining on him, causing him to feel old, just the accumulated sadness of dealing with the worst life had to offer. He popped a Tums into his mouth to quell the fire raging in his gut.

Oblivious to Deluca's personal anguish, the coroner completed his grim task, put the samples collected in his bag and walked toward Segal and Deluca, who remained on the periphery. The little man stopped a few feet from them. "Suffocated. Strangled. Possibly raped," he said in a staccato monotone. "I'll know more once we examine the body in detail."

He brushed past the detectives and made his way back down the path.

Soon after his departure, three members of the PCPD Crime Scene Unit threaded single file down the trail and into the clearing. The team acknowledged Segal and Deluca with nods, but none spoke. The lead tech approached the girl while the others fanned out to collect evidence. Segal and Deluca did not join in. Unlike their TV counterparts, they would not inspect the area until the techies completed their tasks.

As the group worked, Segal leaned toward his boss and whispered. "First homicide in this town in a hellava long time, Skipper."

"Five years to be exact."

"You sure?"

"Does a bear shit in the woods?"

"Not in these woods I hope," Segal said, in feigned shock. "I'm wearing new Nikes."

"Better tiptoe then, big man, you never know what animals may lurk in the shadows."

Chapter 8

Captain William, "Wild Bill," McClusky fumed.

The murder of a young girl riled him. He'd be damned if he'd let the reputation of the city be sullied on his watch. He commanded the Investigation Division of the Pacific City Police Department, which included the Homicide Unit. Word throughout the ranks was the Captain never met a task he couldn't fuck up with gusto or a subordinate he couldn't chew out with equal fervor. Most wondered how he had reached the rank of captain.

McClusky earned his nickname during a 1968 anti-Vietnam war protest. As a young patrol officer, he waded into a group of students demonstrating in front of an Army Recruiting Office and cracked several heads with his baton. A photographer captured the event and the photo appeared in the Los Angeles Times under the caption: "Keeping The Peace, Pacific City Style." McClusky became a local symbol of the divided nation. Pig was one of the milder epithets hurled his way.

"Wild Bill" didn't care. He kept the picture of the incident framed on his wall, hoping visitors or new cops would ask about it. Few did. To most, the forty-year veteran was a dinosaur, an old fart whose eccentricities had to be tolerated, a prime example of the Peter Principle.

McClusky was as wide as he was tall, red veined face, hairline creeping south, belly over-lapping his belt. He had changed little since the nineteen-sixties, spewing profanity often and not concealing his disdain for the growing number of women and minorities now in the department. Behind closed doors he ranted about the goddamned Rainbow Coalition in the homicide unit; he'd opposed hiring any of them but had been over-ruled by the new chief. Another blow to the city and department he loved.

On this Saturday morning, several hours after the discovery of the teenager's body in Wellington Park, McClusky summoned Deluca to his office. The case would be high profile in a city that prided itself on its safety. For the third year in a row it had been named one of the safest cities in America by a national publication. McClusky intended to protect that reputation or heads would roll.

But cultural changes were beyond one man's control. Pacific City, once a white enclave, now reflected the state's changing demographic. An influx of Hispanics had transformed the complexion of some neighborhoods. Middle Easterners appeared to run every 7-Eleven in town. Vietnamese restaurants vied with hamburger joints for customers. Many longtime residents did not embrace the changes. They formed neighborhood watches to protect themselves and expected the predominantly white police force to support them.

Records indicated their expectations were being realized; the percentage of non-whites cited for traffic violations far exceeded that for whites. Hispanic straying into an Anglo neighborhood could expect to be stopped and questioned by police and to be roughed up during such stops. Three Latino males died from injuries sustained while being arrested and restrained by patrol officers, all within the last eighteen months.

Two civil rights groups, the ACLU and MALDEF, the Mexican-American Legal Defense and Education Fund, filed lawsuits and led demonstrations to protest and highlight the circumstances surrounding these deaths.

The apparent rape and murder of a local teenager would be investigated in this charged atmosphere. Lieutenant Deluca knew this when he walked into McClusky's office carrying his coffee cup and sat in one of the two chairs facing the captain's desk. He had since showered, shaved and changed into a new shirt.

JD, Wild Bill began, "we got to close this one fast. The fucking mayor and the other asshole council members are squeezing the chief, a high school kid, for Christ sakes."

"We'll do our best," Deluca said, sitting back in his chair. He took a sip of the hot coffee and circled the cup with the index finger of his right hand.

"Push hard on this one, JD," Wild Bill said, annoyed at Deluca's relaxed demeanor and his fresh, crisp appearance. His own damp shirt clung to his back.

"Put your best people on this," he challenged. His jaw tightened, his jowls puffed out like a frog croaking a warning to someone trespassing in its pond. "Who's gonna work the case?"

"I'll be the primary, with Segal, Willis and Styles as backup."

"Styles? Cara Styles?" McClusky gasped, ignoring the names of the other detectives mentioned.

"Yea! She's a fine detective."

"A goddamn skirt," McClusky said, spitting out the words as his face turned a deep red. "A goddamn skirt," he repeated, shaking his head.

Deluca bristled at Wild Bill's constant profanity, his lack of professionalism, but he remained calm. He had to work with the man or around him.

"Bill," he said, "we need her perspective. We'll have to talk with some female students about rape. They'll feel more comfortable talking to a woman."

McClusky sat back shaking his head again as if to rid such a notion from his mind. He wouldn't challenge his lieutenant though. He feared him, those eyes and his LA reputation; he was unaware of his Marine Corps heroics. "Just get the fucking job done," he said. "Keep me informed at every step."

Deluca nodded and left the office to round up his team. When he was gone, Wild Bill got up and closed the door. He returned to his chair, opened the bottom right hand drawer of his desk and retrieved a bottle of Jim Beam. He filled his coffee mug half way and took a deep, satisfying swallow. "Goddamn skirts," he mumbled, shaking his head for the third time.

Walking back to his own office, Deluca reflected on the conversation with his Captain. Why did he jump to Styles' defense? Was it just because she was a good detective, he asked himself, or because he took delight in antagonizing Wild Bill? No doubt both. He didn't like McClusky. Didn't like the image he projected of the department leadership. Didn't like his history, his antiquated thinking, his heavy-handed approach to police work. Didn't like the man, period.

But Deluca worried he supported Styles because he was attracted to her? She reminded him of a younger version of his wife. She walked on her toes like Kathleen and licked her upper lip with her tongue when lost in thought. That childlike gesture tugged at his heart.

Styles was more vixen than child but, in addition, was tough, bright, enthusiastic and oblivious to the way she flaunted her sexuality or deliberately provocative; either way, difficult to ignore.

Others tried to ignore her and, like McClusky, resented her. She endured hostility from some of the old timers in homicide unaccustomed to a woman in the unit; the same guys who would jump her bones if given the opportunity.

Deluca was not one of them. Despite her physical attributes and the similar mannerisms to his late wife, he adhered to the Gospel as taught by his first mentor, a grizzled sergeant who cautioned his young recruit: "Never dip your pen in company ink."

He had taken that advice, had not chased skirts like many of his married colleagues. Now single, widowed, his thinking hadn't changed.

Still, images of Cara Styles dominated his thoughts.

Chapter 9

Cara Styles covered her eyes as sunlight flooded the room through the open slats of the vertical blinds on her bedroom window. She lay on her bed entwined in the twisted sheets after another fitful night, hadn't slept well since coming to the PCPD.

She rubbed her eyes, untangled herself from the mess on the bed, put her feet on the floor and stood before the mirrored closet door in the well-worn athletic jersey that reminded her of the unusual path she had taken to get here.

First, she was educated at Smith, one of the famous Seven Sisters, which included Vassar, Radcliff and Wellesley. Located in picturesque western Massachusetts, the school touted its academic programs as a route to success in fields not typically the province of women though it's doubtful Smith's famous alumnae Barbara Bush, Julia Child, Julie Nixon Eisenhower or Betty Friedan ever considered patrolling the mean streets of this country as police officers. Neither had Cara Styles.

Her father, a self-made millionaire, owned a pharmaceutical company. Cara attended private schools all her life and was groomed to become an executive in the family business upon graduation. She matched the above Smith graduates in intellect and far exceeded their physical attributes. She had the toned body of a competitive athlete and a face befitting a Hollywood model. Boys flocked to her like mosquitoes to a light bulb.

Her intelligence and quick wit intimidated and deflected most of her suitors, all but one, the captain of the lacrosse team at Amherst College. Ruggedly handsome, he could match wits with anyone. Like Smith, Amherst took only the best and the brightest counting a former president and a Supreme Court Chief Justice among its graduates while Robert Frost had served on the faculty.

Cara's boyfriend no doubt had similar lofty aspirations as she. But intelligence and good looks do not always come with common sense or the will to resist temptation. While they were dating, her lacrosse player became hooked on methamphetamines, overdosed and died derailing Cara's well-planned future.

Angered, inspired and idealistic, she led an anti-drug crusade at Smith and Amherst that won her the support of her liberal fellow students but the enmity of the administrations of both schools who shunned such notoriety. Embittered by the attitude of the college professors whom she considered naïve and out of touch, she obtained her degree but, instead of entering a field more suited to her education and background, she enrolled in a police academy and distinguished herself both for her competence and her physical prowess. Her father was not happy.

Later, as an officer in several different cities, she worked patrol and did the inevitable undercover stint in vice and narcotics. Her performance won her the praise and admiration of her superiors and the attention of those who could assist her career; attention that eventually brought her to the PCPD.

Cara did not forget what led her to law enforcement. She often slept in the now well-worn lacrosse jersey given to her by the boy who would never become a man, his life cut short by drugs.

Cara despised drug dealers, made it her mission to drive them off the streets. Standing before the mirrored closet doors in the faded jersey, she realized she had more than one job to do in Pacific City.

Chapter 10

Lieutenant Deluca occupied a small sparsely furnished office with a department issue metal desk, a metal file cabinet pushed up against one wall and a small table holding a Mr. Coffee machine and several cups. A white board hung behind the desk and the opposite wall held two pictures, one of a young World War II Marine and a high school team picture with Deluca in the back row.

Deluca sat behind his desk waiting for his team to arrive. He smiled to himself. Team! Government agencies, including police departments, liked to name groups organized to solve a problem a "task force." It gave the group a wartime aura conjuring up an armada of ships steaming toward the enemy with guns blazing. A task force would get the job done.

He and the three detectives working the Alex Lyon murder would not be crowned a task force; that would be pretentious and ludicrous. They would crack the case with less bravado.

His brief reverie was broken as Big Tony Segal and Cara Styles walked into his office without knocking. They sat in two straight-backed metal chairs facing Deluca's desk. Styles, her black hair cut short, her round almond eyes, alert and challenging, perched on the edge of her seat leaning forward, eager. Her short skirt revealed toned, muscled legs.

Segal had shed the casual clothes he had worn earlier, and donned a rumpled white shirt and tie but had not shaved. His shirt collar, although unbuttoned, strained to contain his massive neck. A dab of taco sauce from a quick brunch stained the corner of his mouth.

Deluca was signing several reports and purchase orders and had not yet acknowledged the presence of the detectives sitting before him. He signed official documents James Frances Deluca. His father's name was also James so, when he was a child, family and friends called him JD. He'd been JD ever since except in professional circles or on official documents.

No one here was aware he'd earned a different name on the killing fields of Vietnam, a name given to him by the enemy in awe. He never spoke of it. But some, like McClusky, saw the danger revealed in his eyes.

He put the papers aside as the other member of the team strode into the office. Walter Willis was tall and slender, with a pencil thin neck and protruding Adams apple. He looked more like a scholar than a cop. He entered and took a position against the wall behind his seated colleagues. Deluca dipped his head in a silent greeting. He spoke directly to Segal. "What have we got so far?"

Segal brushed what remained of his curly black hair away from his expansive forehead and scratched the back of his head.

"Not much at this point," he said. "We'll get the coroner's report early next week. The kid's name is Alexandra Lyon---nicknamed Alex. Seventeen, senior at East High School, cheerleader, class officer, prom queen, the whole nine yards. Next Friday would have been her eighteenth birthday."

Segal leafed through a thin file resting on his lap and pulled out a sheet of paper with the image of a tire tread. "The CSU team got a good imprint of a tire from the soft mud next to the kid's car. Could be from a car parked next to hers or one that had been there earlier in the day. I'm checking with the city to see what time the sprinkler system in the area came on. Might tell us when the print was made."

Deluca put his hands behind his head, leaned back in his chair. "Doesn't make sense the girl would go to the park alone at that time of night. She either went with someone or planned to meet someone."

"But who?" Segal asked.

"Whoever killed her?"

"No shit, Sherlock, case closed, ipso fatso," Segal said, repeating an old Archie Bunker line.

Segal was one of the few who could rib his former partner.

Willis and Styles chuckled. Deluca managed a wry smile.

Segal grinned and continued. "The area where her body was found was littered with beer cans, whisky bottles, napkins, food containers; popular party area for kids and adults. No telling how long that stuff's been there."

Styles watched the exchange between the two men without comment. Willis leaned against the wall alert, but silent.

"She had to know her killer," Deluca repeated. "Otherwise, why get out of her car or even go to the park in the first place? We all learned in Crime Fighting 101 in a rape or murder you look at someone close to the vic first; husband, wife, boyfriend, co-worker, in this case, classmates. Unless it's a random act, they're all suspects."

"Are we ruling out a random act, then?" Segal asked.

"No. But our evidence so far points to someone she was not afraid to let get close to her."

Styles spoke up. "Sir, three days ago we got a fax warning that Eduardo Ramos had escaped from Atascadero. He's a 24th Street Diablo. He went down for the rape of four women two years ago. All of the women were young. Three of the rapes took place in or near the park. In each instance he took the woman's panties. This fits his MO."

Deluca's expression conveyed doubt. "Yeah but Ramos didn't kill any of his victims."

"Not because he didn't try," Styles countered. "He beat a couple of them bad. Scared hell out of the youngest by threatening to maim her with a pair of pliers. Maybe he's turned up the violence."

Segal snorted. "Man, every so often some chlorine should be dumped in the gene pool."

The remark elicited muffled snickers from everyone but Deluca. "What connects Ramos and the girl?" he asked.

"Possibly drugs."

"What?"

"Yeah. The Diablos sell drugs in the Park. Could be she went there for a buy."

"Alone?"

"Druggies aren't known for their good judgment," Styles said.

"We'll keep Ramos in the equation" Deluca said, his tone skeptical. "Styles dig up what you can on him, talk with his homeboys, you know the drill. Also, interview the school Principal; find out who hung out with Alex. Even if she went to the park to buy drugs, she'd take someone with her. The tire tread might belong to a friend's car."

"Willis, you and Segal canvas the area around the Park again, you might turn up something the uniforms missed. Find out if anybody saw anything out of the ordinary Friday night. I'll go talk to the parents."

Deluca stood up, pushed his chair back. "I don't need to tell all of you that pressure is coming from the top to solve this one pronto. Wild Bill has a hair up his ass and no doubt the mayor is pushing the chief. We need to get this guy and fast."

Chapter 11

Fast was not always the operative word in solving homicides.

Detectives Segal and Willis had knocked on a dozen doors without result. They were now three-quarters of the way down a tree-lined street opposite Wellington Park. Neither detective expected much to come from this exercise since uniformed officers canvassed the area earlier. But both men knew that breaks in a case, despite the advances in technology in the last few years, were still made by old-fashioned legwork, and sometimes, just plain luck. Knocking on doors and talking to people was still part of the drill.

The detectives were truly an odd pairing; Segal, a former football player and wrestler, physical, loud, often annoying, a practical joker, did most of the talking when interviewing suspects or witnesses; Willis quiet, introverted. His thoughtful approach to situations often produced positive results. Today he was especially quiet.

"What's eating you man?" Segal asked.

Willis shook his head.

"Come on," Segal pressed. "What's with the hang dog look?"

Willis stopped, inspected his shoes. "My stepson. I can't reach the kid. He stays in his room, barely speaks to Stephanie and me, hangs out with a bunch of losers. His grades are in the toilet. Steph won't let me talk to him. His room is off limits. We haven't been married long and the kid's affecting our relationship."

Segal brushed off his partner's feelings. "He's a teenager, for Christ sake, man. They're all weird. Get your head out of your ass. We got a homicide to solve."

Willis smiled. He followed his partner up a brick sidewalk to a modest single story home identified by the name on the mailbox as the "Johns" residence. Segal rang the doorbell and took a step backward. After several moments, an elderly woman dressed in a faded pink robe and matching bedroom slippers opened the door. She clutched a cocker spaniel puppy in her arms and regarded both men with suspicion, especially Segal.

"Sorry to bother you ma'am," Segal said, "but we'd like to ask you a few questions. This is detective Willis, I'm detective Segal, PCPD."

"*Speak* up young man," the woman said. "Don't hear as well as I used to, you know."

Segal stole a glance at Willis and rolled his eyes, a gesture that did not escape the woman.

"No need to be rude, young man," she said, fixing Segal with a withering glare.

Segal's face reddened. He lowered his chin to his chest in the manner of a schoolboy chastised by the principal. Willis suppressed a smile, not eager to incur the woman's wrath.

"Taught school for fifty years," she continued. "Taught my children manners and respect for their elders. Don't know what this world is coming to. I'd expect more from a public servant like you. Should be setting the example, you know."

Segal thought even the cocker spaniel glared at him. "Yes ma'am," he said, eager to move on. He raised his voice several octaves. "Are you Mrs. Johns?" referring to the name he had seen on the mailbox.

"Yes, I'm Mrs. Johns," she said, "Although the Mister has been gone ten years now, rest his soul."

"Sorry, Ma'am," Segal said, his expression reflecting empathy. "We won't take much of your time. Were you home Friday night?"

"I spoke to the officers about this already, young man."

"Yes, ma'am, but perhaps you've remembered something since talking to them."

She considered this for several moments. "Well, I did think something odd." She gazed over Segal's shoulder as if in deep thought. "I took Clarence out for his constitutional later than usual. Most often we go out around ten. But I entertained my sister that night; hadn't seen her in quite a while, you know. She'd been sick. I was worried about her, her age and all. She's older than me, you know."

Segal hoped she would get to the point. He kept his expression neutral to avoid another reprimand from the former schoolteacher.

"When Clarence and I went out, I did see someone jogging after midnight, but didn't think much of it at the time. With the Park close, lots of people jog through the area, at all hours, you know."

Segal continued to nod but remained silent; fighting back the urge to laugh at the dog's name each time she mentioned it.

"But the man ran only part way down the street before getting into his car. Most people leave their car in the lot at the park, or after hours, near a sidewalk. No problem finding a space at that hour, you know. Why was his car on this street? A neighbor would just have gone home."

"Could you describe the man?" Segal asked.

"The street is not well lighted. I've complained to the city about the lights being out, but nobody listens, you know." She put the cocker spaniel down and the animal scampered back into the house. She folded her arms and continued. "He wore a dark jogging suit. Beyond that I can't recall much about him."

"Please try, Mrs. Johns. This man might be a witness or may have been involved in the murder. What about his height? Short or tall?"

She shook her head from side to side. "Can't remember. Medium height I guess."

"Age?" Segal pressed.

"Couldn't tell that, either, you know."

"Could you describe his car?"

"Land sakes, young man, might have been able to do that at one time, when there weren't so many of these foreign models around, just Fords, Chevys and the like. But not now, I'm afraid."

"OK, Mrs. Johns," Segal conceded, "We'd appreciate a call if you remember anything else." He reached into his wallet, handed her a business card.

She inspected the card. "You can be assured of it, young man," she said.

The two detectives turned to walk away. "Detective," She called out, causing both men to stop and face her. "Manners are very important, you know. Very important."

"Yes ma'am, "They said in unison.

Chapter 12

The 24th Street Diablos cared little about manners.

The youthful gang hung out at a Seven-Eleven on the fringe of the barrio. The store's clientele consisted mostly of locals and teenagers who knew they could score a beer from the owner who checked ID's like he cleaned the restrooms, rarely. Few outsiders chose to run the gauntlet of the tattooed homeboys and home girls who dropped f-bombs in their speech and in their epithets toward anyone they disliked, which meant those not in their group.

On this day, a dozen young Latinos congregated in the parking lot, standing against cars, leaning out open car windows or sitting on cement curbs. The boys wore the uniform of the day, white sleeveless T-shirts, gray baggy pants cut below the knee, white socks and tennis shoes; most wore baseball hats sideways or backwards. Three sported black watch caps pulled down below their eyebrows, giving them a menacing appearance.

The two girls present also donned a uniform of sorts, short black thigh high skirts and white V-neck blouses revealing ample cleavage. Each carried extra pounds around the middle, accentuated by the skirts stretched tightly over their buttocks and thighs; tattoos adorned arms and necks like their male counterparts. Their heavy facial makeup, blue eye shadow, and rouged cheeks gave them the look of junior hookers.

Styles pulled her unmarked sedan into the Seven-Eleven parking lot and stopped blocking the exit of at least two of the vehicles occupied by the young gang-bangers. Her arrival drew furtive glances from several but most ignored her.

The cool reception was not unexpected. Styles had busted some of them, mostly for drugs and petty theft. Their age reflected the dynamics of gangs everywhere; their elder statesmen, like the escaped rapist Eduardo Ramos, serving time. Many would follow the same dead-end path.

Styles scanned the group as she exited the sedan. Her gaze fell on the bullet-headed Miguel Sanchez, the one homeboy not wearing a head covering and the gang's de facto leader. A gold cross hung from his left ear.

The detective walked toward Sanchez and stopped a few feet in front of him. He gave her an appraising glance but faked disinterest. "Hey Miguel," she said flashing him a brilliant smile.

The gang-banger looked her up and down, undressing her with his eyes. "Couldn't stay away from me, eh! Mama?"

"Oh yeah," Styles said, maintaining her smile. "You know how much I want you."

Sanchez beamed as if he had just scored with the prom queen. Two homeboys snickered, the girls giggled. The good-natured banter relaxed the group. Sanchez exhaled and rolled his shoulders forward. He had been one of the first Diablos busted by Styles, for assault. He was fined and sentenced to thirty days community service, but Styles had not demeaned him, had not made him feel like something you tried to scrape off the bottom of your shoe.

They had developed an uneasy friendship of sorts. She had also worked through him to provide some needy families with food and medical attention for their children. On one occasion, he helped her to head off a planned gang fight when one of his homeboys had been "disrespected" by rivals.

She appraised Sanchez for a moment stepping closer to him. He considered himself a "ladies man" and as leader had bedded more than one of the females in the posse. Styles could see her closeness had the desired effect. He ogled her breasts, shifted his weight from one foot to the other.

"So Miguel," she asked in her most earthy tone, "Seen Eduardo lately?"

Sanchez blinked several times and averted his eyes. He stole a glance at two homeboys who acted as if they had not heard the question.

Sanchez kept silent for a few moments before returning his gaze to Styles. "No ma'am," he lied. "He's at Atascadero; thought you knew that?"

"Not anymore. And you know that"

Sanchez shrugged.

"He's wanted for murder and rape."

"Eduardo don't do murder, mama," Sanchez said, his voice all but squeaking. "He's a lover."

"Rape isn't love, homeboy. You protect him; you'll go down hard. Bet on it!"

Sanchez lowered his head.

Styles wouldn't push further. His demeanor told her he had seen Ramos. If they kept an eye on him, he might lead them to Ramos.

"OK! Miguel," she said, stepping even closer to him so her face was inches from his. "Remember what I said."

She turned away not waiting for a response. She walked to the sedan and, not looking back, got in and closed the door. The gang-bangers ignored her as she drove out of the parking lot. But as the police vehicle disappeared from view, Sanchez ducked behind the Seven-Eleven and pulled out a cell phone. He dialed a familiar number and waited until a formula recording told him to leave a message.

"Call me man," was all he said.

Chapter 13

Deluca pulled to the curb in front of the Lyon residence. The house, a single story California ranch style home with a two-car garage and a manicured lawn, mirrored others on the street and in the surrounding area. A car parked in the driveway was not the one driven by the girl on the night of the murder; it had been impounded and was being inspected by a department forensic team.

Deluca rang the bell and after a short wait the door opened. A tall, wiry man with slight build, stooped shoulders and pale complexion stared vacantly at the detective.

"Mr. Lyon?" Deluca asked.

The man inclined his head.

"I'm Lieutenant Deluca," he said. "I'm sorry for your loss. I know this is a difficult time but I do need to ask you a few questions that might help us find out who harmed your daughter."

He avoided the term "murdered" in the vain hope of lessening the impact. Without a word, Mr. Lyon gestured the detective to a couch in the family room located at the end of the entry hall.

"Can I get you something to drink?" Lyon asked in a voice just above a whisper.

Deluca declined and sat where directed.

"My wife is sedated so she won't be able to join us," Lyon said, as he took a seat in a chair facing Deluca. The couch and chair were arranged in front of a stone fireplace. A photo of Alex in her cheerleader uniform with her arm around a boy in football gear rested on the wooden mantle, brother and sister.

"My son, Brent," Lyon said, when he saw Deluca look at the picture. "He plays linebacker on the sophomore team. It was taken just before the first game this year." He sounded very proud of his son.

Deluca studied the photo for several seconds. It gave him an odd feeling, which he dismissed and focused on Mr. Lyon.

"I know this is difficult, sir, but can you think of anyone who might have wanted to hurt your daughter? Problems at school, in the neighborhood?"

"I haven't thought of anything else these last few hours," Lyon said. "Alex was seventeen years old, pretty, outgoing, everyone loved her. No one I know would want to do something like this."

"Does she normally drive your car?"

"Yes, on Friday nights, to get home after games."

"Any reason for her to be in the park?"

"No! Sometimes the kids party after the game but always at someone's house."

"Did she say she was going to a party last night?

"No, but we assumed she would. It was tradition."

"What time did she usually get home after these parties?"

"Midnight. Any later, we required she call us."

"Did she call?"

"No," Lyon said. "No. I intended to wait up but fell asleep on the couch. Fell asleep while my little girl was being killed." He slumped back in his chair, head down, eyes closed trying to push the reality of what had happened out of his mind.

Deluca sensed that he was at the breaking point. "I know this is hard, sir, but if you can bear with me for a few more questions I'll be on my way."

Lyon nodded.

"Any strange behavior these last few days?" He asked. "Was she moody or worried about something?"

Lyon moaned, rubbing a tear from his eye. "Nothing, nothing..." His voice drifted off.

Deluca did not press further. "Do you mind if I look in her room?" he asked.

"No, not at all." said Lyon. "I haven't been able to go in since it happened." He got up and led Deluca down a short hallway and pointed to a door decorated with a bright yellow and red "Keep Out-Genius at Work" sign.

Deluca opened the door and stepped inside. The room was small, eight by ten, typical of many California homes. A large window with a view of a cinder block wall that separated the tract houses dominated one end of the room. Opposite the window was a closet with mirrored doors. Pictures of Alex in her cheerleader outfit, team photos, and other school paraphernalia adorned the walls.

The room included a bed, a white dresser with yellow rounded knobs on each drawer, a small desk and a freestanding bookcase, also painted white, with adjustable shelves on top and two doors on the bottom. Deluca searched the drawers of the desk but found nothing unusual or helpful to the investigation among the usual pens, pencils, envelopes, tape and writing tablets.

The dresser contained nothing of help either. Along with bras, panties, white athletic socks and panty hose, he found a small box with teenage mementos, pictures, a class ring with the initials TD engraved inside, tickets to a school drama production of "South Pacific," a birthday card signed, "Love Tommy," and a napkin from the Sand Castle Restaurant, a local landmark along the beach. The napkin also was signed, "Love Tommy."

Deluca hesitated before leaving the room, knelt down and opened the doors on the bottom of the bookcase. The shelf was cluttered with school textbooks and several Harlequin romance novels. But, wedged behind two oversized textbooks, was a small leather bound journal---*a diary.*

Chapter 14

Deluca pulled the diary off the shelf and opened it.

The first page contained a poem the girl had written as a warning to those with prying eyes.

This diary is for me and no other,
Not for Mom, Dad or little brother.
Whoever dares peek within these pages
A pox on you for all the ages.

He laughed. Typical teenager. These were her personal, secret thoughts. Her warning made him feel self-conscious but not enough to stop from turning the page. The next lines shocked him.

Sex to me is like scratching an itch,
Although some may think I am a bitch.
I give myself to one and all,
Just for fun—to have a ball.
But love and sex are idle chatter,
Virginity really doesn't matter.

Deluca raised his eyebrows. He hadn't expected such crude language from a young girl. He was further surprised as he read on.

The first several diary entries appeared to be typical of what one would find in a teenage girl's diary, if one dared to look. There were remarks about boys she thought were "hotties," along with notations about school clubs and girls she didn't like. Most names were spelled out but she referred to others by their initials.

Then, beginning on May 8th of this year, her entry read: *Put on a show for JP at school today; gave him an eyeful. Noticed a bulge in his shorts. All Right!!!*

May 10: *Sat at my desk today so JP could see up my skirt. Caught him looking twice. I just smiled. He got red.*

Deluca was curious. Whoever this "JP" was, Alex had tried to turn him on. And from her comments, she succeeded. They needed to ID him. He would be someone of interest.

Continuing to leaf through the diary, he read the entry for May 15. *"Saw Dr. Palmer today. Nice man--but out of it. Told him what he wanted to hear. He thinks he can help me. He almost choked when I flashed him."*

Deluca had the same reaction as the doctor. He wondered if this stuff was real or the kid's fantasy.

As he turned the pages, several other entries recounted visits to Dr. Palmer. But each was brief and didn't reveal much about her thoughts except for the sexual theme.

May 22. *Wore a real short skirt when I saw Dr. Palmer today. Thought the old guy's eyes would pop out of his sockets. Probably went home and jumped his old lady's bones.*

Jesus! The kid was even trying to turn on the doctor. Why was she seeing him? He made a mental note to contact the doctor.

Before closing the book, Deluca noticed an entry for May 30: *TR has a great body. Got goose bumps just being near. Would like to get some of that.*

"Jesus H. Christ," he thought, "this kid had a very active imagination or she was a real tease."

He put the diary on the corner of the dresser and pulled aside a closet door. He found a video camera on one shelf but the camera contained no tapes. He hadn't seen tapes anywhere else in the room.

He put the camera back on the shelf and returned to the family room. Mr. Lyon still sat slumped in a chair, staring into the dormant fireplace. He turned his head when he heard Deluca and stood up to face him.

"I found Alex's diary, Sir," said Deluca. "Do you mind if take it with me. It may contain something that could help?"

Lyon blinked his eyes several times and narrowed them in thought. "A diary? I didn't know she kept one," he said. He lost his concentration for a minute looking off toward the fireplace again. When he regained his focus, he gave permission for Deluca to take the diary.

"Thank you for permitting me to look around, sir. Again, I'm sorry for your loss. I know this is difficult for everyone but at some point soon we'll need to talk with your wife and son."

"Fine," Lyon responded and walked the detective to the door. He watched him leave, then closed and locked the door. His legs felt like rubber and he was unable to stand without shaking. He leaned against the wall for support. Beads of sweat formed on his forehead.

A diary. She kept a diary.

Chapter 13

The diary read like the chronicle of a sexual circus with Alex as the ringmaster orchestrating performers. No lions, tigers or elephants under this big top; only humans eager to act as directed.

Real or fantasy Deluca wondered as he scoured the journal for possible clues to Alex's murder? Several names or initials popped up frequently. Those he jotted down on an 8 X 11 yellow pad: Bubba, JP, SR, TD, D, SD, Dr. Palmer.

He assumed TD stood for Tommy Deerfield, Alex's boyfriend and the quarterback on the football team. His name appeared on the sports pages every week. "Tommy" had signed the birthday card and napkin found in Alex's dresser.

All of them, even the doctor, were mentioned in the context of sexual activity. The girl either had a vivid imagination or she was very sexually active for a seventeen-year old girl. Might be normal adolescent behavior these days, he thought.

Deluca wondered if his own daughter kept a diary. Did she have the same kind of thoughts as Alex Lyon? Would he read her diary given the opportunity? "*No way*," he muttered to himself as he returned his attention to the written pages.

The first entry he wrote down was Sept. 6, of last year. *Turned Bubba on tonight. So easy.*

He continued through the book and captured other dates and incidents:

Sept 14. *Turned Bubba on again. Let him touch me. Wouldn't let him do more so he took care of himself.*

Amazed by this description, Deluca forged on.

Oct 10. *Stopped JP in the hall, he eyeballed my boobs and tight shorts.*

Oct 13. *Bubba couldn't take his eyes off me tonight.*

Oct 17. *SD tries to be so cool but he watches me a lot. Sometimes rubs up against me, by mistake of course. Ha!*

Nov. 18. *SD brushed up against me today. Felt me up. I let him.*

Nov. 15. *Saw TR watching me at the game tonight. Made sure I kicked real high. Lots of people couldn't take their eyes off me, especially TR.*

Dec 13. *Gave SD some special love today, great body.*

Dec 10. Me and *Bubba made out again.*

Feb. 9. *Me and Bubba played hide and seek with some cherries. Read that in a book. Wow!*

Deluca almost dropped his pencil after reading that comment. He read on expecting to be shocked. And wasn't disappointed.

April 4. *Went to math tutorial at lunch. Got wet looking at TR. Love that body!*

April 6. *SD mauled me today, blew his wad in his pants.*

May 8. *First visit to Dr. Palmer. Parents insisted. Think I've got "issues," found out about Bubba. The doc asked questions. Don't know where this is going but gotta do it. The Doc is kinda cute for an old guy.*

June 6. *Snuck around with Bubba, smoked a joint together, naked, his first time. He got high, mauled me. He'll do anything I say.*

June 15. *Last day of school. Found JP in a classroom. Wore a short skirt, low cut blouse. His eyes bulged. Something else bulged too. Ha! Ha!*

Deluca stopped reading. "The parents knew she was sexually active," he said aloud to no one. "Forced her to talk to someone about her behavior. Palmer's gotta be a shrink. Wonder if the parents were aware of the diary? Mr. Lyon denied knowledge but flinched when I mentioned it. He never said anything about Dr. Palmer. Why?"

He read on:

Sept 16. *Messed around with D, the "dickhead" tonight. Didn't want to but he makes it worth my while.*

Oct 6. *Walked by some Goth freaks at school today. Weirdoes. Caught one guy undressing me with his eyes. Fat chance he gets a piece of this.*

Oct 7. *Played around with dickhead again, asshole.*

Oct 10. *Goth freak followed me around at lunch. What a Creep! I should tell SD.*

Why would she tell SD, Deluca thought? So he'd beat the crap out of the Goth kid? Make him back off. Why not tell Bubba or JP?

Deluca sat back, tilted his head to the side, reflecting on what he had read. He had trouble believing; it sounded more like the imagination of a young girl who fancied herself a sex object. But Alex was pretty. She had a great body for her age and flaunted it in the pictures he had seen of her. Maybe she teased the wrong guy. Except for the Goth character, she didn't discriminate. She was pissed at "Dickhead," yet she put out for him, for money, drugs? He cringed.

Puzzled, he returned his attention to the book and noted one of the longer entries: November 10. *Went to Derek's house after the game, parents away for the weekend. We had a Rainbow Party. Sandy, Anna, Kitty and me were the stars, came prepared. It really did look like a Rainbow when we finished. Everyone was wasted. Hope TD doesn't find out.*

What the hell is a Rainbow Party? Deluca wondered.

Chapter 14

Styles waited outside Deluca's door. He stopped reading Alex Lyon's diary, made a note on his yellow pad and motioned her to enter.

"What have you got?" He said.

"Segal checked with the city," she began. "The sprinklers in the section of the Park where Alex was killed were set to go off at ten. So it's possible the tire imprint the CSU found did belong to a car parked next to her Taurus. The lab is checking now to determine the type of vehicle it came from."

Deluca pressed his lips together in a grimace. "OK" he said. "At this point we need to follow up on anything."

Styles waited until the lieutenant had completed his thought. "I talked with the current hefe' of the Diablos," she reported. "He claims he hasn't seen Ramos but he was blowing smoke. He appeared nervous, afraid to say much in front of his homeboys. Ramos is around, I'm sure of it. Also, I attempted to contact the East High Principal at home but talked to his wife. Farraday left earlier in the day for a scheduled meeting in Sacramento with state education big wigs. He couldn't cancel. He's not expected back till Monday morning."

Deluca massaged the slight indentation in his right shoulder. "You need to get to him first thing Monday then," he said. He handed a torn page from his notes to Styles. "Make a copy of this, please. I've listed the names and initials of people Alex mentioned in her diary. Find out if Farraday or anyone else on the staff can ID any of the kids and talk to them as well."

Styles left the office with the sheet of paper and passed Segal and Willis coming in. Segal shook his head seeing the expectant look on his lieutenant's face. "One old gal claims to have seen a jogger come from the Park area and get into his car. She thought it unusual because he parked on her street, not closer to the Park. She's right but she couldn't give us much. Male. Medium height. Age unknown. Could be anybody! No one else saw a damn thing."

"We've got to find that son-of-a-bitch Ramos whether he's involved in this or not," Deluca said

No one spoke but their body language indicated agreement.

Styles returned with a copy of the notes from Alex Lyon's diary. Deluca scanned the sheet and discovered he omitted Palmer's name. "Cara, a Doctor Palmer is mentioned in the journal. Alex had several appointments with him. Check him out, might be a shrink"

"He is," she said.

"What?"

"A friend of mine is a patient of his. He's a psychotherapist specializing in addictions."

"Addictions. You sure?"

"Yeah. Alcohol, drugs, whatever's your poison."

"The kid might have been in the park alone to make a buy," Segal offered.

"Ramos could have been her connection," Styles said.

Deluca wasn't ready to make that leap---not yet. "We need to get the tox screen," he said. "Doing drugs doesn't prove she would go to the park alone; I doubt she was that brave or stupid."

"Let's follow up on the diary leads," he added. "Which reminds me. Anyone know what a Rainbow Party is?"

Blank stares gave him his answer.

Chapter 15

O'Hara's Sports Bar and Grill was a favorite cop hangout.

Located three blocks from police headquarters, cops jammed the place day and night. The restaurant did not serve breakfast but lunch began at 11: 00 A.M. and the bar remained open until two in the morning.

Framed pictures and glass-enclosed uniforms of local athletes who had played college or professional ball adorned the walls. An ornate glass and wooden canopy covered the horseshoe shaped bar, wine glasses hung upside down from an overhead rack. A raised floor and brass railing separated the bar from the dining area. Television sets hanging from the ceiling showed multiple sports events simultaneously.

Since his wife's death, Lieutenant Deluca had become a regular at O'Hara's. He sat alone or with Big Tony Segal. Tonight, Segal regaled his boss with one of his war stories---a pitcher of draft on the table between them.

"I remember when I was assigned to security for a Rock concert at the Anaheim Convention Center," Segal said. "Me, Wilson and Barnes had our arms locked out front holding back a wild mob of teenage girls screaming and shouting."

The big man paused chugging from his glass.

Deluca grinned but said nothing. He knew better than to interrupt his friend in mid story.

"We're doin' OK until someone gets a glimpse of the Rock Star getting out of his limo," Segal continued. "I don't even remember the guy. The kids surged toward us forcing us backward. We all wind up goin' ass over teakettle through a plate glass window. I'm on my back with a fourteen or fifteen year old girl on top of me, her boobs inches from my face; didn't know whether to shit or go blind."

"You didn't go blind," Deluca said, risking a comment. " So I assume you changed your shorts before going home."

"I'm telling ya JD," Segal said, ignoring the jab. "A bunch of teenage girls goin' ballistic over some celebrity hot shot are wild. I spent weeks picking glass shards out of my scalp and earned this battle scar." He pointed to a small jagged white line just above his right eye.

"I hope you at least got a medal of valor for that one," Deluca joked, a grin adding more creases to his lined face.

"Wise ass," Segal quipped. He enjoyed making his friend laugh. "So what do ya think of Styles? Quite a looker, huh?" he said, changing the subject.

"She's a good detective," Deluca said, his face turning the color of the red tablecloth.

"OK to move on," Segal said. "Time ya got back on the dance floor."

Deluca took a sip of beer. "Too early for that, Big Man," he said, twisting the silver band he still wore on his left hand.

"Bullshit," Segal protested, his voice an octave or two higher than necessary. "Ya loved Kathleen. But ya gotta move on. You're too young to be alone."

Deluca didn't respond. It was a subject he and Kathleen discussed off and on over the years. "Would you marry again if I was gone?" She would ask out of the blue. "I can't bear to think of you being alone," she would declare while caressing his cheek or rubbing his back. "People need one another."

Deluca couldn't imagine starting up again with someone new, learning their needs, likes, dislikes; wasn't worth the effort or pain. He didn't want to think about it now. Segal had struck a nerve.

"Since when did you become my shrink, Doctor Segal," he snapped after a few moments. He reached for his wallet. "What do I owe you for the session?"

Segal was surprised and angered by his friend's tone. "Stuff it," he said, pushing back his chair with his legs as he stood up. He threw some money on the table and left.

Deluca remained seated and watched Segal storm out of the bar. He regretted his retort. His friend was trying to help, push him forward. But he didn't get it, tough to shake off the memories of twenty-five years, which ended in an instant without any warning. No time to prepare for a different life.

Deluca shook his head as he recalled how and when it happened. It was a Tuesday. They left for work at the usual time, he to the office downtown, she to her elementary school, where she taught first graders. A cautious driver, she obeyed the speed limit, took no chances. "I'm a very good driver," she often joked, mimicking the Idiot Savant character in the "Rain man" who tried to convince his brother to let him drive a car for the first time.

But being a very good driver sometimes isn't enough, if others on the road are not as good or as careful. Kathleen's route to work each day took her by East High School. She could not know, nor prepare for, the recklessness of a teenager blinded by rage after breaking up with his girlfriend. She had no chance when the kid's car careened out of the student parking lot and slammed into her head on. She and the boy both died at the scene, before Deluca could get there. He was left with the image of his wife lying mangled and trapped in the twisted wreckage.

Deluca took time off for a few days to make funeral arrangements and somehow got through the memorial service. He showed no outward signs of the impact Kathleen's death had on his psyche. But for weeks afterward, he sat alone in their darkened bedroom, replaying in his mind their life together. Eventually he sold the house, bought a two-bedroom condominium, and started going to O'Hara's.

Now, he thought of Segal's words and his relationship with Cara Styles. Hell! What relationship? They worked together. He was her boss. They communicated in the language of the Job. Never went beyond that. Never got personal; a good thing since department policy discouraged fraternization between a supervisor and a direct subordinate.

He drained the remaining liquid from his bottle, added to the bills Segal had dropped on the table and pushed back his chair. Better keep things professional he reminded himself as he hurried toward the door. Yet the image of Cara Styles that flashed through his mind at that moment was anything but professional.

Chapter 16

Jonathon Moser was the activities director at East High School and had grown up in Pacific City. He graduated from Long Beach State University, taught for seven years and then became an activities director, which meant he was responsible for all school functions such as dances, lunch time programs, school elections and student government. Moser also supervised the band, drama and cheerleaders, although they had their own teachers or advisors. An avid surfer, he formed and still coached the surf team.

On this bright, clear Sunday morning, the day after the body of Alex Lyon was found, Moser sat alone drinking coffee on his patio. The Los Angeles Times, which he had retrieved from his driveway, lay unopened on the table in front of him. He hadn't opened it because of the white envelope inserted under the twine that held the bulky paper together. His name, misspelled as Mozer, was on the outside of the envelope printed in black magic marker.

Moser had not slept well. He'd had "night terrors" since he was a boy and last night was bad. The terrors often came after a traumatic event or sometimes even a difficult day at school trying to steer 3500 students into productive activities. He'd had two cups of coffee before going out on his patio. His left eye twitched involuntarily. His hand trembled. Last night was bad.

The envelope worried him but he wasn't sure why. Curious, he extracted it from beneath the twine on the newspaper and slit the sealed edge with his butter knife. A single sheet of folded white paper was inside. Using his fingertips, he pulled the paper out. Printed on the paper, apparently with the same marker as on the outside of the envelope, was a cryptic message:

THE BITCH DESERVED TO DIE. THERE WILL BE OTHERS. I AM THE LAW, IF YOU DONT LIKE IT YOU DIE.

REAPER

What the hell is this? Moser thought. *And who the hell is Reaper?* The crude symbol resembled an upside down cross. He had seen some of the Gothic kids at school wearing pewter necklaces shaped like that—the antichrist. They did it for shock value. And was the printing supposed to be Gothic---some punk kid trying to capitalize on the tragedy? Kids into the Goth scene were rebels or loners, he knew. They didn't fit into the school culture and flaunted their individuality by becoming exactly like each other.

Moser folded the sheet of paper, intended to throw it in the trash; it was crap. He had no trash can outside so he pushed the envelope to the far end of the table. He'd toss it later when he left the patio.

He slipped the newspaper from its encircling twine and searched for the article he knew would be there. He found it on the first page of the California Section.

HIGH SCHOOL GIRL SLAIN

"Police discovered the partially clad body of a seventeen year old East High School student early Saturday morning at Pacific City's Wellington Park. Preliminary reports are that she was raped and murdered. Chief investigator, Lieutenant James Deluca, of the Pacific City Police Department declined to give details regarding the slaying of the popular student. "The investigation is in its early stages," Deluca said, "and we are following up several leads."

"A memorial service will be held for the student, identified as Alexandra 'Alex' Lyon, on Tuesday night in the school gym at 6:00 P.M."

The article concluded by asking anyone with information to call the homicide Unit. A number was provided.

Moser's hand shook. Alex Lyon was one of his students. He met with her daily because she was a class officer. He had watched her cheer at football and basketball games. He'd watched her tease boys with her seductive body language and revealing clothes. She'd flirted with him. He'd talked with her parents about that behavior and dress. Moser skimmed the remaining articles in the California Section until he came to the editorial page where he was surprised to see another item devoted to the Lyon murder:

TOO YOUNG TO DIE

Seventeen is too young to die. But age does not exempt anyone from a force that ultimately claims us all. Death does not discriminate. "It is a slave," wrote

John Donne, "to fate, chance, kings and desperate men." It does not respect wealth, political connections or religious affiliation. It comes to those who expect it and to those who don't. It is sometimes peaceful, often violent. It leaves in its wake sorrow loneliness and fear. When it reaches out to the young, it raises questions of mortality and fairness.

The violent death of Alexandra, "Alex" Lyon, a seventeen year old senior at East High School in Pacific City was not fair. It was not expected, could not have been anticipated. Kids aren't supposed to die---not like this. We know it happens, but we are seldom prepared when it does.

The circumstances of this tragedy have frightened many in the community; a city often listed as one of the safest in the country. Parents fear for the safety of their children. Teenagers worry that there may be a predator in their midst. They've learned from Columbine that even school is no sanctuary. The community at large wonders if we can ever be safe, anywhere.

We urge the police to move swiftly on this. We want answers so that we can resume our lives without fear. We know life is uncertain, that there are no guarantees, but one thing we do know for certain, seventeen is too young to die.

*****

Moser stopped reading. He put the paper down on the glass topped patio table, took a sip of coffee and gazed out on his back yard. But he couldn't focus on his lush, green lawn, the multi-colored flowers that formed its border or his several fruit trees. His thoughts were on the murder of Alex Lyon. His hands trembled; his temple throbbed.

He reconsidered the note he'd just found. It promised others would die. For him, it now evoked memories of Columbine. The newspaper editorial alluded to it and every teacher and administrator in the country remembered or knew of the Columbine High School story---one of the worst massacres to occur on a school campus in modern U.S. History.

The kids who did it had been ridiculed and scorned by fellow students for their Gothic dress and their membership in the so-called "Trench Coat Mafia." Some parents had warned the school and police they were dangerous but their warnings had been ignored---to everyone's sorrow.

Even if this Reaper character hadn't killed Alex Lyon, his dangerous rant might be a genuine warning. Maybe he planned to capitalize on Alex's death and initiate a massacre of his own. Moser's thoughts turned to that of the wounded young boy at Columbine hanging from a second story window in his attempt to escape. That could be one of his students.

My god, he thought, *what if some kid at East High School was planning a mass murder?*

Chapter 17

Was Alex Lyon the first of many who might die?

The possibility of a suicide attack at East High School was unthinkable. Jonathon Moser had to do something. He picked up the cordless phone resting on the table beside the newspaper and dialed a number from memory. The phone was picked up on the third ring.

"Phillips," an authoritative voice responded.

Dalton Phillips was Chief of the Pacific City Police Department---he had been for the past eighteen months. He was also a member of the downtown Rotary Club along with Jonathon Moser. The men had served on several committees together and had become friends.

"Chief, JM here."

"Jon! What can I do for you on this fine Sunday morning, as if I didn't know."

"What do you think you know?" Moser asked.

"I assume you want some information about the murder of one of your students."

"Yes and no," Moser said. "I'd like to hear anything you can share with me. But I have some information for you, might even be evidence."

"I'm all ears, Jon" Phillips said, ignoring his friend's request for information.

Moser understood he wasn't going to get anything out of the Chief, so he pressed on.

"This morning, I found a note stuck in my newspaper. I thought it was a sick joke at first. But now I'm not so sure."

"What did the note say, Jon?" The Chief asked, his voice still indicating his skepticism.

Moser read the note and didn't wait for the Chief to respond. "All of us who work in schools," he continued, "are aware of Columbine and the copycat shootings that followed. And we're familiar with the Secret Service Report, which concluded most kids, who are planning to kill someone, tell their friends, or give out warnings in some way. This might just be a warning? Even if the kid didn't kill Alex Lyon, he could be wacky enough to be planning a mass murder. Christ Chief, who the hell knows what these kids are thinking."

Moser sensed a change in his tone when Phillips spoke again.

"OK, Jon. You're right. Let's get the note to Deluca in homicide. Do me a favor. If you have some plastic gloves, put them on before handling the envelope and note again. Then put them in a baggie and seal it. We might still be able to get some usable fingerprints. I'll have a detective come by and pick up the baggie from you later today."

"Thanks Chief---Dalton. This may be a long shot. But if it isn't, I couldn't live with myself if innocent kids got hurt.

"All right Jon. I do appreciate your concern. I assure you we'll follow up on this."

"Thanks again, Chief," Moser said as he punched the off button on the phone. He took a deep breath and leaned back in his white plastic patio chair. He took a sip of his now stone cold coffee and grimaced at the bitter taste.

Chapter 18

Chief Phillips placed the phone back in its cradle.

"What was that?" Joan Phillips asked as her husband rubbed his brow.

Phillips shook his head before answering. "Activities Director Jon Moser," he said. "He's worried the murder of the high school girl yesterday could be the beginning of a Columbine type thing."

"Why?" Joan Phillips asked, her voice registering surprise, her facial expression doubt. "It didn't happen at a school."

"You don't have to convince me, hon. I don't want to send our guys off on a wild goose chase. But Jon's a school official. They're all supersensitive now about any possible school violence. He doesn't want to be accused of not following up on a possible warning sign that something might happen. And quite frankly, neither do I. The Sheriff's department in Littleton, Colorado got crucified in the press for ignoring what people, with hindsight, said were clear indications that those kids who pulled off the massacre were dangerous. Before the incident, some parents reported that their son had received death threats from one of them. Somehow the report got buried and so did a lot of kids."

"What are you going to do?"

"I'm going to call Deluca and have his guys check out the note Jon got this morning threatening more killings. I'm not going to be standing in front of a bunch of reporters next week---or, god forbid, grieving parents---trying to explain why I let their kids die."

Chapter 19

Deluca thought about his wife.

They had argued often about his working on Sunday. She claimed he spent more time at work and thinking about work than he did about her or spending time with their daughter. For years, he was confused. His role model, his dad, had worked two jobs most of his life. He was the breadwinner. He showed his love to his wife and family by working hard and putting food on the table.

His wife didn't understand. To say women and men did not perceive things in the same way was an understatement. He tried to see things from her perspective but it seldom worked. They argued about this until the day she died in the car accident; too late to change, even if he wanted to.

The phone on his desk rang interrupting his thoughts. He answered and the Chief's voice surprised him.

"JD, Chief Phillips. I thought I might catch you in the office. Why the hell are you working on Sunday morning?

"My wife used to ask the same question Chief."

Both men laughed. Phillips knew Deluca's wife had died but he didn't go there.

"What can I do for you, sir?"

"JD! You know by now I don't meddle in investigations."

"Yes Sir," Deluca said, realizing that was about to change.

"I'm not changing my policy but something has come up regarding the Lyon murder we should look into."

"Yes sir," Deluca repeated, giving no indication he had made a judgment on what the Chief might say.

"I got a call from Jon Moser, the activities director at East High. You know him don't you."

"I've met him sir."

"I thought so. At any rate, Jon found a note attached to his morning newspaper. The note alluded to Lyon's murder and threatened more deaths to follow. Jon's worried about a Columbine type thing. Probably some Wacko; we get enough of them. But we can't ignore this."

"Yes Sir!"

"Is anyone else in the office with you?"

"Yes sir.

"Do me a favor then. Get someone to drop by Jon's house to retrieve the note. We might be able to obtain some usable prints. Someone calling himself Reaper signed the note, possibly a Goth kid at East High School. Our School Resource Officer may be able to identify someone using that name.

"Right sir!"

"Could kids be involved in this JD?"

"Possible, Chief. We doubt the girl went to the Park alone and evidence indicates she wasn't killed elsewhere and dumped there. Our guess is she went with someone, why or with who is unknown. Some of our people like the escaped rapist from Atascadero.

"Ramos?"

"Yes sir."

"OK! I know you're on top of things JD. I'll stay out of your hair. But follow up on this Columbine thing, will ya?"

"Yes sir," Deluca said. He got Moser's address and hung up.

After the call, Deluca leaned forward, elbows resting on his desk; head perched on his closed hands. These were crazy times. Columbine spurred a bunch of copycat incidents across the country. Hell, in nearby Anaheim, two eighth graders planned to blow up their junior high school. Some students heard them bragging and tipped off the police. In a raid on the homes of these kids, cops found bomb making materials, two homemade bombs, rifles and handguns and some Nazi propaganda. The kids might have followed through on their threats if the police had not been forewarned.

Deluca recalled Alex mentioned some Goth kids in her diary; one followed her around and scared her. What if he tried to make a move on her and she pissed him off? He takes her out when he can, plans to get her friends later. But he'd need a reason to lure her to the park, perhaps with the promise of drugs? Big question.

He tore Jon Moser's address from his yellow legal pad and stuffed it in his shirt pocket. He'd follow up on this as the Chief directed, but he promised himself, if this were some wiseass prank, he'd hang whoever did it by the balls.

Chapter 20

Jimmy Phelan sat having breakfast at his favorite restaurant.

The East High School football coach sat in a corner booth where he huddled with his coaching staff each week planning game strategy and greeting well-wishers. The thirty-five year old Phelan was a local celebrity. His teams had won three league championships and two state titles in the last six years. He was in demand as a lunchtime speaker at civic functions and at service club meetings; also was the object of lust by a gaggle of females, students and teachers, who fawned over his tight body and tanned, unlined face.

Phelan handled football and speaking engagements better than women. The young female flesh paraded before him every day tempted the weak willed coach. His hand shook as he took a sip of coffee and glanced down again at the LA Times Article, which rested on the table in front of him. Alex Lyon had been raped and murdered. The thought sickened him; not only because of the tragedy, but also because of the danger he faced in the aftermath. The investigation of her death threatened his career, indeed his freedom.

He first met Alex four years earlier when, as a freshman, she had enrolled in one of his classes. From the beginning, she flirted with him as many of the young girls did. She amused him more than anything despite her obvious attractiveness.

He pictured her in his mind; the tight sweaters and blouses displaying well developed breasts for her age, the short skirts showing off smooth, supple thighs and, sometimes, white cotton panties; the one occasion when she spread her legs when getting up from her desk, and he caught a glimpse of wispy blond hair—no underwear.

Phelan at first dismissed her behavior as that of an adolescent girl becoming aware of her sexuality and did nothing to discourage her.

In retrospect, he wished he had.

Chapter 21

Alex Lyon could not be ignored. Unlike most young girls who had a crush on a handsome teacher, she took things to another level and tested coach Jimmy Phelan's resolve earlier this year. A month after the start of school, a Friday; classes had been dismissed for the day, halls dark and deserted. East High School had been built in the late 1960's to protect students from a nuclear blast still a very real possibility in the minds of many Americans. The architect designed the school as a sprawling single story structure with enclosed corridors and no windows.

Alex approached Phelan outside of his classroom in the darkened hallway. Seeing her there, alone, Phelan sensed trouble. He swiveled his head from side to side as if to catch someone lurking in the shadows. Seeing no one didn't relieve his anxiety.

Lyon was even more striking than she had been as a freshman; her blonde hair pulled back in a ponytail revealing a clear, scrubbed complexion and bright sensitive eyes. Her firm breasts pushed against her transparent white blouse, beige skirt showcasing tanned, shapely legs. She was animated and sincere when she spoke. "Can I talk with you for a minute, Coach."

"Only a minute Alex," he said, "I've got a meeting with the team."

"I'm not sure how to say this, Mr. Phelan," she said in a voice just above a whisper.

Phelan didn't like her tone. Why whisper unless you worried others might overhear? He tried to steer the conversation to something mundane related to school. "If it's the homework assignment," he said, "I can't discuss that with you now."

"Not about the homework. It's personal." She dropped her head but her blue eyes fixed him with a steady, seductive stare.

The hairs on Phelan's neck bristled and he again scanned the halls but no one lurked.

"What I, uh, wanted to ask," Alex said, her voice soft, low, "was, uh, have you ever had an affair?"

Phelan's head snapped back. His face flushed. "That's not something I care to discuss with a student," he said through tight lips, "we'd better not continue this conversation."

He turned to walk away, but stopped when she touched his arm. "Don't go please," she pleaded. "I only asked because one of my teachers has a crush on you and she's too shy to tell you. She'd like to go out with you."

Her response disarmed Phelan. "How would you know that?"

"By the way she looks at you, mentions you and the team in class all the time. She told me she wished you weren't married."

Intrigued, but still wary, Phelan asked, "Ok, who is this mystery teacher?"

Without hesitating, Alex mentioned the name of a matronly English teacher much older than Phelan and, if the truth be known, quite unattractive. Phelan relaxed. He said easily: "No, I would not be interested in her romantically. But she's a fine teacher and a nice lady."

He again turned to leave when Alex blurted out: "How about me? Would you be interested if it was me?"

Chapter 22

The question stunned Phelan. The memory still raised the hairs on his neck. He didn't answer but he hadn't moved either. And, even as young as she was, Alex Lyon knew he was interested.

She smiled and leaned against a group of lockers, which had the effect of thrusting her breasts outward. Her nipples pointed at him---inviting, accusing. Phelan couldn't control his physical reaction and Alex seized the moment.

"Why don't we go into your classroom and talk, Mr. Phelan," she asked, her blue eyes boring into his.

It was a defining moment, in teen speak, a "no brainer." But his brain was not in control. Torn between his attraction for Alex and common sense, he stood transfixed, immobile. He wrestled with his conscience until Alex reached out, took his hand and pulled him into the classroom.

What happened inside the room remained etched in his memory. The girl was skilled beyond her years and touched and stroked him in all the right places. Her fingers danced across his skin, her mouth moistened him. He remembered the feel of her panties---the cool soft skin of the backs of her thighs as she pressed against him when he held her. He hadn't lasted long. Her skill and the sexual tension building within him had pushed him over the edge.

No joy accompanied his physical release. He crossed a line few, if any, would understand or forgive. The consequences flashed before him, like a video replay of a horror movie.

"Alex," he had pleaded. "We have to go. Somebody may come by any minute. The custodian has a key to the room. So do other teachers. They can't find us like this."

"Not yet," she said, her voice firm. She stepped away from Phelan and lifted her skirt. "Now me!"

Phelan had already slipped over the edge of the precipice and was in free fall. He did what he was told.

In the following days and weeks, he continued to do what he was told as Alex flirted with him. Her skirts got shorter and her blouses lower. She lingered after class to ensure he got a close look at her cleavage. She pushed him into dangerous acts.

One day she showed up in his office after the players and other coaches had gone for the day. She closed and locked the door behind her and stood before him in her cheerleader's uniform. Smiling, she raised her skirt to reveal she had removed her panties. She held the pose for several minutes to ensure Phelan could appreciate the view. Then she bent over his desk with her butt thrust outward. She smiled and Phelan succumbed as he always did.

He took her roughly as if to punish her for his weakness but she wasn't discouraged. Other incidents followed: in the back of his car, at Wellington Park, once in her home when her family had gone for the weekend, even on the middle of the football field late at night.

Phelan intended to end the relationship, but he was paralyzed by fear; fear of offending the girl if he broke it off; fear of discovery and the loss of his livelihood and reputation if it continued. He sought refuge in a bottle, which only increased his despair. The affair loomed over him like a precariously balanced weight, which he strained to keep from crashing down on his chest.

That weight pressed on him now as he sat in the restaurant and considered his options. Alex had been murdered. Keeping quiet would make him appear guilty if the affair came to light. Speaking out would expose him to public humiliation, loss of his job, jail? Neither option offered much solace---nor did the events of the night she died.

She asked to meet him. He tried to beg off. To make excuses. Alex would not be put off. She all but threatened him if he didn't show up. He went to his favorite watering hole in Buena Park to bolster his courage. He'd lost count of the number of tequila shooters he'd downed and blanked on everything after that. He found some scrapes on his arms the next day but couldn't remember how he got those. Could he have done something to her? He slammed his hand down on the table and kept his head averted as the noise attracted furtive glances from several other patrons.

Goddam booze. Goddam Alex, he murmured.

Chapter 23

His home was in a walled tract called Silver Lake Estates; no lake and no silver but the homes were spacious and comfortable. The one and two story structures had orange, Spanish style roofs and expansive, well-maintained, front lawns. Captain William "Wild Bill" McClusky of the Pacific City Police Department owned one of the two story models with a three-car garage.

McClusky had remodeled one section of his garage to form a game room he furnished with several card tables and metal folding chairs. A homemade freestanding plywood bar stood in one corner while a large American flag adorned the wall opposite the door. Once a month, McClusky hosted "poker games" in the room although few cards were ever dealt or shuffled there. The games served as cover for meetings of the PCPD's White Aryan Resistance (WAR), a white supremacist group formed by one-time television repairman, Thomas Metzger.

Metzger, a former Grand Dragon of the California Knights of the Ku Klux Klan, once led a band of armed Klansman in a foray to intercept immigrants illegally crossing the U.S./Mexico border south of San Diego. He gained national attention in the late 1980's when his racist comments on the Geraldo Rivera show sparked a studio riot that resulted in a broken nose for the show's host.

Metzger formed WAR after a falling out with KKK national Grand Dragon, David Duke. The former chief of the Pacific City Police Department liked Metzger's rallying cry, "Nothing changes without blood flowing." The chief joined the cause early on and he, in turn, enlisted others of like thought. The group had met secretly for over twenty years.

Metzger's philosophy of hate and organizational strategy fit the needs of racist cops. They couldn't afford to be high profile like the Klan and similar groups who failed because their outspoken advocacy of hatred attracted the attention and infiltration of the Feds. Better to act individually, like lone wolves, or in small cells to avoid detection; covert action would allow them to gain power and financing.

McClusky, adhering to Metzger's teaching, hosted the WAR meetings but kept no written organizational chart, membership list or minutes. No member of the group ever, in an open forum, espoused extremist views or supported an extremist cause. They spread their hate subtly, in the locker room, on patrol with partners, in bars in private conversation—and sometimes in the brutal treatment of those considered inferior or dangerous. Their goal was to preserve the "white" complexion of their city. They also aimed to disrupt any group that threatened the department or to its activities. Intimidation was sanctioned to further their agenda. Some were willing to go beyond that. *Busting a few heads now and then is good for the soul,* McClusky often joked.

Chapter 24

Ten to fifteen cops attended the games at McClusky's each month.

But actual membership in the group was higher. A detective from the homicide unit attended often. The retired Chief dropped in when in the area visiting from his retirement home in Las Vegas to check on his protégé, Wild Bill, the highest-ranking current officer in the group. "My boy," the old chief would fawn as he wrapped an arm around McClusky.

McClusky did no better running the WAR meetings than he did leading his division. Most of the "games" were free-for-all grab-ass sessions with verbal tirades against kikes, beaners, niggers, gooks or rag-heads. Some cops worked themselves into a frenzy when discussing articles from Metzger's WAR newspaper or his on line newsletter, Aryan Update. Violence was often the topic.

"I don't give a flying fuck what you do," McClusky would shout over the din, "but it's gotta look legal—justifiable force when subduing a suspect—shit like that."

The current meeting had none of the theatrics or bombast that accompanied most discussions. Tonight the rape and murder of schoolgirl Alex Lyon dominated conversation.

"Have we got anything to go on in the kid's murder Bill?" asked one of the patrol officers present--a slender man dressed in jeans and a pullover blue sweater.

"Not much yet," McClusky said, taking a deep swallow of beer from the bottle he hoisted to his lips. "The fucking beaner rapist who escaped from Atascadero is my bet." A roar of laughter and several similar epithets directed toward Mexicans followed.

"How the hell does a guy walk out of a maximum security lock up?" asked another cop twisting his mouth into an awkward grin.

McClusky inhaled, tucked his chin into his chest and belched, drawing chuckles from the assembled cops. "Amazing," he said. "Those turds must have had their heads up their asses."

More laughter ensued, then McClusky become serious. "Keep your eyes open for that scumbag Ramos. Word is he's back in town. Arrest him if possible; take him out if necessary." His tone and expression left no doubt as to which method he preferred.

The conversation dragged on fitfully for the next hour. Soon men began to leave. Some had to report for duty. One man stayed behind and waited until the room emptied. McClusky stepped close to him and whispered, "You know what to do if you catch up with the bastard."

The man smiled and asked, "Are we putting him on the list?"

"Damn right," McClusky said. "Put him at the top. Make an example of the fucker."

As the men of WAR left McClusky's in groups of two's and threes, none of them saw a solitary figure sitting in a car across the street. In fact, they weren't looking or particularly worried. The "games" had been held at McClusky's for the past several years. No one had a reason to be suspicious. And they had no reason to suspect anyone would be taking particular notice of them. They were, after all, peace officers in the city.

But they were being watched, had been for some time. Hunkered down in a nondescript vehicle, the individual watching checked the name of each man leaving the house. The watcher recognized some of them; served with them as a PCPD officer as well as a Special Agent for the Federal Bureau of Investigation.

The agent was part of a joint FBI-Justice Department task force investigating White Supremacist groups in police departments throughout the nation. Several civil rights complaints and a couple of high profile incidents involving minorities led federal authorities to focus attention on the PCPD. The agent observing McClusky's house had been inserted into the department eighteen months earlier. Only the current chief knew.

The agent waited several minutes to be sure everyone had left the house before driving off. The man who stayed behind to talk with McClusky stepped onto the sidewalk as the agent's car crawled by. It was dark but the glow from the street lamps silhouetted the driver. For a moment the man thought he recognized the driver but he quickly dismissed the thought.

Couldn't be, he said to himself. *Couldn't be.*

Chapter 25

Eduardo Ramos was high. Nothing unusual. He'd been wasted since his escape from Atascadero. Also horny, he'd gotten his rocks off only once after getting out and barely escaped detection after accosting a young girl.

Miguel warned him the local cops were looking for him. But he was angry and horny. The Puta hadn't visited him the whole time he was inside. A reliable source also told him she hadn't kept her thighs together either. She would do what he wanted, feel his wrath, pay for disrespecting him.

Dressed in a black hooded sweatshirt and black pants, he stood pressed against a wall in the small back yard of the ground floor apartment occupied by his wife and children. He had scaled several wooden fences to get there. The drapes covering the sliding glass door that led to the outside patio were not completely closed. He saw her sitting alone on a battered couch in the family room wearing a short, sheer nightgown, smooth brown legs visible. Her large breasts strained against the material of her nightgown. She'd put on some weight, Ramos thought, but still looked damn good. He wanted her.

At this hour, the kids would be asleep. He knocked several times on the glass before she noticed. She got up slowly, self-conscious. She grabbed a robe, draped beside her on the couch and approached the sound of the rapping. She held the robe closed at her throat. She stopped once but resumed her advance when Ramos pressed his face to the glass. She hesitated before flipping the latch on the door and moving it just enough for him to slip inside. She didn't smile, her eyes wide with fear. Not happy, Ramos thought. No matter. He grinned and slid the door closed behind him.

A 911 call made by her six year old son brought police and paramedics to the apartment. He'd been taught to use the telephone in an emergency. He stood in the open doorway, tears streaming down his face, waiting for help to arrive.

His mother lay naked, spread eagled on her bed, face battered and bruised like a boxer who had gone ten rounds and lost. Blood oozed from between her legs; one arm twisted unnaturally beneath her body, her breathing labored.

Maria Ramos would remember the visit from her husband. So would officer Randy Cunningham first on the scene. No fan of Mexicans, Cunningham resented their presence in his city; writing their fucking gibberish on walls, standing on every street corner, begging for work. Fucking each other up on Friday nights after boozing it up at a local gin mill.

Cunningham expected them to beat up on one another, not surprising. But this particular incident fueled his hatred for Ramos, a scumbag the city could do without. If he got the chance, he vowed to make it happen.

Chapter 26

Deluca ate breakfast at the same place every day.

Mama Rosa's opened in the downtown area when oil was king. Now considered a landmark in Pacific City, it had catered to the blue and white-collar workers whose livelihood depended on the black gold. Walking into the place was like taking a step back in time. The wooden booths were scratched, their finish fading, seat cushions split. Black and white photos adorned the walls. One showed Mama Rosa standing in front of the original building. Several highlighted field workers; faces blackened by the daily grind huddled together smiling, arms draped around each other. A few pictures, in color, showcased local high school baseball and football teams, which had received donations from the restaurant; thank you plaques attached.

The waitresses still dressed in the traditional pink, ankle length skirts, white aprons. The food was plentiful and good if not healthful, biscuits and gravy a specialty of the house.

Deluca's morning routine was unchanged unless interrupted by events such as the murder of Alex Lyon; 45 minute workout at the gym around 4:30 AM, shower at home, breakfast at six or six-fifteen, arrive at work by seven-thirty.

When he walked into Mama Rosa's at 6:15, he waved to the waitress and took a seat at a booth in the back. He opened the morning paper he had carried in and smiled as a waitress brought him his coffee unsolicited. He always started with coffee, a fact known by the wait staff, two middle-aged women. Deluca couldn't remember a younger gal ever being there at this hour.

Pam Gray stood beside Deluca with a pencil and notepad in her hands ready to take his order, an unnecessary ritual since Deluca ordered only two things each morning, scrambled egg whites, fruit and wheat toast, or hot oatmeal and wheat toast, coffee, black.

"Eggs or Oatmeal, lieutenant," Gray asked as she pressed her hip against Deluca's table and balanced her weight on one leg.

Deluca had tried to get the staff to call him JD but to no avail. People like to use the titles of individuals, who are important, a sign of respect. They think a person's notoriety or importance will rub off on them. Deluca's didn't press the issue.

He smiled, and then said, "The eggs please, Pam."

With only a few customers in Rosas's at this hour, Gray returned shortly with Deluca's order. She placed two plates on the table in front of him and refilled his cup from a pot she carried.

As she turned away, Deluca stopped her. "Pam, how's your son Michael doing at East High?"

Gray, a short, thick woman with a round face and kind eyes smiled.

"He's doin' great, Lieutenant. He's starting at linebacker and made the honor roll last grading period."

"Super," Deluca said. Then added, "Did he know Alex Lyon?"

Gray's demeanor changed. She frowned and hugged herself wrapping her arms around her girth careful to keep the coffee pot away from her body.

"So sad," She said. "So sad. They didn't date, or anything but they did go to the same parties."

Gray put the coffee pot on the table and hesitated before she spoke again. "I don't want to speak ill of the dead, mind you, and Alex did not deserve what happened to her, but! She let the sentence hang and scanned the restaurant before continuing.

"Alex had a reputation. Not a good one. She slept around."

"Did Michael tell you that?"

"No. No. Not from Michael. I overheard people talking at football games when I'd sit in the bleachers or go to the snack bar. Some of the high school girls aren't very discreet. You know how girls are."

"I remember," Deluca said then asked, "Who did she hang around with?"

"The athletes and cheerleaders, of course, also with some of those Mexicans, gang kids."

"Why?" Deluca asked.

Gray did a complete pivot around before speaking. She moved closer to the table and bent down so her face was close to Deluca's.

Shaking her head in disapproval, she whispered, "The drugs. The drugs."

Chapter27

Big Tony Segal frowned, shook his head. As he drove to the Monday morning briefing, a group of thirty or more men, women and children with placards marching back and forth on the sidewalk in front of Department Headquarters caught his attention. Demonstrations were rare in Pacific City and he couldn't remember one taking place in front of the department.

Straining to see what was happening, he caught the names on several of the signs being waved around. He recognized them; men who died in police custody. The ACLU made a lot of noise about that along with the group representing Mexicans, MALDORP or some screwy name. Other signs proclaimed "Driving While Brown Is Not A Crime," "Equal Justice For All" and "Brown Pride."

Segal shook his head as he drove his truck behind the headquarters building and pulled into an empty space in the staff parking lot. He turned off the ignition, leaned back against the seat and closed his eyes. This racial crap hit him personally last week. He went to his kid's school for a parent conference; everyone spoke Spanish like he was in another country, his own children in the minority. He and his wife discussed pulling them from school and moving if they had to but he didn't want them held back while all these illegals learned English, not fair.

I'm not a goddam racist, he said aloud. He'd played high school football with plenty of black guys, some low-riders, and even a Samoan kid so huge they called him "Mountain." They partied together, hit the fast food joints as a group after games, and shared the booze hidden in their lockers for a pick me up before heading out to the practice field. They all spoke English or made a fair attempt. The Samoan mostly grunted and the black guys had code words for some things he never did understand. Yet, they got along even if whites were the predominant group. He didn't gloat, but he had been comfortable. He kept in touch with some of those guys. Why should he be made to feel like an outsider in his own country?

I'm not a goddam racist, he muttered again. He gathered the coffee and donuts he had picked up for this morning's meeting, squeezed out of the truck's door and shuffled toward the headquarters' building.

Back in front, the media surrounded the protesters having been tipped off by the sponsors of the demonstration. An attractive blond, who reported on Orange County issues for the local TV station, stood before a mobile mini-cam. Beside her was attorney Antonio Victor Gonzales, a spokesman for the Mexican-American Legal Defense Fund (MALDEF).

The reporter held a microphone in Gonzales' face.

"Sir. What do you hope to accomplish here today?" she asked, in the pompous tone affected by all media types.

"We want to focus attention on what's happening in this city," Gonzales said, looking directly into the camera.

The woman smiled and asked, "And what do you believe that is? By all accounts the city's a safe place to live, isn't it?"

"Not if you're brown," Gonzales said, raising his voice. "Look at the facts. We have a police department out of control, one that enforces the law not based on the statutes but on the color of your skin."

"That's a serious charge, Mr. Gonzales."

"We're prepared to back it up."

"Can you explain?"

"Yes. Check the facts, as I said a moment ago." He held up a sheet of paper he'd been holding by his side. "Within the last fourteen months three unarmed men died at the hands of the police. They all sustained fatal injuries while being arrested and restrained by patrol officers, all of them were Latino."

The reporter shook her head as if agreeing with Gonzales. "So you think the police are targeting Latinos?" she said, giving him the lead in he wanted.

"Wouldn't you? How many white citizens have been treated this way?"

He didn't wait for or expect a response. "I'll tell you. None. These were intentional, reckless acts of excessive force, not accidents. This racist conduct is condoned, maybe even encouraged, by the police hierarchy. These officers, and this department, must be held accountable."

The reporter's eyes widened. "As I understand, sir, a review panel cleared the officers of wrongdoing."

"Of course, by their own people. Do you really think they would find one of their own guilty of anything? It won't happen. That's why we're pursuing this in federal court. These acts are civil rights violations if not outright murder. If this department won't take responsibility for such racist acts someone else will have to force them to; MALDEF and the ACLU have joined forces on this."

The interview ended with the reporter thanking Gonzales, repeating her name and turning the program back to the news station. The anchor, a perfectly coiffed redheaded guy who appeared to be eighteen years old, glared into the camera with a practiced serious expression.

"Pacific City," he announced, "a peaceful community until now, has been rocked by the rape and murder of a teenage girl and a federal civil rights lawsuit filed against the police department. In other news..."

Two patrol officers stood near the Gonzales interview. When it ended, one them, a tall slender man with slicked black hair, leaned close to his companion.

"That greaser needs to be taught the facts of life," he whispered.

Chapter 28

Tony Segal fought to control his anger at the demonstrators.

He climbed the stairs to the detective pen on the second floor and encountered Cheryl Brown, the department secretary, typing on her computer. Pushing aside his feelings, Segal greeted her with a big smile and a raunchy joke.

"Hey Cheryl," he asked. "How do you make five pounds of fat look good?"

Brown did not reply. She stopped after the umpteenth time Segal had trapped her.

"Put a nipple on it," he guffawed as he strode by.

She shook her head but couldn't hide a slight grin.

Segal was still smiling when he got to Deluca's office. He pushed the image of the demonstrators out of his mind. All bullshit.

The others were already there. Deluca had the autopsy file open on his desk leafing through the pages. He accepted a cup of coffee proffered by Segal and returned his eyes to the document. Segal was half sitting on a small conference table, an apple fritter in one hand, coffee in the other. Willis and Styles sat in chairs in front of Deluca's desk. Willis had accepted a donut, Styles had not.

They all watched expectantly, but knew Deluca wouldn't speak until he had absorbed the contents of the report. After several minutes, Deluca pushed away from his desk, took a sip of coffee, tilted his head to the side and gazed off into space. When he turned back, he said, "We've got one big mess on our hands, people."

He didn't follow up on the statement and Segal became impatient. "You going to fill us in, or what?"

"Absolutely," Deluca said. He read from the document in a matter of fact tone, in clipped phrases: "Cause of death, suffocation, the result of having been strangled. Width of ligature marks on the neck and deep penetration indicate a narrow belt or cord of some kind. Toxicology revealed a blood alcohol level of .19, legally drunk in this state. Traces of marijuana and methamphetamine also found."

He turned the page and continued: "Swab samples from mouth and anus show semen residue in both orifices. DNA analysis reveals two different deposits in mouth, no matches in DNA data bank.

"Indications are the victim had sexual contact with multiple individuals, no tearing or abrasion evident in any orifice. Sex may have been consensual, or at least not resisted. Anal penetration may have occurred after death."

There were shocked expressions all around but no comments.

Deluca finished reading, closed the manila folder, and shrugged his shoulders. When he spoke, it was to ask a question: "What's CSU got?

Pacific City was one of the few Orange County communities with a sophisticated crime lab, a multi-million dollar facility recently opened and funded by a municipal bond and a federal grant. Soon it would do its own DNA analysis which was now handled by the County. Currently, the criminologists who worked in the lab gave technical expertise on serology, trace evidence, (such as hair fibers, paint, shoeprints, tire tracks and tool marks), toxicology, blood and urine and alcohol and arson analysis. They used the Cal-ID network computer system to identify fingerprints.

Segal stared at the ceiling for a moment, took a deep breath and recalled several facts from memory: "The CSU team collected beer cans, whisky bottles and the remains of three funny cigarettes. The prints was smudged so they got nothing usable. The ground was hard and covered with leaves, no footprints; panties wasn't found."

Deluca ignored Segal's mangled grammar. "What about condoms?" He asked.

"Three or four but old."

"Did they get any DNA off the joints or cans?" Deluca pressed.

"Yeah! No results yet."

Deluca folded both hands together on his desk, grimaced, and said: "Ok. The girl is drinking and doing drugs. At some point she has sex with more than one guy. She's not raped, simply partying. Everybody's happy until one dude loses control, gets angry, winds up choking her to death. He takes her panties as a souvenir. The other kids just watch all this. Are they so whacked out they can't stop him or they don't realize what's happening."

Segal shook his head. "Don't make sense. Not the drinking, smoking, partying crap, that's the teenage weekend routine these days although I'd kill my own kid if I found out she was doing stuff like that. Thank god," he said, and knocked on the wooden desk for luck, as well as emphasis, "I don't think she is." Segal's daughter was a sophomore at East High School.

"Kids don't go along with this, skipper," he continued, "especially with other girls present, which is probable. Course, they all might a' been as whacked out as Lyon, doing a grab ass orgy like she described in her diary."

"I agree," said Deluca. "These kids are party animals not murderers. But what if the party broke up and everyone left but Lyon and one guy? They continue to drink and fool around; things get out of hand. Alex doesn't, or couldn't, give him what he wants. He loses it. Winds up killing her."

"Why grab her panties?" Segal asked.

Deluca shrugged and shook his head.

"One thing's for sure," Segal said. "She didn't go there with a stranger or to meet someone unknown to her. But I don't buy your scenario. From what we know about her, and the fact semen was found in her mouth, she fucked anyone and everyone. I doubt she was killed because she was a tight ass."

No one blanched at Segal's use of profanity although each of them stole a sideways glance at Styles. Her facial expression did not change but she jumped into the conversation.

"Even if she went with friends to party," she offered, "that doesn't rule out Ramos. Maybe the kids paired up and wandered off leaving Alex passed out. Ramos is nearby doing a drug deal. He sees what's going down, decides to have his own fun."

"That dog don't hunt," Segal said, ignoring the smirks of the others. "When the kids wake up or come back to the clearing and find her body, they're gonna panic, call us or their parents."

"Not if they all were wasted and afraid their parents would find out," Willis countered.

Styles still liked Ramos. "OK! How about this? We know the 24th Street Diablos use the park to do drugs, sell drugs. The kids get their stuff from Ramos and he sticks around after the buy to join in on the fun"

"Goddamn lowlife," Segal muttered, his lips tight.

Deluca ignored the comment but his eyes bored into Segal. "Cara, your second scenario makes more sense," he said. "Everyone partying would explain why more than one semen type was found on her body. It doesn't explain the lack of a match for Ramos. His DNA is on file as a sex offender. Do we have any evidence placing him at the scene?"

Both Styles and Segal shook their heads. "The canvas of the area turned up nada," Segal said. "None of the neighbors remembers seeing anybody suspicious, except the old broad. She places someone running or jogging away from the park around the time of the girl's death. But she's a fruitcake."

Deluca got up from his chair, pushed it under the desk and paced back and forth. He spoke after several minutes. "We need to confirm whether or not the phantom jogger was Ramos."

No one dissented.

Deluca then surprised everyone. "At any rate, we have a new twist in the case." He passed out copies of the note Jon Moser received.

"This was stuffed in the Sunday newspaper of the activities director at East High, Jon Moser. The Chief directed me to pick it up after Moser called him."

The mention of the Chief elicited frowns but no comments.

"Moser took the note as a warning of a Columbine type attack at the high school and that Alex could be the first of many to be killed in a murder plot. The Chief doesn't necessarily agree, and neither do I. We aren't willing to ignore the possibility, though, given the bizarre behavior of kids these days."

"Some shit-bird's idea of a prank," Segal said, as he dropped the note on Deluca's desk.

"Pretty big leap," Styles added.

"Yup," Deluca agreed. "But Alex put an entry in her diary about being followed around campus by a kid into the Goth scene. He frightened her. Remember when the fingers started pointing in Colorado, the Sheriff's department took a lot of flack for ignoring warning signs. We're not going to repeat that mistake."

He made eye contact with each detective. Willis looked away, dropped his head jamming both hands into his pants pockets. Deluca thought his behavior odd but did not comment. Then he continued. "So here's what we're going to do:

"First, Willis and Segal. Follow up on the Columbine idea and talk with the SRO at East High. He may have a lead on kids angry enough to follow up on the threat, might even be able to ID Reaper. Also, do what you can to find Ramos and/ or the mysterious jogger.

"Second, Styles. Interview the high school principal. He might be able to ID the kids in Alex's diary. Chances are if she partied at the park one or all of them were with her.

"I'll talk to Alex's shrink. Perhaps he can tell us about her friends, fears or enemies. She may have revealed things in therapy she didn't chronicle in her journal. Maybe she mentioned this Reaper character. We've got to narrow the field of suspects pronto."

No one disagreed.

Chapter 29

A concrete ampitheater was the centerpiece of the East High School campus. Its floor sloped downward into a six-foot depression, which culminated at the base of an elevated stage. The theater was much used, from senior commencement exercises to lunchtime skits sponsored by the student body leadership. Sometimes bands entertained the kids and annoyed the faculty.

At lunch, on the Monday following Alex Lyon's death, groups of students sat huddled together on the benches discussing, in hushed tones, the murder and rape of one of their classmates. In one such group, three football players and two cheerleaders, all friends of Alex, talked quietly each of them looking around furtively, afraid of being overheard.

Derek Johnson, the team's bulky fullback and a high school All-American, said nervously: "We better plan on what to do? They're going to find out we was there."

"Oh my god!" one of the girls almost shouted covering her mouth with her hand.

"Relax," said Michael Bryant, a slender African-American with two silver earrings in each ear. "How're they gonna know?"

"Don't be stupid," Johnson said. "They'll find out. Not like we didn't leave stuff behind."

"The paper says she was raped," chimed in Kitty Richmond, co-captain of the cheerleaders and Lyon's best friend.

"Yeah but we know differently, don't we?" Johnson scoffed.

"Man, we're in deep bandini," said Floyd Warner, the team's place kicker and probable school valedictorian.

"Don't get you're panties wet," Johnson snapped. "We just need to have our stories straight."

"Stop blowing smoke, man," Warner retorted, "This ain't about cutting class or getting home late after a party. We're talkin' murder. Fuckin' murder, man."

"We killed her! We killed her," Richmond said her voice quivering, tears forming in the corners of her eyes.

"Shut up," Johnson snarled, pointing his finger at her. "We didn't kill nobody."

Nancy Holmes, the other girl present, came to Richmond's defense. "Kitty's, like, right," she said, as she put her arm around her friend and stroked her hair. "We should, like, tell the police what happened. It wasn't our fault." She too began to cry.

Johnson ignored their tears and tried to take control of the situation. "Look! So what if the cops find out we was there. They can't prove nothing. Lots of kids party in the park. We open our mouths and we'll get booted from school. We could go to jail."

His words did little to comfort the girls who stood clinging to each other, tears flowing. Johnson's frustration was evident as he all but shouted, "Hell! You want to risk our futures, our reputations?"

Bryant, the team's only black player, spoke up. "Jesus, Derek, we both got scholarships to SC man! They'll cut us loose if they find out about this."

The conversation stopped and all eyes turned as Tommy Deerfield, Lyon's boyfriend, approached the group. Deerfield's head was down, his gait slow. When he reached his friends, the two girls put their arms around him in an affectionate embrace. The bell sounded and everyone picked up books and backpacks and started walking back to class. No one made eye contact.

Chapter 30

The principal watched as kids trudged back to class.

His office overlooked the central quad. It was a large square room. One wall, dominated by windows, provided a view of the inside of the campus. Plaques, various awards won by the school over the years and pictures of championship sports teams covered two walls. Above the Principal's desk, butted up against one wall, he had hung his personal awards and academic degrees. Along the opposite wall, under the various plaques, a couch and two chairs faced each other with a coffee table between. Detective Styles sat on the couch.

Principal William Farraday turned away from the window and sat beside his Director of Activities, Jonathon Moser, who occupied one of the chairs. Farraday stood several inches over six feet. He had a large angular face with deep brown eyes accentuated by bushy brown eyelashes.

The diminutive Moser, on the other hand, may have been five-six, with soft green eyes, a smooth, pleasant face and sandy blond hair flowing over his ears and shirt collar; still a surfer at heart. Both men wore gray slacks, black school blazers and school ties displaying the head of a snarling panther.

Farraday leaned forward in his chair and offered the detective coffee from a silver carafe resting on the table. When she declined, he poured himself a cup, smiled and opened the conversation by promising he and his staff would do anything to help the investigation. Then, he dipped his head in an obvious invitation for Styles to begin.

"Thank you for seeing me with such short notice," she said, smiling warmly. She wore a blue skirt cut two inches above the knee, a white blouse and blue blazer. Seated on the couch with her legs crossed, a wide expanse of her toned, muscled thigh was exposed. Both school officials struggled to keep their eyes above her waist.

Cara Styles, unlike many of her female counterparts, did not attempt to disguise her femininity. She considered her physical attractiveness an asset, particularly when dealing with men. They relaxed around her, sometimes would tell her things, things they might say only in intimate conversation with a loved one or someone they hoped to seduce. No doubt many thought of seducing her. Cara used this to her advantage aware of the possible danger but confident she could protect herself. She was aware of the effect she was having on both school administrators as she posed her first question to Farraday.

"How well did you know Alex Lyon?"

"Not well. There are almost thirty-five hundred students here, so my interaction with individual kids is limited."

"Anything you can tell me will help," Styles said, taking out her "Palm Pilot" having long discarded the traditional notebook for the more convenient pocket computer.

"That's why I asked Jonathon to join us," said Farraday. "He's responsible for student activities, including athletics and cheerleading. He still helps out coaching the surf team."

He turned toward Moser who picked up the cue.

"Alex was a good student," he said, "cheerleader, vice-president of the senior class."

"May I get a list of class officers and the girls on the cheerleading squad," Styles asked.

"Sure."

"I'd also like a roster of the football team."

"I can give you both before you leave," said Moser, as he jotted a note on a yellow legal pad he held in his lap.

"Did she have any problems with anyone?"

"Alex was outgoing. Well liked," Moser said after a brief hesitation. "She flaunted her looks; pushed the limit on the school dress code, showed a lot of skin."

"To your knowledge was she sexually active?"

Both men eyed each other, silent. Sensing their reluctance, Styles prodded, "Gentlemen. This is a murder investigation. We need your help."

Moser sat up a little straighter, adjusted his tie. "I can't tell you anything definitive, you understand, just snippets I pick up from the kids conversation."

"I appreciate that," said Styles, again smiling and displaying her white teeth. She adjusted her position on the couch exposing more thigh as she did so.

"Why don't you let us determine what is relevant," she continued.

Moser struggled to keep his eyes from wandering downward, shifted in his chair, straightened his tie again. "As I said, I just pick up things here and there, most of it kids' stuff, juicy girl type gossip. On at least two occasions I overheard girls on the cheer squad talking about the parties after the football games. If what they said was true, things got wild---drinking, drugs, group sex. Alex was involved."

"To what extent?"

"Again, I'm not sure."

"Who attended these parties?"

"Mostly cheerleaders and football players."

"Where did they take place?"

"At the homes of students whose parents are gone a lot. Many of these kids lead independent lives with little or no parent supervision."

East High School's attendance zone included Pacific Harbor, an area of exclusive homes. Each had docking facilities on a series of canals, which snaked through the housing complex. The owners were professionals whose careers often took precedence over their families. Their children fended for themselves with not unexpected results.

Styles own experience had been similar. Her dad, a self-made businessman, was an absentee parent. Her mother preferred social gatherings to rearing her daughter. Left by herself for much of her youth, Styles knew such freedom could lead to trouble.

"Can you give me the names of her close friends?" she asked.

"Her boyfriend is Tommy Deerfield," Moser said, "the quarterback on the football team. Kitty Richmond, Nancy Holmes and Anna Lawrence are cheerleaders who hung around with Alex."

"What kind of a kid is Deerfield?"

"Super. Excellent student. Fine athlete. Model citizen," said Farraday, as if promoting the kid for student of the year.

"Would he be at any of these post game parties?"

"He's the star quarterback on the team," Farraday said, "so I would guess he'd be there. But I doubt he was doing drugs or drinking. He's very religious."

"What about the girls?"

"Yeah, I'm sure they liked to party. I'd be speculating about the drugs and drinking though," said Moser.

Styles then took from her purse the copy of the notes Deluca had made from Alex's diary and handed it to Moser. She had lined out "dickhead" for obvious reasons. "These are the initials of some people Alex mentioned in her diary, can you put names to any of them?"

Moser examined the list while rubbing his chin. "JP could be Jeremy Peters, a senior on the football team. SR might be Steve Richey or Scott Roland both on the team. TD, I would guess, is Tommy Deerfield. The others don't strike a chord of any kind. Heck, half the athletes on campus call each other Bubba." He handed the list back to Styles.

"Any problems with students into the gothic scene?" Styles asked, folding the list in half, leaving it on her lap. "Particularly someone named Reaper."

"Every school has such a group," Farraday said. "They get into scrapes sometimes, nothing serious to my knowledge. If this Reaper is a student here, I don't know him. Jonathon told me about the note he received and I'm concerned. I'm glad you're following that up."

"Since Columbine," Moser added, "We can't take any chances with this stuff as off the wall as it may sound."

"I understand," Styles said, turning the conversation back to the athletes. "I want to talk with Peters, Richey and Roland. May I use an office to speak to them and the other students you mentioned, especially girls friendly with Alex?"

"Sure, you can use my office," Moser offered. "Right down the hall."

"Should we notify the parents?" Farraday asked. "School district policy requires us to do so whenever kids are interviewed by the police."

"OK by me," Styles said. "We have nothing to hide."

"Yeah! I hope the kids don't either," Farraday said.

Chapter 31

Jeremy Peters felt confident he had nothing to hide.

He was the first student interviewed in the Activities Director's office. Moser sat behind his desk, allowed to sit in on the conversation to head off future parent complaints. He would not ask any questions.

Moser's small office had room for a desk and small conference table. High walls were adorned with photos of athletic teams, the band, drama club, present and past student officers and varied banners emblazoned with the school name. Behind his desk, hung several pictures of the surf team, with Moser in each one as the coach. A glass wall, like the principal's, looked out on the quad.

Styles and Peters sat at the small, round conference table. Peters was a little over six feet tall, California bleached blond, blue eyes. His broad shoulders, short haircut and strong jaw "shouted" athlete.

"Jeremy," Styles began, "thanks for talking with me."

The boy smiled. "Call me Jay. Everybody does," he said clasping his hands together.

"OK, Jay. I want to ask you a few questions about Alex Lyon."

The boy tensed; exhaled audibly and sat up straighter in his chair, as if steeling himself against what might come next. Styles picked up on his body language.

"Relax Jay. We don't suspect you of anything. We're talking to some of Alex's friends. You were her friend, right?

"I suppose so," the kid replied. "She partied with us after games, hung around practice with other cheerleaders."

"Did you ever date her?"

"We hooked up a couple of times but she was Tommy D's girl."

"Hooked up?"

"We, ah, fooled around."

Styles nodded. "Alex made several references in her diary to someone with the initials JP. Is that you?"

"What, what did she say?" the boy asked. His face reddened and he clasped his hands tighter.

"What do you think she might say?" Styles asked, keeping her voice calm, soft.

The kid twisted in his chair and dropped his eyes to the table. "I didn't think she'd write that stuff down."

"What stuff?"

Peters stammered: "Ah! Ah! What she, ah, did with me, with other guys."

"Jay. I'm not here to pass judgment. What you tell me is confidential. No one will know. Not even your parents."

She was on shaky ground with that promise depending upon what the kid revealed.

Jeremy took a deep breath, his head down. "She gave me, us, ah, oral sex."

He slipped lower in his chair, reddened again, and clasped his hands together.

Styles let the boy compose himself before continuing. "Did she do this more than once?"

"Yeah."

"With other guys on the team?"

"Yeah," he said averting his eyes.

"Did she do it with someone named Bubba?"

Peters chocked back a laugh. "Bubba's a nickname we give all the offensive lineman, ah, like they're big, dumb rednecks. Not mean, though, fooling around, you know."

"Did Alex do any of them?"

"Yeah, some."

"Did she like one of them more than another?"

"No. Um. I don't want to be mean, but Alex had, ah, sort of a reputation, you know. Most of the cheerleaders did."

Styles changed her line of questioning. "Jay. Did you go to the party after the game Friday night?

"Yes!" He said eager to move on to something else, shifting his body toward Styles regaining his confidence.

"Did you see Alex there?

Peters thought for a moment before answering. "Yes. She didn't stay long though."

"How long did you stay?"

"Around twelve or twelve-thirty. Most everybody had left by then? Alex wasn't there."

"Jay," Styles asked. "Do you know Eduardo Ramos?"

The boy tensed, the color drained from his face and he kept silent.

"Jay," Styles prodded. "Up to now you've been cooperative. That's good; this is a murder investigation. I'm not looking to hurt you or your friends but if you don't help I might wonder why."

Jay hesitated, thought better of it. “Ah, when he’s around, some of the guys get Roids from him. Ah, other things too.

“What other things?”

“Anything you want, Meth, Ludes, Coke.”

Styles sat back in her chair, waited a moment: “Where do the kids go to get their stuff from him?”

The kid’s eyes widened.

“The Park,” he said.

Chapter 32

William Bradford was the East High School resident cop.

The school district called him a Resource Officer and provided him a small windowless office in the counseling wing of the administration building. The cramped space had room for the standard issue metal desk, two straight-backed chairs and a freestanding bookcase containing yearbooks and several tomes on the state education code. A two-tone red and gray IMac computer on his cluttered desk contained the student database. Bradford had access to the academic transcripts, daily schedule and home address and telephone number of registered students.

Bradford was in his office now writing an incident report of a fight that had occurred that morning. Students caught fighting were suspended, received a citation and had to go to court and pay a $250 fine.

Things hadn't changed much since his own high school days, Bradford thought as he filled in details of the altercation. Most fights on campus still involved boy/girl issues or someone from one group looking sideways, "mad-dogging," at someone in another group. Two girls, scratching, pawing, clawing each other earlier in the day attracted a crowd of admirers who egged them on rather than intervene. Bradford's cheek had been scratched stepping in to separate the girls. He touched the wound with his fingertips and shook his head as he sought to remember the specifics of what had happened.

Bradford finished the report and looked up to see two men he recognized as detectives standing in his open doorway. He stood up as both men crowded into his office. He did not know the name of either man so he waited for introductions.

Segal spoke first. "Officer Bradford, Detectives Willis and Segal. The string bean is Willis."

The men shook hands and Bradford signaled them into the two chairs facing his desk. Both detectives felt awkward. It reminded them of their days in school when sitting before the principal. They understood why Bradford had arranged the chairs and desk this way. And it wasn't only because of space concerns. Many authorities on leadership discuss the placement of furniture; a desk between office visitors and the principal or business manager establishes a position of authority for the person behind the desk. In the case of the Resource Officer, it put offending students or belligerent parents on the defensive. Willis and Segal occupied chairs reserved for student miscreants.

"What can I do for two of Pacific City's finest?" Bradford asked, his mouth twisting into a grin.

Again, Segal spoke first. 'We're following up a lead in the Lyon murder. Did you know the girl?"

"Yeah! I'd see her around campus. Pretty, showed off her assets, called on the carpet a few times for dress code violations. Never got into serious trouble."

"Was she popular?" Willis asked.

"Sure! With the leadership and jock crowd."

"Anyone not like her?"

"No doubt. She was stuck up. Boys panted after her like a pack of dogs in heat. Some girls got their noses bent out of shape when their boyfriends did the panting. Kids stuff, though."

"Any students on campus into the Gothic scene?" Segal asked.

"Yeah, ten or fifteen. You can't miss them; Black clothes, white faces, black lipstick, black fingernails. Lots of piercing everywhere, no doubt in some places we don't want to know about. No trench coats allowed since Columbine."

Segal noticed the chagrin on his partner's face similar to the look he got when Deluca mentioned the Goth note. "Any of these kids go by the name Reaper?"

Bradford's head snapped back. "We've had graffiti in the heads with a joker using that name. I've been trying to nail the bastard but so far I've got bupkis."

Segal fished in his pocket, handed a folded note to Bradford. "That was stuffed in the Sunday paper of the activities director, Jonathon Moser."

Bradford studied the note for several seconds, puzzled. "Something's familiar about this," he said.

"The name?

"No! The content."

Bradford gazed at the ceiling in an effort to recall where he had seen the words. He reached down, opened the bottom right hand drawer of his desk, pulled out a manila folder and thumbed its contents. He found what he was looking for halfway through the file, took a sheet of paper out, examined it one more time and handed it to Segal.

The paper was a copy of a report published about the Columbine school shootings. Segal located what Bradford wanted him to see, then gave the page to Willis.

"I'll be go to hell," Willis said. Eric Harris, one of the Columbine shooters, had posted the statement on his web site before the massacre. "I am the law, if you don't like it you die. If I don't like you or I don't like what you want me to do, you die."

"So! Our Reaper character is an admirer of Eric Harris," Willis observed, handing the paper back to Bradford. "Not good."

"No," Bradford said. "But does the asshole plan to do a Columbine or is he jerking us off?

"We'd better find out."

Everyone nodded agreement.

"Can you locate this kid?" Willis asked, looking at Bradford. "We got to assume he's a student here, someone who didn't like Alex Lyon, or her whole group."

"Give me a couple of hours," Bradford said.

"Don't take too long." Segal said. "The pin may already have popped on the grenade this kid plans to throw."

Chapter 33

Dr. Jeffrey Palmer's office was located in a strip mall the type that had proliferated in Pacific City and southern California in recent years. They were a pot pourri of fast food restaurants, boutiques, hair salons, greeting card stores and other small businesses. This particular L-shaped mall dominated the northeast corner of Wellington and Cedar avenues downtown; an Albertson's grocery store anchoring one end and a café the other. Several businesses and offices, including Palmer's, had their names emblazoned in white across darkened glass fronts. Deluca found a parking spot in front of Palmer's office.

Deluca pushed the door open and a soft bell sounded alerting a receptionist who slid back an opaque glass partition in one wall. The receptionist was a buxom, bleached blond in her late forties with rouged cheeks. "May I help you?" she asked, flashing a wide, white smile, her fleshy face wrinkling in the process.

Deluca flashed his badge. "Lieutenant Deluca. I have an appointment."

The woman nodded, left her seat and disappeared from sight for several seconds before reappearing by opening the one door in the reception area and gesturing for him to come ahead.

Dr. Palmer, in tan slacks and a blue polo shirt, sat behind a large mahogany desk. He rose and greeted Deluca cordially. His soft, moist, handshake led Deluca to drop it quickly.

The doctor was not quite six feet tall with delicate features, thinning brown hair and green eyes. His narrow lips and smooth, pale skin evoked an effeminate image.

Gesturing toward a couch against the wall opposite his desk, Palmer said, "Please have a seat."

Palmer sat in a flowered, winged back chair facing the couch. "How can I help you," he asked.

Deluca took a notebook from the inside pocket of his jacket, placed it on his right leg and said. "I'm investigating the murder of Alex Lyon. I understand she was a patient of yours."

"How did you come to that understanding," Palmer asked, inclining his head to the side and bringing his fingers together in the shape of a steeple in front of his chest.

Deluca studied the good doctor, wondered if he planned to stonewall him. He opted to be direct. "She made several entries in her diary, indicating visits to your office."

Palmer flinched at the diary reference, fixed his stare over Deluca's right shoulder and dropped his hands into his lap. "You know, ethically, even though she's dead, I'm bound by doctor patient privilege to respect the confidentiality of our discussions. Other family members must be considered."

"Doctor. I'm investigating the murder of a seventeen-year old girl. I need to know as much about her life as possible to help us find her killer. I have no desire or intent to publicize anything you say. It will give me a better picture of Alex Lyon and perhaps fill in some pieces of the puzzle surrounding her murder. I can get a court order if necessary."

Palmer pursed his lips and bowed his head in resignation. "Fine. I do want to help. What happened is tragic, tragic."

"Thank you," Deluca said. "Can you tell me why she came to you?"

"Lieutenant, you're making it difficult for me. Surely you can't expect me to reveal that."

"Dr. Palmer, I understand your desire to maintain confidentiality. But we're beyond that now. Surely YOU can understand that. A youngster has been murdered. We need to get the killer off the streets."

Palmer slouched in his chair, exhaled and opened his hands wide, "Her parents were concerned about her sexual behavior. I treat various addictions, chemical and otherwise. I treated her for what we now refer to as sexual addiction."

Chapter 34

Sexual addiction!

Deluca shook his head. "You treated a seventeen year old for a sex disorder? Reminds me of some dirty old man in a trench coat exposing himself in a movie theater, like the guy who had that kids show on television."

"Your reaction is common," Palmer said. "Most people don't understand the concept of sexual addition because there's no physical substance like drugs or alcohol. A chemical addict needs the substance to feel normal and, in his or her mind, to function normally. The same is true of a sex addict. Sex provides the high."

"How do you determine if someone is addicted to sex? Hell! As a kid we all tried to get laid as much as possible. Some girls even liked it."

Palmer smiled. "There's a fine line between normal and abnormal. Everyone's appetite for sex is different. We look for a preoccupation with things sexual. For an adult, frequent random affairs might indicate someone out of control, as might an obsession with pornography or masturbation. In many cases the person engages in risky behavior, which opens them to public exposure. They can't stop despite the risks. In fact, in some instances, the possibility of exposure adds to the pleasure and excitement. A rapist could be a sex addict although we consider rape more of a violent act."

Deluca wrote something in his notebook and paused before continuing his questioning. "But teenage hormones are always raging, even girls if I'm not mistaken. They experiment. They sometimes go too far unable to control their impulses. How do you separate a kid's normal desire and experimentation from addiction?"

"The same as with adults. Preoccupation with things sexual, sleeping around, other risky behavior."

"All right, then. What can cause this?"

"This is more difficult to pinpoint than chemical addiction," Palmer said, in a professorial manner, as if instructing a college class on human behavior. "Some people are genetically disposed to drugs or alcohol, or may be driven by depression or the desire to experience a high which will make them more socially acceptable to peers."

Palmer paused. "The causes of sexual addiction are less clear but most professionals believe a childhood trauma to be a major factor. For example, a recent article published by the University of Pennsylvania reported on a study to determine factors contributing to child prostitution. The study concluded these kids had been abused, 47% of them by relatives, 49% by acquaintances and 4% by strangers. Prostitution sometimes is a manifestation of sexual addiction although other factors contribute."

"Alex was sexually abused then?"

"Don't jump to conclusions, please. She did not confide much in our meetings. The only thing I'm certain of is she was exposed to some traumatic sexual experience, which manifested itself in overt and dangerous sexual behavior. She didn't share anything about such an experience and neither did her parents. They described her as sexually aggressive, no details, no one identified. They wanted me to help her. I doubt they would have brought her in if the abuse took place in their own home or if one of them abused her."

"OK. What did Alex tell you?

"She admitted 'fooling around' convinced everyone did it and her parents had forgotten what it was like to be a teenager."

"Did she mention the names of anyone she might be fooling around with?"

"Again, no. She became silent whenever I tried to push for names."

Deluca flipped through his notebook and stopped at a page he had flagged. "Do the initials TD, JP, SD or TR mean anything to you?"

Palmer pursed his lips once again, a mannerism irritating to Deluca. "No. We barely scratched the surface of her situation and, quite frankly, she was uncooperative."

"How about someone called Bubba?"

"I'm no expert on names." Palmer said, smiling, "but I understand athletes sometimes refer to each other as Bubba. I can't believe any parent would name a child Bubba."

Deluca grinned. "Can you tell me anything else? Did she have trouble with anyone, fear anyone?"

"No! Nothing like that," Palmer responded. "As I said, she was quite cavalier. She perceived her behavior as normal as if everyone did it."

Deluca closed his notebook and stood up. "Thank you for your time doctor. Please call me if you remember anything helpful."

He handed Palmer his card, shook hands, turned to leave, then stopped. His eyes met the doctors and held them.

"We need your help on this doctor," he said, "We really do."

Chapter 35

Jeffrey Palmer wiped his brow with a handkerchief and waited several minutes to be sure the detective had gone. Then, he got up from his chair, walked to his desk, picked up the phone and punched the intercom button.

"Yes, doctor," his receptionist, said.

"Joyce, Cancel my appointments for the rest of the day. I need to leave the office in a few minutes."

He offered no explanation for his abrupt departure and none was expected. Last minute changes happened often.

Palmer replaced the phone in its cradle and slumped down in his chair. The visit by Deluca unnerved him. He grabbed the edge of his desk with both hands. He didn't like discussing patients with police. A potential lawsuit for breaching a patient's confidentiality would be ruinous.

He hoped Lyon's case would enhance his standing in the professional community by blazing new ground in the study of sex addiction. But if it surfaced he had divulged confidential information about a client forget it.

He needed time to think. He hadn't told Deluca everything. He was sure what he knew was not critical to a murder. Revealing the identity of some of those in Alex's diary could only cause harm to them and to himself since he should have notified child protective services a long time ago.

He sat up straight, placed his elbows on his desk and steepled his fingers under his chin. Hell, he had to protect doctor/client privilege, didn't he?

Chapter 36

Deluca's visit to Dr. Palmer produced more questions than answers. He needed some clarification from someone he trusted. Twenty-minutes after leaving Dr. Palmer, he walked into the carpeted office of Joan Weston PhD. Weston did the psychological examinations on all candidates for employment with the PCPD. She also worked with veteran officers involved in traumatic events like a shooting or an accident involving violent death. Despite the disdain most police officers had for psychologists, Weston had a solid reputation. She gave sound advice and maintained confidentiality with a religious fervor.

In her late forties, Weston was a tall, slender woman with black hair peppered with gray, which she did not attempt to conceal. She stood beside her desk with her hands folded in front of her as Deluca entered her office.

"Thanks for seeing me on such short notice, Joan," Deluca said, addressing her informally and extending his hand. He and Weston had been friends for years and their professional relationship was cordial and relaxed.

"No problem, JD," Weston said, taking his hand and signaling with a sweeping gesture for him to sit on a couch butted against the wall opposite her desk. She sat in a comfortable stuffed chair facing him.

"What can I do for you?"

"I'm investigating the murder of the East High Cheerleader," he said.

"Yes, I've read the Times stories."

"She was a client of one your colleagues, Dr. Palmer."

"Jeffrey and I run into each other at conferences occasionally. He was the guest speaker at one recent workshop I attended---spoke on sexual addiction."

Deluca's reaction did not escape Weston.

"He treated her for that?"

"Yes. We've discovered she was sexually active, maybe with adults. I'm having trouble accepting a seventeen year old as a sex addict. What's your professional opinion?

"Well, first sex addiction is not recognized as a legitimate psychiatric disorder although research does indicate many individuals, primarily men, have displayed the signs of addictive sexual behavior. A woman or girl might also show such signs. But, second, I couldn't make such a judgment without talking with the patient."

"Joan. I need your help here. What would be your best guess?"

Weston considered the question for a few moments before offering an opinion. "From my experience, and the published studies, most adolescents who exhibit anti-social sexual behavior have been victims of abuse."

"Can we narrow down who it might be?"

"Depends. Any adult within the child's circle of relatives or acquaintances--a parent, an aunt, an uncle, an older sibling, a teacher, a member of the clergy could be the abuser. Need I recount the recent troubles of the Catholic Church and its priests?

Deluca rubbed his chin and his left hand went to his right shoulder.

"So! Any particular clues to look for?" He asked.

"That's difficult to say, JD, without speaking to the child, which is obviously not possible here. Sexual predators are clever and careful. They win the confidence of their victims. Sometimes they convince them what they are doing is normal or it's the victim's fault. Give me something specific to go on and I might be more able to help."

She spread her hands in front of her inviting Deluca to elaborate.

Deluca didn't respond so Weston offered another view.

"You know, JD, today's mores and attitudes towards sex have changed, particularly among teenagers. Kids are experimenting at younger and younger ages. Some sex acts are not even considered sex. Anything short of vaginal intercourse---oral sex and anal penetration---for example, are in the category of "non-sex." The kids think they're safer because they don't lead to pregnancy. They discount STD's."

She shook her head and continued. "Let me illustrate what I'm talking about. A few days ago, some parents brought in their daughter caught by an assistant principal performing oral sex on her boyfriend in a vacant classroom. The girl was mortified, not by what she had done, but because she had been caught. The parents couldn't, didn't understand."

"I'm with the parents," Deluca said. "What you're saying is that Lyon's behavior, in her own mind, and from what she was exposed to, was OK---not abuse.

"I'm afraid so. The culture is more open now. Porn is easily viewed and downloaded from the Internet. TV shows are more explicit. Kids aren't living in a vacuum. They're aroused. What some of them are doing would curl your hair. The girl I described whined about how her parents overreacted. Many of her friends had done the same thing. It was OK as long as you liked the boy. Abuse clearly did not influence this girl's actions. Nor would I characterize her as a sex addict. Sorry!"

Deluca exhaled, his frustration evident. He got up from the couch to leave, then remembered something. "Joan. Alex put an entry in her diary about a Rainbow party. Any idea what that is?"

Weston's face drained of color. "Yes. I'm afraid I do."

Deluca held out his hands encouraging her response.

"Ok. Something else you won't believe. A Rainbow party is when several girls, each wearing a different color lipstick, perform fellatio on a group of boys. When they're finished, the boys line up and the result resembles a Rainbow."

"Sorry I asked," Deluca said, his face crimson.

"Thought you would be."

"Thanks again Joan, I appreciate the time and insight. Wish we had more to give you on Alex's background."

"So do I, JD. Call me if you get more specifics." She extended her hand, which Deluca clasped with both of his.

In the car, on the way back to headquarters, Deluca shook his head in frustration. First, a psychologist talks about sex addiction in a kid. Another says this may be normal behavior. Then lipstick can turn a party into an orgy. He found the spot on his right shoulder. We still better follow up on the abuse angle. At least rule it out. Check family members who might be in the system or if there have been any reports taken by Child Protective Services. He pulled out his cell phone to call Segal.

His shoulder ached more than usual.

CHAPTER 37

Everyone crowded into Deluca's office.

Deluca, in a starched white shirt with sleeves rolled to the elbows, a black tie and gray slacks, stood in front of the white board behind his desk with a blue marker in his hand poised to write. Segal, also without a jacket, leaned against the opposite wall while Styles, in black skirt and white blouse, sat in a metal folding chair to the right front of the desk. She had a "Palm Pilot" in her lap, writing notes on the screen with a small plastic stylus. Willis sat next to Styles.

"O.K," Deluca said, breaking the silence. "Let's go over what we've got. Styles. You're up!"

"I checked the file on Eduardo Ramos, besides the four rapes that sent him to Atascadero, he was the prime suspect in at least three others. None of those women could, or would, ID him; but same MO: Women out jogging alone at night, attacked from behind, dragged off the road or trail, raped and in two instances, sodomized, all beaten and threatened, panties taken. The rape of his babysitter was different, target of opportunity, took her panties as well."

Deluca jotted down notes on the white board. Segal stole a glance at the expanse of thigh exposed by Styles' crossed legs

"Ramos was arrested twice at his home for assaulting his wife," Styles continued. "She took a bad beating but refused to press charges each time. He struck again last night. Put the wife in the hospital. She may not recover. Certainly confirms he's back in town and capable of murder."

"Bastard," said Segal.

"We get anything at school?" Deluca asked.

"Maybe," said Styles. "I contacted the principal, the activities guy and several football players and cheerleaders, friends of Alex."

She scrolled through her notes. "Alex partied hearty like most kids her age, some sex and drugs. She went to the post game party but no one knew how long she stayed, when she left or if she left with anyone, people coming and going. Some in the group paired off for sex. One of the guys claims he and Alex played touchy feely, nothing more. The boyfriend wasn't there, injured in the game.

"Also. Get this. One of the football players, Jeremy Peters, admitted kids knew Ramos. They got steroids and almost anything else from him, including meth. And, they met him in the Park to make their buys.

“This kid, Jeremy,” she continued, “might be the JP in the diary. He said he and Alex hooked up a couple of times. But we can scratch him off as a suspect. Other kids verified he was among the last to leave the party, around midnight.”

Deluca paused in thought for a moment, then on the white board under the words SCHOOL in block letters, he wrote and underlined: party, sex, drugs, Ramos. Turning back toward Styles he asked, "What do you think?"

"The kids’ stories, except for Peters, are too similar. Had to be rehearsed. A couple of them mentioned Ramos when pressed."

"You think one of them did it and the others are covering up?" Deluca asked.

"No,” Styles said. "But they're hiding something."

"Which one can we break?" Segal asked.

"One of the girls," Styles said. “Nancy Holmes. She was frightened. Won't take much to get her to talk.”

Deluca turned toward Willis and Segal. “Did we turn up anything on Reaper?”

“Yes and no,” Segal said. “The Columbine angle might not be as far-fetched as we thought. Turns out the Reaper note to the activities guy was copied from one of the Columbine shooters and a tagger at East High has been going by that handle. The SRO, Bradford is trying to ID him. He promised to get back to us fast but nothing yet.”

“OK!” Deluca said. “Stay on that. Cara, interrogate the Holmes girl, break her story.”

“I talked to the shrink, Dr. Jeffrey Palmer,” Deluca continued. “After some coaxing, he admitted to treating Alex for what he called sexual addiction. Parents brought her in concerned about her behavior.”

“Ya got to be kidding,” Segal blurted.

“Nope. That’s what the man said. We can accept it or not. The girl whored around, why doesn’t matter. Her reckless acts put her at risk, and widens the pool of suspects.”

The room became quiet, each detective wrestling with their own thoughts. They had seen many different manifestations of human behavior, some violent, some bizarre, some comical, some sad. This was hard to categorize.

Deluca broke the awkward silence. “Let’s turn up the heat, people. McClusky’s in my face and the Chief called me again. ‘Just checking,’ in his words; the mayor’s no doubt turning the screws. The politicians want Ramos for this. Might get the ACLU and MALDEF to back off.

“Let’s forget politics people, not in our control. Our job is to get this guy off the streets.”

Chapter 38

Reaper worried the note had been a bad idea. The school dude probably pissed his pants, which was good. Then he probably told the police, not good. He wasn't ready. He counted on the fact he had only been at East High a short time and that none of his crew would give him up to get the time he needed.

He turned on his computer and accessed his email account. He didn't use Reaper as his screen name so they couldn't track him that way. He hoped the local cops were not very savvy about the Internet.

Once online, he pecked out a message to his crew:

Get ready. The time has come. Meet me at the mall in the usual place tomorrow at 3:00. We will rewrite the history books. No one will ever forget us. We are the LAW!!!!!

*****

Reaper exited his account and shut down his computer. He reached into his desk drawer and pulled out the list of targets along with the newspaper accounts of Alex Lyon's murder. The guy who wrote the stuff about Columbine didn't know how close he came to the truth. He laughed aloud.

Shifting his attention to the list, he made a notation next to Lyon's name, crossed it out and put the paper back in the drawer. The cops would find it later and discover the truth.

Reaper sighed, leaned back in his chair and closed his eyes.

The bitch deserved to die.

Chapter 39

They called themselves Raven and Spyder. Their real names were Jamie Dressler and Ron Spivey; the friends Reaper counted on to help him carry out his plan. They hunched over a workbench in the back of Raven's garage, cluttered with boxes, old furniture and hundreds of odds and ends his parents had accumulated over the years. The main door was closed and even, had it been open, the boys couldn't be seen from the street.

Good thing. They were cleaning the two Glock 19 semiautomatic pistols they would use when Reaper gave the word. Two loaded fifteen round magazines lay beside each weapon. The pistols belonged to Raven's father who had left an extensive gun collection behind after a messy divorce.

"The murder of that bitch might ruin everything," Raven said as he wiped down the barrel of his Glock. "The cops aren't stupid. The pig at school knows where we hang out. What if they drag everybody in, start asking questions."

"So what. No one else is aware of the plan," Spyder said, shaking his head and completing the reassembly of his pistol. "You think he offed her?"

Raven smirked. "Offed her? What are you, a Mafia hit man?

Spyder's face flushed. "I'm just saying. His idea. Would he do something to fuck it up?"

"Maybe. The fucker is crazy."

"What's that make us?" Spyder asked.

Chapter 40

Monday night meant football.

They sat on a couch in Tony Segal's den facing a big screen TV; two bottles of beer, a bag of chips and a container of onion dip rested on the low coffee table in front of them. Segal wore a multi-colored Hawaiian shirt, baggy tan shorts and sandals; Deluca a gray, short sleeve polo, jeans and running shoes.

The game, Raiders versus Eagles in Oakland, was a circus. Cameras focused on the stands as much as the field panning the seats occupied by the "Raider Nation." Most sported silver and black outfits like the guy now caught in a close-up. His face painted half-silver, half black, he donned a spiked helmet, spiked shoulder pads, and a silver breastplate.

"Christ, can you picture going to a game looking like that dumb bastard?" Segal asked.

"Only if I was zooted," Deluca said. "Which he undoubtedly is."

Segal snorted, reached for a chip, swiped it through the onion dip and changed the subject. "What's your take on the kid's murder?"

Shoptalk was verboten during Monday night football, a ritual since the death of Deluca's wife. Sports and women topped the list of hot topics. Segal, though married, flirted with most gals he met; his banter with the secretaries and female officers at work bordered on sexual harassment. He got away with it because of his easy-going, disarming manner characteristic of many fat men. His quips were laughed off, often returned in kind. Other officers would have been braced before their supervisors facing discipline. And, of course, Deluca was Segal's supervisor.

Segal was relentless in his attempt to hook-up Deluca. He often broached the subject when they were alone as he had at O'Hara's. Not something Deluca cared to discuss so he was more than happy to talk about the case.

"The girl's recklessness disturbs me. But this sex addiction stuff is crap. The shrinks come up with some phantom disease to explain everything and to keep people from taking responsibility for their actions; a kid's a jerk, he's ADD, he's truant, school phobia, screws around, sex addict. What crap. I can believe raging hormones, lack of parent supervision, too much time on their hands, drugs."

Segal grinned. "I'm with ya. If my daughter has a diary, I don't want to see what's in it."

Deluca felt the same about his own daughter. He remembered some of the sexual fantasies he'd had as a kid, glad his parents couldn't read his mind. No way he'd keep a journal.

Cheering coming from the TV distracted them. Oakland had scored and the camera focused on a big-breasted woman in a low cut black and silver blouse, jumping up and down and waving her arms.

"Man," Segal said, "get a load of those jugs. I'd like to bury my face between 'em."

"You'd suffocate," Deluca said, grinning.

When the noise subsided, and the TV station switched to a commercial, Segal returned the discussion to the case. "We're going in all different directions on this thing, friends, some Goth wacko, a dickhead rapist. We need to focus on the old reliable trio, means, motive, opportunity."

"OK," Deluca said. "We know the means, a belt or cord possibly from a sweat suit."

"Yeah! But here we go again. Every guy in the world has a belt, several belts. Every damn Joe jock jogs."

Segal opened his arms wide. "Hey! What is that?"

"What's what?"

"What I just said. Joe jock jogs; a kind of literary thing poets or writers use. Something we learned in high school English."

"You actually paid attention in class?"

"Don't bust my balls, college boy. At least I speak English, not like some of the turds we deal with. These mopes run down this city, this country. You need a translator to talk to most a' them. You go into a store, sounds like Tijuana with all that jabbering. They speak more Spanish than English at my kid's school."

Deluca turned and looked his former partner in the eyes.

"Don't give me the stare, JD. You know I'm not blowing smoke. You're too politically correct to admit it."

Deluca took a swig of his beer and put it down on the coffee table. "You sound like a jerk spouting that nonsense, big man. What I believe or don't believe about immigrants or immigration is irrelevant. We took an oath to protect this community, English speakers or not. We both look bad when you talk like that. I'm your boss and former partner. You sound like a skinhead"

"True is all," Segal said. He grabbed a fist full of chips and turned back toward the TV.

After a moment, Deluca said with a grin, "Alliteration."

"What?"

"Alliteration. Joe jock jogs is an example of alliteration."

"I knew it," Segal said. "I coulda been a poet."

Deluca laughed and they were soon distracted by the game action, an Eagle player dancing in the end zone after returning a kick-off all the way. The Raider Nation was quiet. Only the sporadic clapping and cheering of the few Eagle fans in attendance could be heard.

"Man! Those bastards better watch their backs after the game," Segal announced taking a swig of his beer. "You don't cheer for the Eagles in Oakland,"

Chapter 40

Deluca drove home after the game at Segal's.

He pulled into the parking lot of the Sea Breeze Condominium Complex and parked his 1965 classic Mustang convertible, his one extravagance, into his designated garage. He paid thirty dollars a month extra for the privilege of securing his car in a locked garage instead of under an open carport like most residents. He didn't want to risk having it vandalized. He knew few of his neighbors and couldn't count on any of them to watch the car.

Deluca squeezed out of the driver's side door, grabbed his battered black briefcase from the back seat, and locked the car. He secured the garage and walked from the parking lot fifty feet to the stairs leading to his second floor apartment. He opened the door, flipped on a light switch and kicked the door closed behind him. He put his briefcase on one of the chairs around a small glass-topped table adjacent to the kitchen, then got a wineglass and a bottle of burgundy from the cupboard over the sink. He returned to the table to review his notes on the Lyon murder and to scan the diary again.

Sitting alone, he reflected on the quiet, which enveloped him like a warm blanket. The only discernable sound came from the low hum of the refrigerator. He liked his solitude, used it to recharge his energy. He didn't need someone around him all the time. The noise, crush of people at work every day drained him.

His wife, on the other hand, had been gregarious. She pushed him to socialize. She once had him fill out one of those inventories, which assigned personality types a series of letters. He couldn't remember all of the letters and their meanings, except that "I" stood for introvert and "E" extrovert. He and Kathleen turned out to be opposites. But unlike the old saying that did not "attract" them to each other as much as pushed them apart.

His work consumed him and was another point of contention. Once embroiled in an investigation, he often neglected family responsibilities. They didn't fight about this, no yelling and screaming. Kathleen showed her displeasure by extended periods of silence; she spoke only when asked a question. Eventually, they would have a long discussion; Deluca would apologize and promise to do better.

He and Kathleen had been high school sweethearts. She followed him to California. Her death created a void in his life. He missed her more than he could say---or have imagined. He didn't brood. If he thought about it too much, his work suffered and he couldn't support his daughter who had her own problems coping.

His daughter, a student at San Diego State University, lived on campus. He drove down the coast once a month to have dinner with her. Their former close relationship was now strained, neither eager to discuss Kathleen's death. Small talk dominated their conversations, the weather, her grades, a roommate's boyfriends. He wished it were different but not enough to change things.

He leaned back in his chair and shook his head to clear his mind. He opened Alex's diary again and spent the next hour scanning the pages. Nothing new caught his attention.

He closed the diary and studied the names and incidents he had written on his legal pad; those he felt were significant or at least could be helpful. Something did strike him as odd. Alex had been murdered on a Friday night, possibly while partying with friends. Football games were on Friday's, as were the post-game parties. Presumably, Alex would attend with boyfriend Tommy Deerfield, the quarterback. Yet the sexual romps between Alex and Bubba happened on Saturday nights. Mr. Lyon hadn't mentioned Alex going out on Saturday's.

Confused, Deluca opened his briefcase and rummaged through the papers inside until he found East High's football schedule. With one stadium in the city, and three high schools, teams alternated game nights. But with the exception of one Thursday and one Saturday, all of East High's games had occurred on Fridays. He checked his notes and the date of the Saturday game. No encounter with Bubba on that night, unless Alex did not record it, which didn't make sense given her penchant for highlighting her sexual activities. Deluca made a note to check with Mr. Lyon about Alex's Saturday night dates.

He rubbed his eyes, took his wine and stood before the sliding glass door, which led to his small, seldom used balcony. The curtains were open. Several spotlights illuminated the carports below. The full moon glided between fast moving clouds. When it did show itself, Deluca thought the old man's face etched in the surface mocked him for not having found the murderer of Alex Lyon. The veteran detective raised his glass in a salute.

We're going to get him old man, he said, drained the remaining liquid and shuffled toward the bathroom to shower.

Chapter 41

Jimmy Phelan leaned over and kissed Peggy Deerfield on the lips.

He licked his way down her neck to her breasts and began sucking on her right nipple when she arched her back and turned away. Phelan and Deerfield had been seeing each other for several months, ever since she split from her husband. Her son was the quarterback on Phelan's team but that did not keep them apart. Yet something had been nagging at Deerfield since the murder of Alex Lyon

"What happened that night," she asked without preamble.

"What night?

"The night Alex was killed."

Phelan, who had been nibbling on her shoulder and rubbing her arm, stopped and rolled on to his back. He stared at the ceiling a few minutes before asking: "What do you mean?"

"You came over really late, half in the bag, scratches on your neck and arms. And, you couldn't."

She didn't finish the sentence. It had been one of the few times "Mr. Happy" did not perform. Phelan, embarrassed, blamed the booze but suspected something else, something he couldn't reveal to Peggy.

"Sorry I disappointed you," he said, "I was drunk, blowing off steam. We had just won a big game, made the playoffs."

Deerfield didn't buy it. His reputation as a ladies man worried her. "What about the scratches? Were you with someone else before coming here."

"No. No," Phelan said and snuggled into her from behind. He got hard as he pressed into her. She had self-esteem issues since her husband dumped her. Phelan's attention flattered her. She knew he had his choice of many women. Still, she worried.

"You didn't have anything to do with Alex's death, did you, Jimmy?" she blurted. She propped herself up on one elbow, turned, and looked at him in the dim light cast by the one night lamp she always kept on during their lovemaking.

"Baby, you can't believe that," Phelan said as he brushed a strand of hair from her forehead and rubbed her neck. "Alex was a kid; I'm a teacher. I wouldn't go there," he lied.

Phelan saw the indecision on her face, pulled her toward him and kissed her hard, dropping his hand to her breast. Peggy gave in to the kiss and asked no more questions as Phelan pushed her on her back.

Phelan moved his body in rhythm with the woman beneath him, but his thoughts wandered. He couldn't account for the time between leaving the bar and showing up at Deerfield's. He kept thinking about Alex. He feared the worst but felt he could never hurt anyone. Yet, why couldn't he remember?

Maybe he didn't want to.

Chapter 42

They sat alone on concrete benches at the back entrance to the mall. The only people who came this way were workers and those who couldn't find a parking space when the place was crowded.

Reaper leaned into Spyder and Raven and outlined his plan in a barely audible voice. "The quad at school is locked at night," he explained, "but only by four iron gates ten feet high. Dudes scale those all the time."

Raven smirked, making him look like a nerd, which everybody called him when he wasn't around.

Reaper shook his head and continued: "The night before it goes down, we'll climb over a back gate, one behind the school facing out onto the playing fields. We'll stash our weapons and ski masks in our lockers and take off."

"What if someone sees us?" Raven asked, raising his eyes to face Reaper.

"Not gonna happen," Reaper said, grabbing the front of Raven's shirt, his glare penetrating.

"Ok. Ok, he's right Rave," Spyder said to break the tension and reassure Raven, the weak link in the plan.

"The roving security patrol goes from school to school," he said; takes them a couple of hours to hit all the schools and come back. We can be in and out in a few minutes. Piece a' cake."

"Right," Reaper agreed. "The next day, at lunch, we go to our lockers in the quad, and grab the weapons and masks. One guy is going to start a food fight. He's not aware of our real plan. When it hits the fan, and the noon duty aides are distracted, we go after everyone on our list. Easy."

"Then" Reaper continued, "we head over to the social studies wing for the teachers."

"Why there?" Spyder asked.

"Two reasons," Reaper replied. "Half those teachers are jocks, like that bastard Phelan, who's been on our asses all year. I can't wait to see his face when I blast him."

They all laughed. "Yeah," Raven said for emphasis.

"A second reason," Reaper explained, "is that the back door to that wing opens out onto the maintenance road behind the school where a drainage ditch runs all the way to the park. We'll be sheltered from the main road."

Raven and Spyder admired Reaper. Their faces lit up. He had thought this out.

"We'll run out the back door to the drainage ditch once we're through messing up as many fuckers as we can," Reaper said. "We drop our guns, masks and sweats in the ditch and walk back to school across the baseball field to the gym. Everybody will be so fucked up on campus nobody will be looking at us. They never lock the back door to the Gym so guys can go to the crapper during PE."

"Damn," said Spyder. "We can pull this off."

"What about the list? Everybody on it won't be in social studies?" Raven asked. He moved a couple of steps back from Reaper afraid he might get mad again.

Reaper remained calm. Raven had a point. "Yeah, you're right Rave, but this is the only way we have a chance to get away. Like the army, dude, plans change."

"Damn," Spyder repeated. "We can do this."

"I told you I was smarter than Harris and Klebold!" Reaper said, smiling.

He didn't tell them things wouldn't go quite like he explained. You can't be alive and be a martyr.

Chapter 43

The detective/FBI special agent hunched over a computer keyboard in an all but empty squad room. Some privacy was afforded by six-foot high partitions separating cubicles. The interrogation rooms, down the hall, kept suspects out of the area.

Most of the day squad had gone and the night detail straggled in. The agent, positioned to block the screen from passersby, glanced around but doubted anyone would pay attention to a colleague on a computer. These days, detectives spent much time scrolling for information on-line or within the department database. Still, it paid to be careful.

The agent typed in the code word to gain unrestricted access to all department records. The database had been created three years earlier when paper files were scanned into the system. Criminal records and personnel information was now available electronically. Crimes were listed by type, known criminals filed alphabetically and local gangs identified. Searches could be conducted by in-putting a keyword like "rape," which generated a chronology of rapes committed in the city for the last five years. Another feature permitted senior staff officers, and others with the proper authorization, to view an officer's arrest record.

A patrol officer or detective could view only his or her own file while lieutenants had access to any record within their division. The Chief and division captains had unrestricted access, as did the agent; hence, the desire to conceal the screen from those who might be curious.

After in-putting the six-digit code and scanning the main menu, the agent opted to do a search entering the phrase "deaths, officer involved" in the oblong box provided. In seconds, an Incident Report Form dated April 12, fourteen months earlier, appeared. It contained details of a traffic stop during which a man named Juan Alomar died. Alomar had become belligerent, struggled with officers and was subdued by pepper spray after being placed in a chokehold. He went into cardiac arrest at the scene and died at the hospital.

All deaths in police custody required a review by an in house panel and the result was included with the incident report. The panel, chaired by Captain William McClusky, cleared the officers of any wrongdoing. The Orange County DA's office concurred.

The agent made several notes then scrolled down to the next document. Dated three months after the report just examined, it detailed events leading to the death of one Edgar Salazar, who died in police custody after a routine traffic stop. Salazar bolted from officers after being pulled over for running a red light. Officers chased him down and subdued him with their batons. He collapsed and died in a holding cell at police headquarters. The autopsy report, while indicating the cause of death as a ruptured spleen, also listed cirrhosis of the liver as a contributing factor. Officer Randy Cunningham signed this form, like the first, along with Officer Riley Jones. The review panel, again chaired by McClusky, found no cause for further action or discipline. The Orange County District Attorney's office determined "justifiable force" had been used restraining Salazar.

Voices could be heard several cubicles away but the agent, reluctant to stop, scrolled down to see how many files remained. There were four, all related to an incident last May, a disturbance in Wellington Park. The agent did not print them for fear the noise might attract attention but continued reading and taking notes.

The next file detailed a Cinqo de Mayo celebration attended by five hundred people, mostly Latinos. During the festivities, several men became enraged when the toilets overflowed in the public rest room. Drunk, the men smashed urinals and other facilities with baseball bats. Officers dispatched to the scene claimed they were confronted by at least two bat-wielding Latinos later identified as gang-bangers. Officers pummeled one man, Julio Peter Vargas, when he refused to drop a bat. Kicked, punched and tasered Vargas died at a hospital.

Despite the beating Vargas had taken, the coroner established the cause of death as persistent use of methamphetamines, which were in his system at the time. Officers Randy Cunningham, "Pops" Parker, Riley Jones and Donald Williams filed identical reports on the incident. The review panel led by McClusky found no culpability on the part of the officers for the death. The district attorney's office concurred.

What the hell!

The agent examined the records further and found a Los Angeles Times Article on the three incidents. Several representatives of MALDEF charged that the deaths reflected a pattern of abuse by the PCPD. One man, attorney Antonio Victor Gonzales, claimed these incidents were civil rights violations and a disturbing example of how the PCPD routinely exceeded the use of force guidelines.

The agent finished taking notes, exited the program and shut down the computer. As the screen went from blue to black detective John Goodman strolled into the squad room. He peered over the top of a cubicle close to the agent.

"Hey douche bag," he shouted, "You're makin us look bad. What'ya still doing here?"

Big Tony Segal smiled. "Tryin to pick up something cheap on E-bay, what else?"

"Yeah! Some new sex toy I bet," Goodman said. He stepped into the cubicle and thrust his hips forward to simulate sex.

"Bite me" Segal said good-naturedly, stood up and brushed passed Goodman.

"Ok," Goodman called out as Segal headed for the door. "Just keep your hands above the sheets tonight."

His guttural laugh echoed through the squad room.

Segal looked around as he left. He thought another detective had been in the room with him but was clearly gone now.

CHAPTER 44

The memorial service was held in the East High gym.

Deluca stood by the door, as the family, friends and classmates of Alex Lyon filed past. Next to him, on a tripod, stood an enlarged color photo of Alex in her cheerleader uniform, her smile radiant, her blue eyes alive and alert. Deluca eyed each mourner as they walked by in hopes of learning something from their demeanor. Many of those entering the gym looked from the picture to Deluca, as if anticipating an explanation of what had happened. Others shuffled by, eyes averted, staring straight ahead or at the ground.

The East High Gym seated two thousand people but only one section was used tonight. The large sliding doors dividing the Gym into separate facilities for P.E classes were closed and served as a backdrop for the ceremony. Ten chairs were set up, centered facing the bleachers, flowers positioned at each end of the chairs. A podium with a microphone also faced the stands. Seated were Mr. And Mrs. Lyon, Brent Lyon, the brother, Principal William Farraday, the Lyon's pastor, Reverend Reinhardt, three cheerleaders, football coach Jimmy Phelan and Tommy Deerfield, the boyfriend.

Before the ceremony, a man approached Mr. Lyon and the two engaged in a heated exchange. Lyon gesticulated with his arms, pushed his face close to the other man's jaw, seemed about to strike him when pulled away by his wife; the man slinked away and found a seat in the stands. Deluca observed the confrontation, wondered what prompted it but before he could think on it further, the ceremony started.

Principal Farraday rose from his seat and walked to the microphone. He welcomed all those who had come to honor Alex and nodded his head in the direction of one of the side doors. On cue, the door opened and the school choir of fifteen boys and girls, dressed in black and white, marched in and formed around a piano placed to one side of the bleachers. The choir director, a short, balding man in a black suit, white shirt and black tie, raised his hand. When he dropped it, the group began to sing:

Did you know that you're my hero
You're everything I wish I could be

Tears flowed as individuals in the audience felt the pain of losing a loved one

I can fly higher than an eagle
For you are the wind beneath my wings.

The lyrics hit home to many, especially Alex's parents; grief stricken, eyes lowered, teary. They sat transfixed, bodies rigid, as if the slightest movement would disrespect their daughter's memory.

The voices of the choir reverberated with intensity as they finished their salute to Alex:

Thank you, thank you,
Thank God for you, the wind beneath my
wings.

Sobbing punctuated the quiet of the gym; cheerleaders sitting next to the family embraced. The minister, a veteran of many similar ceremonies, sat, lips pressed together, hands folded in his lap. He waited a few moments, stood up and walked to the podium, scanning the crowd.

"We are here to celebrate the life of Alex Lyon," he began, his eyes widening, the corners of his mouth turning upward, "not to mourn her death. At times like these we ask God why he would take from us one so young. We become angry with God, doubt his wisdom and compassion; challenge him to give us a reason for such a tragedy. But I hope you believe, as I do, when we leave this earth life is not over. We enter a new phase of existence with God and all of our loved ones who have gone before us. Death is not the final word. It is the door to eternal life and happiness."

He paused for a moment before continuing, his voice sharp, firm, confident. "Take pleasure in the short time Alex Lyon spent with us, in the joy she brought to family and friends. Yes, she was here all too briefly but long enough to leave an indelible mark on our hearts. She remains a shining light in our memories. We will miss her. We will meet her again."

The minister sat down, followed to the podium by coach Phelan and Principal Farraday. Both praised Alex and declared how much she meant to the school and the football team. Phelan returned to his seat after a few words, head bowed, elbows resting on his knees.

The last to speak was Kitty Richmond, a cheerleader, and Alex Lyon's best friend. Two other cheerleaders offering moral support flanked her.

Richmond had written a poem. She began in a barely audible voice, her sadness reflected in every word:

For Alex

Life is a gift
Which can be taken away
Come what may.
At any time,
Before we know what we have.

Your life was our gift
Which you shared
Come what may.
Joy, fun, laughter,
It was over
Before we knew what we had.

We cherish the memories of what you brought
To all of us.
And we will regret forever,
That it was over,
Before we knew what we had.

When Kitty finished, the three girls embraced and were joined by Principal Farraday who engulfed them with his long arms. He held that position for a few moments, turned to the microphone and announced the end of the service.

In the car, on the way back to police headquarters, Deluca reflected on the ceremony. He wondered who the guy arguing with Mr. Lyon was but he dwelled more on the pastor's words, particularly the phrase, "Death is not the final word." Deluca, although baptized a Catholic, was not religious, had not been since his college days when, as a history major, he learned of the machinations of the early Pope's and the corruption rampant among church leaders. Disillusioned, he never again went to confession or attended mass. Vietnam convinced him of the futility of prayer and the unlikely existence of a just God. Nevertheless, he knew many people took comfort in the belief in an afterlife. He would never criticize their faith. But as a pragmatist and detective, his slant on life differed from theirs. He expected to ensure that in the case of Alex Lyon, justice and not death, would be the final word, whether an afterlife existed or not.

Chapter45

Antonio Victor Gonzales was a local attorney.

He worked primarily for MALDEF, the Mexican-American Legal Defense and Education Foundation. A dapper little man of forty-two, he sported a thick, black mustache and wore his long hair in a ponytail. He eschewed the usual business attire for faded jeans, loafers and outdated string ties. But his outward, laid back appearance was deceptive. He did his homework, knew the law, was tenacious in court. He tangled often with the Pacific City Police Department over discrimination and harassment claims. Many officers bristled at his recent excessive force comments on TV.

Gonzales had a small two-room suite in Pacific City on the second floor of a strip mall adjacent to a personal storage facility. The cramped reception area had space for five straight-backed metal chairs, a freestanding magazine rack and a secretary's desk. A portrait of civil rights activist Cesar Chavez hung on one wall.

Gonzales' windowless office was sparsely furnished with a couch, a stuffed chair, a large mahogany desk and a black leather swivel chair. One wall held built-in floor to ceiling bookshelves containing an assortment of reference books, criminal codes and California histories. The other walls were bare except for the one behind his desk, which displayed his UCLA diploma.

Gonzales often worked late; his secretary had gone home three hours earlier. The outer office was deserted. He stood by his desk, placing several file folders into his black attaché case when he heard the outside door open. His own partially closed door blocked his view into the reception area.

"Is that you Maria," he called. His secretary lived nearby and sometimes came back to shoo him home. When he got no response, he tensed but quickly dismissed his fear. He had the reputation of seeing anyone, regardless of the hour or lack of an appointment.

But Gonzales was startled when his office door swung open and two young men appeared in the doorway; in their early twenties, dressed in ragged jeans, white t-shirts rolled up over their shoulders, black Doc Marten boots. Multiple rings adorned their pierced ears and shaved heads. One had two silver studs in his lower lip.

"Kind of late guys," Gonzales said, in a controlled voice, hoping he would appear unconcerned by their presence. "I'm on my way out," he added. "Drop by tomorrow, I can help you then."

"Don't need no help from you," two studs in his lower lip said as he stepped toward Gonzales. "We ain't wetbacks."

"Oh, oh," Gonzales thought. *"These guys are not friendlies. How the hell do I get out of this?"*

Ignoring the wetback comment, he asked, "How can I help you?"

"You can get out of this city, motherfucker," two studs in his lower lip said, putting his hands on his hips. His partner kept silent but twisted his mouth into a sneer." Look guys," Gonzales said, still trying to sound like the voice of reason. "I'm not out to piss anyone off. I just do my job."

He took a step toward the men. He did not see, nor did he react to, the roundhouse right hand delivered by two studs in his lower lip. Staggered backward by the blow, Gonzales tried to get his hands up to protect himself. Never a fighter, he was driven to the floor by multiple blows and kicked several times in the side.

"Jesus, they broke my ribs" was his last conscious thought before a kick to the head brought on darkness.

Laughing uproariously, as if their behavior was the funniest thing in the world, the two skinheads emptied desk drawers and filing cabinets, scattering the contents. They swept books from shelves, ripping pages. As a coup de grace, two studs in his lower lip slashed the cushions of the couch with a switchblade carried in his boot.

The men left the suite and descended the stairs to the parking lot. They did not run; just two guys out for a stroll. When they reached the sidewalk, two studs in his lower lip stopped and looked across the street. A man sitting in a blue Ford minivan nodded. Two studs in his lower lip returned the nod, slapped his buddy on the shoulder and they walked away.

The man in the blue van jotted several notes in his spiral notebook, slipped the book into his jacket pocket and turned on the ignition. He pulled his jacket over his badge and gun, put the car in gear and drove off.

Chapter 46

Four men sat in a corner booth of the dimly lit bar.

They met in different restaurants, in different cities, once a month. This group, minus one, constituted the leadership council of the PCPD Chapter of the White Aryan Resistance. One of the men was a detective, two patrol officers. The leader was Captain William, Wild Bill, McClusky. The group set the agenda for the cell although most members were unaware of its existence. They kept their voices low though they were the only customers.

McClusky took a typed sheet of paper from a manila folder resting on the table in front of him. It contained a list of names the first of which was Antonio Victor Gonzales, the attorney for MALDEF.

"Where are we on the Gonzales matter," he asked, looking at detective John Goodman.

"The beaner is in the Hospital," Goodman answered. "He got roughed up good."

McClusky smiled. "I trust the culprits will be difficult to find," he said, pronouncing the words like a British barrister.

Goodman rolled his eyes, a comedian ready to deliver the punch line. "I caught the case, not making much progress."

The group laughed while Goodman sipped his beer.

McClusky reviewed the list and shook his head. "We'd better cool it. A friend in the LAPD tipped me off the fed's have been sniffing around. "They wanted a look at your personnel file, Randy."

"Did they get it?

"Don't know for sure, my guess would be yes."

Cunningham tensed, sat back on the bench seat, swigged his beer, face etched with concern. The group fell silent as Goodman grabbed the pitcher and filled each man's glass.

Their attention was drawn to the front door as it opened and a shaft of light split the darkness. A heavy-set man stood silhouetted in the light for a moment before the door closed behind him. Once his eyes adjusted to the room, the man weaved his way through the empty tables to the group and slid in beside Cunningham who was perched at the end of the booth.

"Nice of you to join us," McClusky said.

"Took a while to break away. Chasing turds takes time," the big man joked.

The remark broke the tension.

"We hate to take you away from work, detective" McClusky said smiling. "Where are we on the kid's murder? Your fucking boss is not keeping me informed despite my order to do so."

The big man yanked his shirt collar outward, his bulging neck trapped by his tie. "We're all over the place; Styles likes Ramos, the escaped rapist. We're also looking at the Gothic assholes at the High School, some kind of Columbine replay. We're chasing our tails though one of those tails I wouldn't mind catching."

The obvious reference to Styles drew laughs. McClusky shook his head. "Can we tie that wetback Ramos to this, might shut those liberal assholes up."

The big man shrugged, "Who knows, could go that way? He's back in town. Beat his wife up good after raping her with the kids in the house."

Cunningham grimaced, his jaw tightened.

"OK," McClusky said. "Make it happen. Whatever it takes."

McClusky slid out of the booth, the other men following.

"Let's get the fuck out of here," he said, like Sundance to Butch Cassidy running from the relentless posse.

Chapter 47

The Pacific City Rotary Club met on Wednesdays at the Sand Castle restaurant, a popular eatery on the beach side of the coast highway. Diners had a panoramic view of the ocean and the usual cadre of wet suited surfers dancing on the crest of waves as they coasted effortlessly toward the shore.

Today's Rotary meeting opened with everyone standing to sing God Bless America. The group remained on their feet, heads bowed, for the invocation by Pastor Scott Reinhardt. "We ask your blessing, father," Reinhardt said "on these men and women who do your work in the community. Bless this food to our use and us to your service."

He paused, and his voice trembled when he continued. "We ask also, father, that you confer blessings on the Lyon family as they struggle to deal with the pain of losing a daughter. We ask this in your name."

Reinhardt sat down to an "amen" spoken in unison, even from those who were not Christian or particularly religious. The opening prayer ritual had not been challenged as the club's demographics changed from white, protestant male to a mix representative of a multi-cultural community.

Seated at the table with Pastor Reinhardt were local psychotherapist Dr. Jeffrey Palmer, and two men from East High School, football Coach Jimmy Phelan, today's guest speaker and Activities Director, Jonathon Moser.

"Thank you for mentioning the Lyon family, Scott," Moser said. "How're they doing?"

"Not well, I'm afraid, they're in shock, as we all are, especially her brother Brent. They were close."

"Such a tragedy," Moser said, taking a sip of his coffee.

"How are the students at school doing?" Palmer chimed in, directing his question to Phelan and Moser.

"Everyone's shook up," Phelan answered. "The memorial service last night made it real for many of the kids. Some are scared, especially the girls."

Moser concurred. "I work with many of Alex's friends; they're having a hard time. Like Jimmy says, they're frightened."

"And maybe they should be," Moser continued. His words jolted the men who straightened in their chairs, eyes on Moser.

"What do you mean, Jon?" Reinhardt said.

Moser realized he had misspoken. He had knowledge, confidential information, possibly evidence in Alex Lyon's murder. But he was among friends, didn't see the harm in sharing with them. He leaned in dropping his voice. "I shouldn't say anything but I know I can trust you to keep quiet."

Everyone nodded.

"The day after Alex was killed," Moser said, "Someone calling himself Reaper stuffed a note in my morning paper taking credit for Alex's death and threatening more killing."

"Reaper," Phelan said. "Sounds like a kid's prank, Jon."

"Come on Jon," Pastor Reinhardt added. "You can't be serious."

"I'm very serious," Moser said. "I was also skeptical at first. Then I thought about Columbine. A Secret Service study after the incident found that kids who kill at school often tell somebody beforehand. I worried that if we didn't take the warning seriously other kids could die."

"This didn't happen at East High, Jon," Reinhardt pressed. "Seems far-fetched to me."

"I know I'm probably paranoid. We have a Goth group at East. These kids are weird. But those boys at Columbine were into the Goth scene too? I gave the note to Lieutenant Deluca. The police are going to follow up. At least I'll sleep better."

The men remained skeptical. He tried one last time to convince them. "I can't get the note out of my mind." He recited from memory: "The Bitch deserved to die. There will be others. I am the law. If you don't like it you die."

"I hope I'm wrong, but I won't put other kids at risk."

"You did the right thing Jon," Phelan said. "All of us who work at schools are hyper sensitive about possible violence." He didn't add this might help him avoid police scrutiny.

Moser thought he knew why Phelan had done an about face. The coach couldn't keep it in his pants. Moser long suspected he might be diddling some students along with a teacher or two. Nevertheless, his support helped him gain credibility with the men at the table.

He had compromised evidence for reasons they would never guess.

Chapter 48

A slate pool table dominated the center of the oak paneled game room. A bar was built into one wall and two comfortable chairs and a couch were arranged along the opposite wall. A large, tinted picture window overlooked a canal, which snaked its way through the exclusive Park Harbor housing development and emptied into the Pacific Ocean.

Kitty Richmond, co-captain of the East High Cheerleaders, lay spread-eagled on the pool table. She wore a pink bra and matching panties, nothing else. She moaned and moved her head from side to side as Derek Johnson, East High's football All-American, stroked her thighs.

Kitty and Derek were not alone. Cheerleader Nancy Holmes and football player Floyd Warner sat huddled on the couch. Nancy's pleated white skirt had been pushed above her waist as Warner ran his fingertips along her legs.

Four empty beer cans rested on a nearby table with a small compact mirror containing the residue of a white powder. The teenagers had been drinking and snorting meth since coming to the house two hours earlier. Johnson's parents, who owned the home, were once again out of town.

As she lay back with her eyes closed, Nancy Holmes felt the combined effect of the booze and drugs; her body shook, tears ran down her cheeks.

"I'm so scared," she said, in a high-pitched, whining tone.

Warner, eyes glazed, face contorted in a stupid grin, giggled, "Like, why?"

His gaze fell on Nancy's thighs. He brushed his fingers across the front of her panties. Nancy moved her hips against Warner's hand but she managed to stammer, "Because of Alex. We're going to get caught. We could go to jail."

"No way," Warner said. “She liked everything we did."

Nancy whimpered out of fear and her rising passion. Warner had pushed her blouse above her bra; his tongue played on the crests of her small, firm breasts.

"But, like, what we did after...we, like, shouldn’t have done that...we shouldn’t. The cops are going to find out. I'm not sure that lady detective believed me," Nancy whined.

Warner ignored her, intent on freeing her breasts from the constriction of her bra. "Don’t worry," he said, as he squeezed her nipples. "We'll be O.K. if we stick together."

Johnson, who had been watching the pair on the couch, suddenly shouted, "Damn right. Nobody says nothing."

Johnson's tone startled Warner and Holmes.

Still irritated, Johnson asked, “Did anyone mention her brother?”

Warner and Holmes shook their heads.

“We can point the finger at him” Johnson said. “The little fucker was there. Maybe he stayed after I slapped him around, got pissed his sister gave it up to everyone.”

“Yeah,” Warner said, as if Johnson’s idea was the best thing he’d ever heard; his head fell on Nancy Holmes bare chest, she moaned.

Johnson stripped off his shirt and shorts and stood clad only in black sports briefs. The effects of the booze and drugs and his fondling of Kitty Richmond aroused him. He broke into a big grin. "Hey, like, what are we talking about Alex for? Let's party."

Throwing his head back, he took a sip of the beer he had placed on the rim of the pool table. Some of the liquid splashed on his face. He wiped it off with the back of his hand. Then, returned his attention to Kitty Richmond's thighs.

Chapter 49

Brent Lyon thought about thighs too but not Kitty Richmond's. He lay on his bed, head propped on a pillow, eyes focused on the ceiling fan rotating above him. The low hum mesmerized him as he thought of his sister.

Brent had not returned to school. He didn't know when he would have the strength to do so. He secluded himself in his room, leaving only for the funeral, the memorial service and to eat. He responded to his parents' questions and solicitations with a shrug of his shoulders or a monosyllabic word or two. He was both devastated by his sister's death and guilty about their relationship. He doubted anyone would understand. Dr. Palmer had been sympathetic but clueless, friends and teachers would be shocked; coach angry.

Brent remembered back to the Saturday two years earlier when it began, Alex sixteen, he fourteen, his parent's night out. They attended hockey games in the winter months at the Pond in Anaheim, home of the Mighty Ducks. Ardent fans, they had season tickets, one of Mr. Lyon's few extravagances. When hockey wasn't an option, the couple had dinner with friends, attended theater productions at the Orange County Performing Arts Center, or window-shopped at the malls within driving distance.

The Lyons were "helicopter parents" so when the kids were young, Mrs. Lyon's brother David and his wife Judith were the only ones allowed to babysit. They did this for several years until Alex turned sixteen and Brent and Alex stayed home alone for the first time.

Brent remembered every detail of what happened. At about ten o'clock, he walked down the hall to his room to go to bed. The door to Alex's room was ajar and he peeked through the opening. Alex, in white cotton panties, lay on her stomach on top of her bed clad in a shear baby-doll nightgown. She massaged her breasts as she read a book, pulling on her nipples with her thumb and index finger.

The sight awed Brent. He stood transfixed outside the door, like a peeping Tom, unable to move. Alex noticed him but was not shocked and didn't yell at him as expected. Her smile sent shivers down his spine. She patted the bed and motioned for him to come inside.

Brent's young life changed that night. Alex introduced him to the pleasure, joy and excitement of sex. She taught him things that had been mere fantasy. He hadn't known you could do some of those things.

He also became more aware of his sister; her deep blue eyes, her smooth, soft skin her smell.

He couldn't wait for Saturday's to come. Alex opened herself to him; let him poke and prod, lick and suck, every opening, every way. She played him and he loved it. Saturday brought new pleasures, new wonders, until the night it all unraveled.

Alex lay on her bed on her stomach clad in only a pair of high cut pink panties. Brent straddled her from behind, stroked and kissed her calves, her inner thighs. Rock hard, he slipped off her panties, the twin mounds of her buttocks supple and inviting. He paused a moment, raised himself above her. With some effort, moving his hips back and forth, he entered her. Alex let out a little cry but urged him on.

Engrossed in their sex play, they did not hear the front door open and close. Mrs. Lyon suffered a migraine during the movie she and her husband attended. She asked to return home early. Mr. Lyon, once inside the house, went to the kitchen for a cold drink and something to eat. Mrs. Lyon walked toward the bathroom to get aspirin from the medicine cabinet. As she passed Alex's room she heard strange sounds, thought Alex might be having a nightmare. She opened the door to comfort her daughter and was confronted with a nightmare of her own.

She screamed and collapsed against the door jam, her legs wobbly.

Horrified by the sudden appearance of his mother, Brent pulled out of Alex, but too late to stop his orgasm. Mrs. Lyon fainted.

Recalling those incidents now, lying on his bed, Brent felt guilt and shame--- Guilt for having engaged in such behavior with his sister in the first place and shame for having been caught by his parents, who no doubt, hated him. He blamed Alex for his weakness and despised himself because, despite being discovered, he and Alex had continued the intimate relationship.

"I want you," she said at every opportunity until he gave in.

He loved her; cared for her, but everything came crashing down around him the night she died. He'd heard Alex on the phone planning the party. Their home was just a few blocks from the park. He snuck out of the house when both parents were asleep. Hiding in the woods, he seethed with rage at his sister for behaving like a slut. Other boys doing to her what he thought only he had done.

He acted without thinking.

Chapter 51

The football players straggled off the field carrying shoulder pads, practice jerseys and helmets; their gray t-shirts stained with sweat, pants streaked with grass stains blood and dirt. Quarterback Tommy Deerfield strolled over to one of the student managers grabbed a water bottle and squirted his head and face with the cool liquid. The young manager threw him a towel and Deerfield dried himself off.

"Good practice, Tommy" coach Jimmy Phelan said walking over to the two boys.

"Thanks coach," Deerfield said as he draped the towel over his head.

Deerfield kept to himself since Alex Lyon's death. Never talkative, he was more reserved than ever. He went through the motions at practice but his competitive fire was dampened.

"How're you doing Tommy?" Phelan asked as he draped his arm around the boy and guided him away from the manager.

"I'm OK, coach," he said, without much emotion.

The boy was hurting, Phelan could see it in his eyes; in the way he moped around campus, his shoulders stooped, his gait slow.

Phelan leaned into his Quarterback. "Tommy. Are you friends with any of those Goth kids at school?"

"Not really," Deerfield said. "I know where they hang out but they're weird dudes."

"How about somebody called Reaper? Ever heard of him?"

Deerfield pulled back, puzzled. "I've seen his name scribbled in the bathrooms. What's this about coach."

"I shouldn't tell you this but there's a rumor he might, uh, have been involved in Alex's death."

Deerfield took the towel off his head, wiped his face, stunned. His eyes hardened.

"I don't understand coach. What do you mean involved?"

"That's all I've heard, Tommy. He's a suspect."

Deerfield's eyes welled with tears. He sprinted off the field.

Phelan felt a pang of guilt watching his quarterback disappear into the locker room but said to himself, *You're toast Reaper.*

Chapter 52

The detective/FBI special agent couldn't understand it.

The department computer files revealed an obvious problem if not an outright cover-up. Red flags should have gone up when three men died in police custody, particularly since all three incidents involved the same officer. That was a command staff problem not one for MALDEF and the ACLU who focused on police conduct in general, not the actions of specific officers. Those groups had issues with the whole department and were not trying to place the blame on rogue individuals. But why the blind eye by the chief and other upper echelon staff?

The agent made a mental note to review the personnel file of Officer Randy Cunningham then decided to check the file labeled, "extremists and extremist organizations," now rather than later to avoid suspicion by staying late again. Could be overreacting, but in this business, mistakes were fatal. Staying alive was high on everyone's Christmas list.

Now seemed a good time; Deluca was in his office buried in paperwork while other team members were out chasing leads. The agent typed in the access code to the department's restricted files. The main menu appeared in seconds and the agent clicked on the designation for "extremists and extremist organizations." A cover page described the document's purpose. "The groups and individuals noted here," it asserted, "present threats to public order and safety. Some groups have attempted to undermine the effective operation of the PCPD; the individuals are agitators, members of dangerous organizations, gangbangers or others who bear watching."

"Others who bear watching." Jesus Christ, shades of Big Brother.

The agent moved the cursor to the right and clicked on the down arrow to move to the next page. Twenty-five organizations appeared. The agent scanned the groups, surprised at those included. The ACLU, MALDEF, Greenpeace and the Anti-Defamation League made the list along with local gangs. Students for A Democratic Society (did they still exist?), the Knights of Columbus (the Pope would be surprised), and the Committee Against Police Brutality were also named.

The next page contained names of individuals and a rationale for their designation as an extremist. Three stood out: Julio Peter Vargas, Juan Alomar and Edgar Salazar, the men who within the last fourteen months had died while being detained by the PCPD. Vargas was identified as a gang member with ties to the Mexican Mafia, Alomar and Salazar as agitators with possible gang affiliation. It had not been reported at the time of their arrest, or during the subsequent investigation that these men had been on the department's watch list.

More like hit list.

The agent rose up and looked around to ensure privacy before continuing. The last name, Antonio Victor Gonzales, an attorney for MALDEF and organizer of the Committee Against Police Brutality, seemed familiar but the agent could not recall why.

The agent scrolled down to see what else the file contained. One other document remained, an internal memo.

PACIFIC CITY POLICE DEPARTMENT
Memorandum
To: Captain William McClusky
From: Detective John Goodman
Date: May 18, 2001
Subject: Surveillance of Antonio Victor Gonzales

Information has been received by some of our detectives that Antonio Victor Gonzales, a local attorney, has been working to mobilize several organizations in the Orange County area to actively protest and lobby government agencies. Their goal is to limit law-enforcement authority and to establish "watchdog groups" to publicize what they consider instances of police brutality. These organizations would then file federal lawsuits alleging civil rights violations.

The surveillance of Gonzales and the questioning of his associates revealed the following:

1. A rally is planned in June at the Anaheim Convention Center to bring attention to this issue (police brutality).
2. Chapters of a group calling itself The Committee against Police Brutality have been formed in the Orange County area, including Pacific City.
3. MALDEF, which Gonzales represents, plans to ask the District Attorney to investigate the PCPD and three other police departments.

4. Gonzales met with representatives of the Police Brutality Committees on Oct 1,2, Nov. 7,8, Dec. 10, 2000 and Jan 24, 2001.

The continued surveillance of Gonzales and his known associates will help us prepare to combat the activities of these ant-law enforcement organizations, which threaten to undermine our ability to enforce the law.

Respectfully submitted,

Detective John Goodman #670111
cc. Sergeant Anthony Segal

The memo went directly to McClusky, not his immediate supervisor, Deluca. The Lieutenant was not even copied, as was customary, although Sergeant Segal had been. Did Segal inform Deluca?

The agent, needing more time to examine the list of Organizations and individuals, printed the entire file, taking care not to be observed. The agent then exited the program, shut down the computer and walked out of the detective pen still trying to figure out why the name Antonio Victor Gonzales resonated.

Chapter 53

Deluca was seated at his desk when the phone rang.

"Deluca," he said.

"Lieutenant. Jeffrey Palmer here."

"What I can I do for you, doctor?" Deluca said, surprised by the call. Palmer had not been forthcoming when questioned earlier.

"I, uh, I wanted to apologize for being obstinate the other day. Alex's murder shocked me and doctor/patient confidentiality is critical in my profession."

Deluca smiled to himself but remained silent forcing Palmer to fill the void, which he did. "Have you made any progress?" he asked. "Alex was a good kid---confused---but didn't deserve what happened to her."

"I appreciate your concern, doctor. But as you might expect, I can't discuss the case."

"I understand, I understand," Palmer responded. I only…"

"Did you remember something," Deluca asked, cutting him off.

"I'm not sure it's relevant."

"Why don't you let us evaluate whatever it is, doctor?"

"Well, in our last session, Alex mentioned being followed around campus by one of those kids into the Goth stuff. Stalked was how she put it."

"You didn't think that relevant? Come on, Doctor."

Palmer remained silent for several seconds. When he spoke, he sounded like a child chastised by a parent. "I recently re-read my notes of the meeting, Lieutenant. I honestly didn't remember it then. I was in shock, I guess. I've never had a patient murdered."

"Ok, doctor," Deluca, said. No use shooting the messenger. "Did she mention any names?

"Not a name, really. She didn't know him. She thought one of his friends called him Reaper or something similar."

Deluca's kept silent for a few moments. "Thank you for calling, doctor," he said hoping his voice did not betray his anger. "This may be of help."

"You're welcome," Palmer said. He placed the phone in its cradle and leaned back in his chair, a wry smile on his face. He still hadn't told Deluca everything but consoled himself with the thought that perhaps this Reaper kid actually did kill Alex.

Chapter 54

Eduardo Ramos sat alone at the beach. His homiest didn't want him around anymore; too much heat. The visit to his wife had been a mistake, necessary, but a mistake. Now the cops knew he was in town and looking at him for doing the cheerleader. Sanchez gave him the word.

"Dude," Sanchez explained, "you got to get far away from here. Cops are messing with everybody. They want you bad. Homeboys can't risk hiding yak."

Ramos shook his head but understood. "I need some grip, a car. I'll go to TJ, get lost."

That had been two days ago. Sanchez came up with money, no car. Ramos would have to find one himself. His so-called amigos turned on him.

"*Fuck them.*"

Ramos sat on the sand, his back against a low, decorative sea wall, far from the public restrooms and fire pits, where people might congregate though that was unlikely this time of year. Clouds blanketed the sky and offshore winds were cold, biting. A few brave, or dumb, surfers ventured out into the raging water, whipped into frenzy. The current could suck you down. No matter how good a swimmer, you couldn't win if the ocean wanted to claim you. Ramos felt like he was being sucked into something he couldn't fight, like a riptide. He needed to get away.

He wore an Oakland Raiders jacket over a black hooded sweatshirt, his cap pulled low over his eyes. A backpack containing everything he owned rested on the sand beside him. He held a large paper coffee cup from a near-by Jack in the Box. The coffee warmed him but he knew he must keep moving.

He'd get out of the city tonight. Steal a car. Drive down close to the border then walk across mingling with tourists seeking the bargains and pleasures in Tijuana. He'd stay with friends, if he still had any, and pay off the local police. Money talked in Mexico.

Ramos was pissed though he had no one to blame but himself. Meth clouded his thinking, led him to take chances. He should have gone straight to Mexico after the escape, not try to settle with his wife, or sample again the pleasures of the women in Pacific City.

The cheerleader flaunted her tits and ass a lot. And she wanted what he offered---meth. He took a sip of his coffee warming his insides as much as thoughts of the girl. Her soft white skin, her legs, got him hard.

He had some meth left; he fumbled in his backpack for the mirror and baggy. He snorted it all and leaned back, wild thoughts running through his mind; fine women in this city. He might stick around a little longer.

But he needed a car.

Chapter 55

Kitty Richmond walked along a tree-covered sidewalk alone; her gait unsteady, stumbling when her foot came down on the edge of the curb. High on a combination of alcohol and crystal meth, she had partied again at Derek Johnson's who lived only two blocks away from her.

Her house was set back from the street surrounded by a six-foot tall hedge. Kitty opened the gate and staggered down the stone path toward her front door, straying onto the grass a couple of times. She giggled, fumbled in her purse for her keys; the house dark, her parents away again, she didn't know where, didn't care.

Absorbed with trying to locate her keys, the black clad figure slipped behind her, unnoticed. His gloved hand covered her mouth before she uttered a sound. She felt herself being pulled backward behind a tall shrub, forced to the ground, a heavy weight on top of her.

"Do as I say, you won't get hurt," he hissed into her left ear, his face inches from hers, and the whisky on his breath overpowering.

Paralyzed by fear, her eyes wide, she sensed his free hand move down her leg, the cool air on her hips as he pushed her skirt above her waist. She whimpered, her voice muffled against his gloved hand, as her panties were pulled down and off, her legs forced apart.

Tears cascaded down her cheeks, her chest heaved. She had trouble breathing. The booze and meth rendered her helpless. She cried out as he plunged into her. He moved his hips like a piston, intent on inflicting pain rather than arousing pleasure; dry and tight, each thrust agony, like sandpaper scraping her insides.

To her surprise, it ended quickly. He didn't groan or shout, as boys did when they came, just stopped. Her lower body ached and her head pounded from her earlier partying.

She thought the worst over until the cord encircled her neck. She opened her mouth to cry out, twisted to break away, but made no sound, could not move against his weight pressing on her. She heard a distant gurgling, then nothing.

He had killed for the second time; this planned, unlike the first. The body would be dumped where it would be found; the police would know who killed her.

He would make sure of that.

Chapter 56

Deluca spent the weekend with his daughter in San Diego.

They had dinner Saturday night in the Gas Lamp district and shopped at Seaport Village on Sunday. Deluca pushed thoughts of the Lyon case out of his mind while he talked with his daughter about college and her messy roommates. She had never been "Miss. Clean" either, but the savvy detective tactfully did not mention this. His visit boosted his own spirits; thankful she was happy even while grousing about the foibles of her friends.

As Deluca drove back to Pacific City on Interstate 5, he passed Camp Pendleton, the sprawling Marine Base located between Oceanside and San Clemente. The north access road to the base was named after World War II Medal of Honor winner, Gunnery Sergeant John Basilone, "Manila John;" a legendary Marine hero who almost single handedly repelled a Japanese regimental assault on his position at Guadalcanal. He killed over one hundred enemy soldiers in the process. Home on leave, Basil one rejected a promotion to lieutenant and an offer to tour the US selling war bonds to return to the Pacific. He refused to let his buddies go in harm's way without him and died on the beach at Iwo Jima.

Deluca kept a picture of Basilone on his office wall as a reminder of the strength of the human spirit, of what one man could do with courage, perseverance and loyalty. He hoped the group of detectives working on the Lyon case would learn to care for each other as much as Basilone cared for his fellow Marines. But he knew it often took the pressure of war or the threat of life and death to promote such feelings. A homicide investigation did not rise to those lofty heights nor was it likely any of them would die working on this case.

Back in his office on this Monday morning, Deluca was not prepared for the news delivered by Cara Styles who stood before him, face ashen, back rigid, hands clasped in front of her.

"What?" he asked, sure he didn't want to hear the answer.

"We have another one," she said.

"Another what?"

"Murdered girl. A jogger in Wellington Park found the body this morning. Willis and Segal are on the way. Preliminary reports indicate similarities to the Lyon murder."

"I'll meet you there," Deluca said, pushing his chair back and standing up.

The task force members arrived in Wellington Park within minutes of each other. A small crowd gathered, held in check by several patrol officers. No press, but that would soon change. The spotlight on Pacific City, and the homicide unit, was about to become brighter.

The patrol officers parted the crowd to let Deluca through. The girl's body was sprawled several feet down an incline just off the trail leading to the clearing where cheerleader Alex Lyon had been killed. She lay on her back, legs askew, skirt above her hips, nude from the waist down, her blouse torn, white bra visible.This time the coroner, the same man who had examined Alex, was on the scene completing his examination of the body. Willis and Segal had joined the CSU team nearby ready to move in. Styles chatted with a woman in shorts and T-shirt, the jogger who stumbled onto the body.

The coroner snapped his bag shut and struggled up the incline to where Deluca stood. "Looks like she was raped and strangled; ligature mark on her neck similar to the one on the other girl. Won't know for sure, of course, until a closer exam at the lab."

"Fast track this, will you?" Deluca said, as the small man pushed past him toward his County van.

Deluca caught Segal's eye, waved him over. "Too many cooks in the kitchen right now. Tell Styles to work with CSU. You and Willis continue with what you were working on. If it's connected to Alex, we need to be ready to put the pieces together."

"OK skipper," Segal said.

As Deluca drove out of the parking lot, a group of people had gathered on the sidewalk across from the park attracted by the sirens, police and emergency vehicles. Deluca kept his eyes locked on the road.

He did not see Edwardo Ramos peering over the shoulder of one of the men in the crowd.

Chapter 57

The detective team converged on Deluca's office after returning from the latest murder. Styles and Willis took seats while Segal stood against the wall opposite Deluca's desk.

Styles took the lead. "We might not be spinning our wheels on this Reaper thing. The murdered girl is Kitty Richmond, a cheerleader at East High School, a friend of Alex Lyon."

"Yeah." Deluca said. "I remember her. She spoke at the memorial service."

Styles held up a plastic bag with a slip of paper inside. "CSU found this a few feet from the girl, a note from Reaper; same wording as the one stuffed into Moser's newspaper. This guy is picking off kids at East High."

"Shoots down our Ramos theory," Deluca said. "A rapist turned serial killer doesn't fly."

"Maybe," Segal offered. "Ramos might know this Reaper character. Supplies his group with drugs like Lyon's crowd. He's aware Reaper hates athletes, cheerleaders, be a good scapegoat."

"Why no note on Alex?" Deluca asked.

"Walker scared him off. He resorts to slipping the first one into Moser's newspaper."

"Either of you buy this?" Deluca said, looking from Styles to Willis.

Styles jumped in, "Ramos can be violent. Attacked his wife, left her for dead. If he is supplying high school kids with drugs, he would know the various groups, who likes each other, who doesn't. And," she paused for effect, "Kitty's panties were not found. Ramos' MO."

"C'mon," Willis countered. "Ramos is a rapist and drug dealer, high most of the time; knocking the wife around was personal, revengeful; his rapes spur of the moment, opportunistic. These murders smack of planning ahead. Not his style. I doubt he has a clue about Columbine or anything those killers might have said or written.

"And if it is Reaper," he continued, "he's stupid. He takes credit for two murders, leaves his name plastered around school. Somebody's going to give him up."

"What if he doesn't care?" Deluca said. "What if he's prepared to do his Columbine thing soon? Like Harris and Klebold, ready to die.

"Dr. Palmer called me on Friday," Deluca added. "Told me that Alex was stalked by one of the Goth kids. Nice of him to wait this long to tell us."

The sarcasm was not lost on the group.

"We'd better find this asshole---now," Deluca said, emphasizing the word now.

Chapter 58

Seventeen-year old Jared Spacey strolled home from his girlfriend's house only a few blocks from his. Even in his own neighborhood, his appearance still caused passing motorists to gawk. He was dressed in two-tone jeans, one leg blue, the other white. He wore a sleeveless denim vest over a short-sleeve black T-shirt, a spiked choker around his neck, jet-black hair streaked with red. Rings adorned each ear his lower lip and nose. He bounced down the street walking on his toes, arms swinging as if flaunting his looks. Tonight he, Raven and Spyder would hide their weapons on campus. Tomorrow they would do it.

Soon people will know he was someone to be reckoned with---soon.

He stepped on to the walkway leading to his front door when a white Mustang convertible pulled to the curb. Four boys jumped out and surrounded him.

One boy stood nose-to-nose with him and spit out a challenge: "Hey asshole. Coach told me about you. What did you do to Alex?"

Spacey was not a big kid; stick thin he weighed a hundred and thirty pounds on a good day, no match physically for the boy facing him, at least six inches taller and sixty pounds heavier. But he did not back down from his bigger adversary and made the youthful mistake of throwing back the challenge. "Who the fuck wants to know?" he said, his fists clenched, his mouth twisted in anger.

His answer was a blow to the jaw. It knocked him backward into the arms of one of the other boys, who pushed Spacey back upright forcing him to absorb several more swift punches to his head and body. His nose was flattened against his face, a nasty gash opened above his right eye. Blood gushed in torrents from his nose and mouth as he fell to the ground. His assailant kicked him in the rib cage several times; Spacey felt searing pain before a kick to the head ended any conscious thought.

"Fucking asshole, scumbag, freak," his attacker screamed as he stood over Spacey's crumpled form like a prizefighter that had pummeled his foe to the canvas. "Rot in hell, dickhead," he shouted giving him another kick as a parting gesture.

One boy grabbed him and said, "Let's get the fuck out of here before the cops come."

The boy dragged him into the car with the other members of the East High football team. They drove off as fast as they had arrived leaving Jared Spacey, "Reaper," lying face-down on the sidewalk.

Chapter 59

Willis and Segal were at a Taco Bell.

Segal's cell phone rang as he placed his two fish tacos on a corner table. He pulled the phone from his inside jacket pocket, flipped it open and said in a tone that reflected his annoyance at being disturbed. "Yeah! Segal."

"Detective. This is Bradford at East High. We've got a problem."

"What's up?"

"The good news is we located Reaper."

"Yeah! Drop the shoe."

"Someone got to him before we did. They beat the hell out of him."

"How bad?"

"Unconscious when patrol found him. He's at Pacifica Hospital. I'm on my way now."

"How'd ya find him?"

"I put out the word at school. Didn't say why. One of the girls I've been working with, a Goth, her family life's horrible, came to see me. She told me a new kid called himself Reaper and bragged about how cool the Columbine shooters were. Made noises like he was gonna do something similar. Most of the kids ignored him."

"What's his name," Segal asked, breaking into Bradford's monologue.

"Jared Spacey. He's a junior. Got kicked out of Kennedy High across town and transferred here. That's why I hadn't seen the graffiti before."

"Why was he booted from Kennedy?"

"No info yet. Haven't gotten a call back from the Kennedy SRO.

"OK!" Segal said. "Willis and I will head over to the hospital. Appreciate it if you'd notify Lieutenant Deluca. We need to get a search warrant for Reaper, Spacey's, house. If he can't talk maybe we can find something to connect him to the dead girls."

"Uh! We got another problem detective. Is your partner there?

"Yeah! Why?

"Uh! The kid's name is Jared Spacey. But his records folder lists his step-dad as Walter Willis, Pacific City PD."

"Oh, man!"

"Yup. What do you want me to do?"

"Call Deluca. I'll handle things on this end." He hung up without waiting for a response.

Willis slipped into a chair opposite him. "I hope you got something you can eat in the car," Segal said. "Let's go. I'll explain on the way."

Willis sat in his seat, back stiff, hands on thighs, nodding when Segal explained what had happened and who the victim was. He stared straight ahead, said nothing on the trip to the hospital.

Officer Bradford, the East High School SRO, met them. "The kid, Uh, Jared, is still unconscious," Bradford said to the two detectives as they pushed through the double doors of the corridor where Reaper's room was located.

"The usual tubes coming out of every orifice," Bradford continued by way of explaining the kid would not be talking for a while.

Segal winced; Willis' face went white.

Bradford realized he'd screwed up and whispered, "Uh! Walt, I'm sorry, I, Uh."

Willis held up his hand as he and Segal pushed past.

Stephanie Willis stood outside the door to her son's room talking to a doctor in the manner people do when confronted with a crisis. She was a looker, a decade younger than Willis, with brown hair cascading to her shoulders. She wore a low cut white blouse, blue blazer and short matching skirt two inches above attractive knees. Her arms were folded across an ample bosom.

As Willis and Segal approached, she turned away from the doctor and fell into her husband's arms. "Who did this to my son?" she spoke into his shoulder.

"We don't know yet, Hon, we have some ideas."

"What ideas?" She asked, stepping back, her face hardening into a withering stare.

"Something to do with the Gothic group at the high school," Segal said, in an attempt to rescue his partner.

Stephanie Willis expected that response, she lowered her eyes, shoulders slumped forward. She moved into her husband's embrace.

Segal spoke again. "Did any of your son's friends refer to him as Reaper, or something similar?"

She shook her head. "I'm embarrassed to say we don't know much about this Gothic stuff. Jared's been somewhat of a loner. We, I, thought the weird clothes, the dyed hair, the dark music was a phase; at least he had some friends. I didn't let Walt interfere."

Segal smiled. He had a thirteen-year old boy; had his share of disagreements with the kid over choice of clothes, taste in music, friends. Teenagers either tried to blend with the crowd or rebelled like the Goths. As a parent, you're torn between tightening your grip or backing off to wait it out. He wasn't about to judge his partner or his wife.

"Doesn't appear we're going to be able to speak with Jared anytime soon," he said, regretting his choice of words as he spoke them. They were worried enough without him suggesting the boy might not recover.

He tried to back track. "What I mean, ma'am, Steph, is we don't want to slow our investigation. Something in his room at home could steer us in the right direction, help us hold someone accountable."

Willis and his wife looked at each other, their faces reflecting anguish or a secret. "We never go into his room," she said. "Something I asked Walt to respect. He didn't like it. I only wish." She didn't finish the sentence as tears cascaded down her cheeks.

Segal felt his partner's pain, the awkwardness of the situation. He spoke to Mrs. Willis. "I understand but it may lead us to whoever hurt your son."

"You know he's right, Steph," Willis said, holding her close.

Resigned, she said, "You go. I'll stay with Jared."

Willis kissed her on the forehead and motioned Segal to follow as he turned to leave. They walked down the hall together toward Bradford who had stayed a respectful distance away.

Chapter 60

Jared Spacey's room was a shrine to evil.

Willis and Segal stood in the open doorway stunned by what faced them. Posters of Nazi's, white supremacists and Klansmen screamed from the walls. A scowling Adolf Hitler, arm raised in the Nazi salute, towered over a wooden desk. The image of David Duke, a former Grand Dragon of the KKK, hung on the opposite wall above his oft quoted epithet: "Hitler was right."

In contrast, the rest of the room was tidy; the bed made; the small trash receptacle beside the desk empty; no clothes scattered about, no clutter. "Unlike my son's room," Segal thought, but was grateful the only posters on his teenager's walls featured Joe Montana and Jerry Rice.

Segal and Willis exchanged glances. "You don't have to do this, Walt," Segal said

Willis shook his head. "I can do my job," he said and led the way into the room.

The search yielded results at once. Segal opened the middle drawer of Jared's desk and found five copies of the note sent to activities director Moser. The boy obviously intended to send them to others and made no attempt to hide them, confident his mom and step-dad would not invade his space.

Segal also found a black notebook in the drawer containing a single sheet of paper with twenty-five typed names. Stashed under the book were old Internet downloads of the Columbine Massacre along with several Los Angeles Times articles on the murder of Alex Lyon. Jared had scribbled "Good. Saves us the trouble" in black pen on the margin of the newspaper, Alex's name crossed off the typed list.

Segal sifted through the boy's desk, while Willis inspected the neat closet--shirts and jackets, all facing the same direction, hung from hangers. The one overhead shelf held computer games, stacked one on top of the other, corners aligned. Several pairs of boots and running shoes, all black, toes pointing outward, lined the bottom of the closet.

Pushing aside some jackets, Willis noticed a large grey athletic bag he had not seen before in a corner on the floor. He grabbed the handles and dragged it out into the room, struck by its weight.

"What does the boy have in there, dumbbells?" he thought as he unzipped the top. He let out a soft whistle when he eyed the contents,

"What?" Segal said.

"Have a look, partner," Willis directed, as he stretched the bag open.

Segal peered inside and saw a shotgun and two forty-five-caliber military style pistols, several boxes of ammunition arranged around them.

"Quite an arsenal," Willis said, as he ran his right hand over his forehead and back through his hair. "I was stupid, went along to get along. My stepson is Reaper; he planned to kill people."

"Yeah! But don't blame yourself, man," Segal said. "You tried to give the kid some space, your wife peace of mind. Despite what he might have planned, I don't think Jared killed Alex Lyon or Kitty Richmond."

"You want to enlighten me?"

"The note scribbled on the article about Lyon's murder."

"Yeah!"

"It said, "Good. Saves us the trouble."

Willis put his hands on his hips and cocked his head to one side catching the meaning of his partner's words.

"Why would he write that if he had killed her?" Segal said. "Somebody beat him to it."

"What about Richmond?" Willis asked wanting to believe his stepson wasn't a murderer.

Segal shrugged. "Not on the list."

Willis exhaled, relieved. "Yeah. By the looks of this stuff," he said, looking toward the bag of weapons, "he intended to use heavy artillery on his enemies like Harris and Klebold. Alex and Kitty were strangled. I don't know much about my stepson but he's not the type to get that close to his victim. He's too neat."

"I agree. We still got a problem, though."

"What do you mean?"

"The note scribbled on the article."

"Yeah!"

"It said 'Saves US the trouble'."

"Damn."

"Do you know any of his friends?"

"No, I'm ashamed to say. He seldom brought anyone around here and I never asked."

"We better find out who his pals are, pronto."

Segal made two quick calls on his cell phone as they drove away from the Willis home. One to Deluca to advise him of their find at Reaper's and why they didn't now believe Jared Spacey killed either Alex Lyon or Kitty Richmond.

Glancing sideways at Willis, he said, "I have something else to tell you but I'll wait to talk to you in person."

Willis kept his eyes averted.

Segal then called Officer William Bradford at East High School. "We're in deep guano," he announced without preamble.

"How so?" Bradford asked.

"You need to get to your Goth snitch again. We found an arsenal at Jared's house. Confirms he and his buddies planned a Columbine attack. With Reaper on the shelf, they may decide to go ahead without him."

"I'll get on it," Bradford assured him.

"Good. We need to get warrants and hit their homes fast."

Segal did not wait for another response. He punched the end button on his cell phone and turned to Willis who was driving.

"Hope we're not too late."

Chapter 61

Brent Lyon called from a cell phone and after three rings received a recorded greeting: "Hi. You've reached the surfer dude. Leave a message, I'll get right back to ya. Chow."

"Uh, this is Brent Lyon, you said to call if we needed to talk. I, Uh…" A man interrupted the message. "Hey Brent what can I do ya for?"

"I need to talk with someone I can trust."

"Where are you?"

"By the snack shop at the Park."

"Is anyone else around?"

"No."

"I'll be there in fifteen minutes. Sit tight."

Twenty-minutes later, a blue late model mustang convertible pulled up to the curb at Wellington Park. The driver lowered the window and waved Brent Lyon over. "Get in buddy," he called out.

Brent walked to the car, head down, opened the door and slid in. He slouched down in the seat, did not make eye contact.

The surfer dude reached over, put his hand behind Brent's neck and gave it a gentle, affectionate shake. "Not to worry, pal," he said. "We'll go somewhere and talk."

Brent nodded as the man drove toward the beach, pulled off the main highway and maneuvered up a steep dirt road. He reached the top of a hill then turned into a gravel area big enough for three or four cars. Locals who sought to get a great view of the Pacific and teenagers who had other ideas favored Eagle Point, which overlooked a hundred foot cliff with jagged rocks below. More than one person strayed too close to the edge and plunged to their death despite warning signs.

When the surfer dude parked the car, Brent began shouting and rocking back and forth, spittle forming on the sides of his mouth. "I killed her, I killed her," he said, slamming himself against the seat.

"Whoa! Easy Brent," the surfer dude said to calm him, his tone measured, soothing. "Not your fault. You couldn't predict what happened."

"You don't understand. I was there. I should have done something, taken her home."

Brent's outburst and confession stunned the surfer dude; his mind raced, eyes widened. He hadn't known the boy was in the park that night. He doubted the police knew either.

"What did you see?" he asked, his voice calm, even. He didn't want to spook the boy.

Brent spit out his answer, disgust evident in his voice. "Guys on the team, cheerleaders. They were, they were, with Alex."

Brent shook his head as if trying to purge the memory. To describe what he saw would sully the image of his sister. He loved her. She loved him. He buried his face in his hands. His shoulders convulsed.

The surfer dude placed his arm around the teenager. They remained like that for several minutes until the man broke the silence. "Brent, let's get some fresh air; walk to the Point. Go on ahead. I'll follow. We'll talk more. Work this out."

The kid nodded, pushed the door open, slid off the seat and shuffled toward the cliff. He didn't close the door.

The surfer dude gripped the steering wheel with both hands. Brent had been in the Park, observed his sister with her friends, doing drugs, having sex. If he'd seen the murder he had somehow repressed the memory, blamed himself. Would he continue to repress the events of that night or go to the police when he recalled what actually happened?

The surfer dude frowned, slumped back in his seat, remained like that for several minutes. He hated himself for what he must do. He hadn't planned any of this. Things just spiraled out of control—Alex and Kitty.

He reached into the glove compartment and pulled back the black cardboard installed to conceal a space behind. He grabbed the baggie with the objects stowed there, opened it, smiled as the perfumed aroma filled his nostrils, still strong. He shoved the baggie into his pocket, left the car and walked up toward the Point.

He couldn't take the chance the kid had seen him in the park.

Chapter 62

O'Hara's Sports Bar and Grill was crowded.

Deluca, McClusky, Big Tony Segal and two secretaries from the Investigation Division were seated at one of the round tables adjacent to the bar. One of the women, a buxom blond wearing a low cut beige V-neck sweater and short white skirt, sat close to McClusky, whose hand was active under the table. The woman feigned rapt interest in the conversation; showed no sign that her boss's caresses were not welcome; a smile pasted on her face. She sipped her beer delicately, although her bright red lipstick left a smudge on the rim of her glass.

The other woman, a petite, slender brunette in a short brown dress with matching wide belt, sat wedged between Deluca and Segal. Her thigh pressed against Deluca's but he made no attempt to disengage from the contact, considered it a casual, inadvertent touch caused by the close positioning of their chairs.

Two half-filled pitchers of draft and several orders of O'Hara's famous beer battered fish and chips littered the table in front. Talk shifted back and forth between the basketball game on T.V. and the Lyon investigation. Deluca did his best to keep the chatter light and focused on the game but McClusky, fortified by several drinks, insisted on discussing the murder.

"C'mon JD," McClusky demanded, slurring his words. "Whaddya doin to wrap this thing up? You got to find that prick Ramos. The bastard's good for these murders, rapes. The chief's on my ass and I don't have dick to give him."

The blond smacked McClusky on the arm and giggled. The brunette smiled and sipped her beer.

Deluca shifted his attention to the TV pretending to be mesmerized by scantily clad snow bunnies prancing in a commercial for something or other. Actually, he thought, the bunnies were cute.

"JD," McClusky said once again, raising his voice to the point that several nearby patrons stared. The blond put her hand on McClusky's forearm, leaned close to whisper in his ear to quiet him down. McClusky pulled away and glared at the woman. About to speak, he stopped, smiled self-consciously. He raised his glass, drained its contents and slammed it on the table. He pushed his chair back, grabbed his gal by the arm. "Let's get outta here," he said, scowling. Turning toward Deluca, he said, "Call me in the mornin."

As he and the blond walked away, she struggled to pull the hem of her skirt down over fleshy thighs. Her attempt attracted lascivious glances from more than a few of the men in the bar.

The other woman took that opportunity to leave also; placing a hand on Deluca's thigh for support, she stood up. "See you tomorrow guys," she said, waving as she threaded through the crowd. Deluca admired the way her dress clung to her thighs and buttocks as she glided toward the exit. Before he could comment on the view, he noticed a familiar figure squeeze past the departing secretary. Coach Jimmy Phelan, dressed in his signature orange and black coaching regalia, strode into the restaurant smiling and waving to several men who shouted his name.

Phelan scanned the room for a seat then wended his way toward a slender, raven-haired women seated at the bar staring into a glass of wine. He slid onto the stool next to her and touched her on the shoulder. She turned, returned his smile, both in surprise and recognition. Phelan ordered a beer and chatted her up.

"Wonder who the broad is?" Segal mused, taking a slug of beer, wiping froth from his mouth with the back of his hand.

"Not his wife, I'll bet." Deluca said. He remembered something, took out his ever-present notebook and scribbled a note. "Coaches are tuned in to what's happening with kids, we need to push him hard for information. Did Styles talk with him?"

Segal shrugged and reached for the last piece of fish in the basket on the table.

As Segal devoured the fish, Deluca's phone vibrated against his hip. He extracted the phone from its case, flipped it open, tapped the talk button and said, "Deluca!"

He covered one ear with his hand as he strained to catch what was being said, nodding several times in response to the message. "Ok," he said and pushed the end button to disconnect.

He sat back in his chair, sighed and rubbed his forehead with the fingers of his right hand. Regarding Segal with a look somewhere between astonishment and resignation, he spoke in a voice so low Segal leaned toward him to hear.

"Brent Lyon, Alex's brother," he said. "They found him at the bottom of Eagle Point. He's dead; note pinned to his jacket, may have killed himself."

Chapter 63

At the bottom of Eagle Point Officer Mike Walker greeted Deluca and Segal as they navigated over slippery, jagged rocks. Brent Lyon's mangled body lay face up and bent backward over a moss-covered boulder, head and face a mass of red. A bloodstained piece of folded white stationary, held in place by a small safety pin, clung to his torn jacket.

"Not much loose dirt on the ridge," Walker said to Deluca's back as the Lieutenant pulled on a pair of plastic gloves and stooped to unpin the note from the boy's shirt.

"He could have fallen but more of the ridge should have been disturbed had it given way," Walker continued, intimating the kid had jumped.

Deluca kept silent. He stood up grasping the note by the thumb and forefinger of his right hand, flipped it open and squinted trying to decipher the words in the dim light cast by a crescent moon. After holding the paper up in several different directions, he ordered Walker to shine his flashlight towards him. The note, signed Bubba, scrawled in bold black print was brief, "I'm sorry for what I did."

Detective Cara Styles clambered over rocks to dodge the tide lapping back and forth against the ridge bottom. She dressed casually in jeans, white tennis shoes and a turtleneck sweater. Even without makeup, Styles looked great, Deluca thought.

He held the note up by one corner for her to read.

"What do you think?" he asked.

Walker stood nearby, hands on hips, head cocked toward the detectives in an effort to hear their conversation.

After a moment of awkward silence, Styles spoke. "I'd say we just found the Bubba in Alex's diary. She used the nickname to conceal her brother's identity. Even his initials would have been a giveaway.

"She didn't need to go out on Saturdays because Bubba, little brother, was home. His guilt could have pushed him to jump, guilt for playing around with his sister or guilt because he killed her."

"Makes sense," Deluca said. The deep lines in his face twisted into a grimace. He stared off into the darkness, several thoughts and questions colliding in his mind. Alex's parents, alarmed by her sexual behavior, took her to Dr. Palmer. She admitted this in her diary and confessed it was because they found about she and Bubba (Brent). Did the parents tell Palmer this or were they as vague as the good doctor suggested? Were Brent's words a confession of murder, an apology for taking his own life, a plea for forgiveness for an incestuous relationship with his sister, or did somebody want us to think that?"

Before Deluca could voice any of his thoughts, Walker's radio blared, "Shots fired Sea and Main, officer involved. All available units respond."

Walker asked, and was granted permission, to go.

Deluca directed the remaining officers to seal off the area and motioned Styles to join him several feet away from Brent's body.

They scrambled over the slick rocks and stood on a stretch of sand soon to be reclaimed by the onrushing tide. "Brent was Bubba, no doubt," he said to Styles. "The Saturday night time frame clinches it. I can understand now why the dad didn't say anything but it pisses me off that Palmer withheld that from us, assuming he knew."

"Assuming he knew," Styles repeated.

"Is the kid a murderer or a victim of this sordid mess?" Deluca asked.

He didn't wait for a response. "I don't buy it. No way Brent hurts his sister, let alone Kitty, her best friend, then jumps off a cliff in remorse."

Deluca stepped back and looked up at the ridge, water now lapping at his shoes. "Brent didn't jump, but someone has gone to a lot of trouble to convince us he did. A real son-of-a bitch; a real son-of-a bitch."

Chapter 64

Yellow crime scene tape cordoned off sea-street for two blocks, blue and white police cruisers parked inside. Officers with reflective vests diverted traffic to Main Street, which ran perpendicular to Sea and through the business district in downtown Pacific City.

Fifty-year old massive Maple trees, beginning to shed their orange, brown and red leaves, lined sea-street. The trees shielded from the street new condominiums and nineteen-fifty's style stucco homes clustered together. The prostrate body of a man, clad in a black running suit lay beside a parked vehicle. The man's torso was twisted so that he lay on his side with his arms outstretched and flat on the pavement. His sightless eyes stared upward, shirt and pants saturated with a dark liquid oozing from two chest wounds. A metal rod, of the type used to pop car door locks, lay inches from his right hand. A black backpack with one strap partially looped over a shoulder nestled beside his head.

Two Pacific City police officers, Mike Walker and Stanley "Pops" Parker, the oldest officer still working a beat, hovered over the body. "Pops" was as tall as he was wide, with a round face and massive gut. Officer Randy Cunningham stood several feet away, arms folded across his chest, a blank expression on his face. Tall and wiry, the thirty-nine year old Cunningham fired the shots that felled the victim. A refugee from the LAPD, Cunningham was a department marksman and former firing range instructor.

As Walker and "Pops" Parker stood vigil, detective Cara Styles approached them. Like Walker, she left the mangled body of young Brent Lyon lying at the base of Eagle point.

"What have we got," she asked, her eyes darting between the officers and the man on the street?

"Cunningham shot the guy," Walker said, pointing toward the tall officer not looking in their direction but staring into the darkness. "He was on foot patrol," continued Walker. His voice snapped the heads of the detectives who had been studying the statue like figure of Cunningham.

"When he turned on to Sea Street, he observed a suspect dressed in dark clothing peering into a parked vehicle. Suspicious, Cunningham identified himself and warned the man to stand still. Instead, he whirls around toward Cunningham with an object in his hand. Cunningham thinks it's a gun, cranks off two rounds. Dead car thief."

Styles leaned over the body. "Hey, shine your flashlight over here, Walker."

The man had shorter hair than she remembered and no moustache but she was sure it was him. "This is Eduardo Ramos."

Styles took a pair of plastic gloves from her pants pocket and searched through the zippered compartments of the backpack. She opened a small side pouch, and said in mock surprise, "What have we here?" and pulled out two pairs of women's panties; one bright Orange, the color Alex Lyon wore as part of her cheerleader's uniform; the other white, possibly Kitty Richmond's.

Intent on her discovery, she didn't catch the furtive glance shared between Walker and "Pops" Parker.

Chapter 65

Wild Bill McClusky called the meeting the morning after the shooting of Eduardo Ramos and the death of Brent Lyon. The group gathered in a small conference room adjacent to the Captain's office. The only furniture was a long wooden table and six chairs. Pictures of the President of the United States and the current chief hung side by side on one wall. The other walls were bare.

Wild Bill sat at one end of the table, Deluca the other. Styles and Segal sat on opposite sides facing each other. Willis had taken a personal leave to handle the situation with his wife and stepson. Ed Stankovich took his place temporarily and perched next to Segal.

The seated detectives all had paper coffee cups in front of them while McClusky had his own blue mug with "CAPT" in white old English style letters painted on the side, no donuts.

McClusky opened the meeting in his usual abrupt, direct, irreverent manner. "People, we got the fucker who killed and raped those high school kids. I'm gonna recommend the chief call a press conference this morning to get the fucking media off our backs and wrap this up. I knew the fucking greaser was good for this."

No one flinched at Wild Bill's profanity, but they all became very interested in their coffee cups or spots on the carpet, everyone except Deluca. "I'm not sure we're ready yet, Captain," he said keeping his tone respectful.

McClusky's face flushed. He leaned forward. "Why the hell not?" He challenged. "We got hard evidence linking the goddam pervert to the kids."

Deluca chose his words carefully to avoid appearing to question Wild Bill; otherwise his point would be lost.

"Captain, some evidence does connect Ramos to the murders; good chance he's our guy. But we need to tie up some loose ends. If we jump the gun on this the press will crucify us and embarrass the Chief. MALDEF is making noises about how we took down Ramos."

"Fuck them. Who cares what they think? We got the panties in the greaser's backpack."

"That's true, Sir," Deluca said. "But we can't put Ramos at the scene of either murder and the note on Lyon's brother raises some sticky questions. Alex Lyon had sex with multiple partners at the Park, maybe even her brother. We don't have much evidence from the Kitty Richmond crime scene. We need to take it slowly. Ramos' DNA on the panties of either girl could cinch it."

McClusky hesitated. Acting too quickly would not be in his best interests. MALDEF would piss and moan over the way Ramos was killed. Not that he cared. But he did not want to aggravate the chief and endanger his upcoming retirement.

Wild Bill took a gulp of coffee and furrowed his brow. "We got to move on this people. This was a righteous shoot. I don't want Cuningham hanging out there while we fiddle fart around. Wrap this up. Ramos was a scumbag. Good riddance. We owe it to the families of the two girls and to this community to bring an end to this. You got forty-eight hours." He got up, grabbed his cup from the table and left the room.

"You heard the man," Deluca said. "My office in fifteen minutes.

Chapter 66

The three detectives assembled in Deluca's office. Their lieutenant gazed at the picture of Manila John Basilone on his wall perhaps searching for answers in the young, resolute face staring back. He did not at first acknowledge the presence of his two remaining team members and newest addition. Finally, he leaned forward, elbows on his desk and rested his chin on his folded hands. "Cara you wanted Ramos for this. Is McClusky right? Do we wrap this up?"

"I detest drug dealers," she said. "But some things don't add up. Nothing concrete places Ramos at either murder scene, other than his possession of the panties. Odd he would be carrying them around? He's not that stupid.

"The brother's note might be an admission of guilt for killing his sister, or simply shame for getting it on with her. Perhaps he killed her out of rage or jealousy. But if he did, how did the panties wind up on Ramos? Nothing connects Brent and Ramos. No reason at all for Brent to rape and murder Kitty Richmond. Doesn't add up."

She paused for effect; "Alex had sex with more than one guy the night she was killed. Who were they and where did they go? The semen found on Alex did not match Ramos or with any other samples in the DNA data base."

"We're having both sets of panties checked for semen and prints, although getting prints of that material is difficult." Segal chimed in.

"As much as we want to nail Ramos for this, we don't have enough to tack his scalp to the wall," Deluca stated. "Like Cara said, why would the guy still be toting panties around, the very items to implicate him?"

"The guy's a pervert," Segal shouted as he spat out the words. "He had the panties because that's how he gets off."

"Maybe," Deluca said. "We've got forty-eight hours to fill in the missing pieces. Cara interview the cheerleader you think you can break. Big man, you and Ed press the lab for the fingerprints; dig up anything to connect Brent Lyon and Ramos. The Peters kid said football players got all sorts of stuff from Ramos, including steroids. Brent was buff for his age; he might not have been so ripped from lifting weights alone. At any rate, I'm going to talk to Mr. Lyon again, see what he knows about the relationship between Brent, Alex and Kitty."

Deluca paused, then said. "This is too neat. Ramos gets killed with the panties in his possession; a note is pinned to Brent's shirt. Everything gift wrapped for us. Somebody's jerking us around. First Reaper, then Brent, now Ramos. And whoever it is may pull this off if we can't hold off McClusky."

Chapter 67

Deluca pulled up to the Lyon residence and parked at the curb. A television news van was stationed in front. The same attractive blond reporter who had covered the protest at police headquarters stood on the sidewalk. The blond and her cameraman rushed him as he got out of his car. She thrust her microphone in his face.

"Lieutenant Deluca," she shouted breathlessly, as if she had just run a mile. "What happened to young Brent Lyon? Rumors are he committed suicide."

Deluca held up his hand, kept walking.

"Lieutenant," the blond persisted, "did he leave a note? Was the boy involved in his sisters' death, with Kitty's?"

"Come on Lieutenant," she called after him, "tell us something."

Deluca fumed. He detested the "fourth estate" and its intrusion into the lives of families who suffered a tragedy; their only interest to create thirty-second sound bites to fill an evening news slot; "Ken and Barbie" clones exchanging frowns and solemn words, quickly forgotten in the haste to get to a commercial break and the next "sensational" story.

He didn't say this, of course, wouldn't matter. Tragedy sells; tragedy tinged with sex sells even more. So he kept silent as he walked up to the Lyon house and rang the doorbell.

Mr. Lyon, looking frailer than on Deluca's first visit, opened the door, recognized the detective and let him in. This time he did not invite him to enter the family room. Deluca understood the man's desire to get this over-with. "I'm sorry for your loss, Sir, this must be devastating coming so closely after Alex' death."

Lyon's face was drawn, eyes drooped, mouth quivered. He didn't respond so Deluca pressed on.

"I'll be brief, Sir, but I do need to ask you some questions."

"I, I understand, detective," Lyon said, voice cracking. He folded his hands together in front of him, sagged against a wall, made no move to go further into the house.

"We found a note on Brent, sir," Deluca continued. "It said: 'I'm sorry for what I did.' Any idea what he meant?"

"I don't. Lieutenant. I don't."

"Did Brent know Kitty?"

"Yes! She hung out here a lot, but with Alex, she didn't talk to Brent much. None of the seniors gave sophomores the time of day."

Deluca paused a moment, struggling for the right words, couldn't find any so he plunged ahead. "Sir, we must consider every possibility. Uh, could Brent have had something to do with Alex's death? Could his note, uh, have been an apology for hurting her?"

Lyon's body stiffened; his head snapped back as if he had taken a blow. "I can't believe that, detective, I can't. He had no reason? He loved his sister."

Close to the truth, but I doubt he wanted me to take it literally.

"Mr. Lyon, again, please understand we've got to pursue all avenues. I, uh, I read Alex's diary. She implied she was sexually active. Were she and Brent, uh, intimate"

Lyon didn't answer. His eyes gave him away although he averted them. He knew. Whether he was willing to admit it or not, he knew.

As the man stood there, eyes downcast, body sagging, Deluca did not press the issue. "Well," he said, breaking the brief silence, "if you remember anything you think might be helpful please call me. Again, I'm sorry for your loss. We'll do everything we can to find out who killed Alex. And, what may have happened to Brent."

He handed Lyon one of his cards, turned, then stopped. Something had bothered him for a while.

Mr. Lyon, at Alex's memorial, I observed you in a heated argument with another man; appeared you might strike him. Who was that?"

Lyon's eyes flickered for a moment, his face twisted into an awkward grin. "My dick-head brother-in-law, family matter, is all."

"You looked pretty riled."

Lyon waved him off. Deluca did not pursue it and let himself out.

John Lyon stood transfixed, tears streaming down his face.

Chapter 68

Raven and Spyder lay on their stomachs on the baseball field behind East High School. It was 11:30 PM, pitch black; night-lights glowed dimly on several of the school buildings. A ten-foot high metal gate, fifty yards from where the boys lay, blocked entrance to the school. Not a problem; they had practiced climbing the gate a few nights earlier and scaled it easily.

The attack on Reaper angered them. They were on the way to his house when the car full of football players pulled away from the curb leaving their friend unconscious and bleeding. At that time they vowed to carry out the plan---Reaper's Plan.

Laying on the grass each boy grasped a large garbage bag with weapons scrounged from Raven's dad's collection---two shotguns, two glock semi-automatic pistols. They had also cobbled together several homemade Molotov cocktails, enough firepower to do some damage. Not as much as anticipated but with Reaper gone they had little choice unless they abandoned the attack altogether.

The bags also contained ski masks. They still believed they could escape without being caught or identified.

"OK," whispered Spyder. "Get ready. When we get over the gate, the cafeteria is a few yards to our left. We'll stash the bags behind the two dumpsters at the rear of the cafeteria. Garbage isn't collected for another two days. We can go back there at lunch."

Raven nodded and clutched his bag to his side.

Spyder got up, grabbed his bag and ran to the gate. Raven followed seconds later.

When they were sure all was clear, Spyder placed his foot on one of the giant hinges holding the door and hoisted himself over. Raven then slipped their two bags between the wide vertical bars and climbed over.

Shadows played off the walls of the dimly lit quad and outside corridors. A breeze whistled through the school carrying sounds that spooked Raven. Spyder gripped his chin. "Be cool," he whispered. "No one's around. We'll be out of here in a few minutes.

Raven's eyes were wide with fright.

Spyder led the way as they ran to the area where the dumpsters were stored behind a cinder block wall. Wooden planks bolted to the wall prevented the containers from banging into, and damaging, the wall. The planks left a gap wide enough to stash their bags where they would be hidden from view. Anyone seeing the bags would think someone had carelessly dumped them there.

Catching their breath, the boys smiled, so far so good. Spyder punched Raven playfully on the shoulder and flicked his head to indicate they should leave. They sprinted toward the exit gate as two night custodians riding an electric cart came around a corner headed straight for them.

"Hey," one of the men yelled as the boys stopped. Raven grabbed Spyder's shirt paralyzed with fear.

"Split up," Spyder shouted as he pushed away from Raven and darted across the quad to another gate. Raven, shaken but now moving, sprinted off in another direction.

The custodians sped after Spyder hollering, "stop" as they careened along an outside walkway, the quad on their left, lockers on the right, like an episode from an old "keystone cops" movie.

Spyder easily outdistanced the slow electric cart, vaulted over the gate in seconds and scampered across the field leaving the custodians far behind.

"Dammit," one of the men said as he watched the boy disappear into the darkness. "Goddam kids."

His partner shrugged.

Chapter 69

Officer William Bradford checked his mailbox at East High School each morning. He often found notes from teachers about some problem with students they were sure he could resolve better than they. He also got incident reports from the previous night from the custodial staff regarding graffiti or other incidents of vandalism. Bradford took pictures of graffiti for his notebook and shared it with patrol officers, who used his Intel to identify taggers in the city.

Bradford emptied his mailbox, walked back to his office down the hall and sifted through the notes and forms he had retrieved; a report from the night before caught his eye. Custodians reported chasing two students on campus but the kids got away. They couldn't identify the boys but believed they dressed like Goths.

Bradford picked up his phone and dialed Tony Segal.

Segal answered on the third ring. "Segal," he said.

"Detective. This is Bradford at East High."

"Brad, What's up?"

"Custodians chased two kids on campus last night who might be part of our Goth contingent."

"Are they sure?"

"Haven't talked with them but can we take the chance? They might have been preparing something big for today"

Segal was silent for what seemed a long time to Bradford.

"No we can't take any chances," Segal said finally. "Styles and I will be right over. I'll get patrol to send some units to the school. Notify the principal but let's keep a low profile. We don't want to spook them or cause a panic if we're over-reacting."

Before Bradford could respond Segal asked: "Any idea who they might be?"

"My informant, the girl I told you about, gave me the names of a couple of guys tight with Reaper. I planned to check them out today."

"OK," Segal said. "Find out what classes they're in and keep an eye on them."

"Roger that," Bradford said as he dropped the phone back in its cradle, got up and walked toward the principal's office.

Chapter 70

Lunchtime at East High was organized chaos.

Kids formed groups all over campus. Some ate in the enclosed cafeteria; others bought food from large windows open on the side of the cafeteria. Still others bought pizza, hot dogs and hamburgers from carts spread around the quad. They ate on metal tables or sat on the wooden seats in the open amphitheater. Cliques ate with cliques---the jocks and cheerleaders, gang wannabees, surfers, bandos, geeks, Goths.

Officer William Bradford surveyed the groups from a raised cement walkway in front of the administration building. The noon aides, who all carried radios tuned to a school frequency, circulated among the students chatting with them, sharing jokes, reminding others to pick up their trash. Today they were extra vigilant. Bradford briefed them prior to lunch.

Principal Farraday and activities director Jonathon Moser also walked the campus acting nonchalant. But Farraday's shirt was soaked through at the armpits and beads of sweat formed at the small of his back. His head swiveled from side to side to pick up anything unusual or spot the two Goth boys. Moser spoke with some of the jocks and cheerleaders but he wandered near the benches where the Goths lounged acting indifferent to everything going on around them. *Nothing unusual for them*, Moser thought.

Segal and Styles watched from office windows that opened onto the quad; two patrol cars parked at the north and south ends of the school. Cops were on campus for one thing or another so often their presence did not raise concerns. In fact, some students stopped to banter with the officers in the cars.

The staff, except for the administrators and noon aides, was oblivious. Teachers ate in the faculty dining room or in department offices. Farraday took a calculated risk and not alerted them for fear someone would inadvertently reveal the potential danger. His head would roll if anyone were hurt or worse

Ten minutes after lunch began, Raven and Spyder walked together toward the back of the cafeteria, both boys anxious. They avoided the area where their fellow Goths congregated. They didn't want to be held up from their mission for any reason. And they had abandoned the idea of a food fight to distract attention for something better.

A noon aide spotted the boys and alerted everyone. "They're on their way toward the cafeteria," he whispered into his radio.

Officer Bradford picked up the transmission and relayed it to Segal and Styles, who left their office perch and strode through the quad at a fast pace.

Raven and Spyder stopped before reaching the dumpster; checked to see if anyone was watching, then walked to where they had stored their weapons. Each boy reached into a bag, pulled out a ski mask and slipped it on. They also grabbed a Molotov cocktail, which they planned to launch into a group of students to create panic. They would then shoot those on their list and other targets of opportunity.

Before they could act, a booming voice braced them.

"Stop right there," Big Tony Segal shouted as he, Styles and two patrol officers trained their weapons on the boys.

"Nooo!" Spyder screamed. He raised his arm and stepped toward the officers.

Chapter 71

It ended almost as soon as it began.

Spyder cocked his arm to throw his Molotov cocktail when a hail of bullets ripped through his body throwing him backwards. As he fell his homemade bomb hit the ground and exploded engulfing he and Raven in flames.

Then Raven's cocktail ignited. The officers, and a group of students, watched in horror as the boys writhed in agony. Some girls shrieked and ran while other students sprinted toward the action.

Officer Bradford raced into the cafeteria, returned with a fire extinguisher and doused the flames dancing on the bodies of both young boys. Raven screamed; Spyder was still.

The paramedics arrived in minutes along with two ambulances and spirited the boys off to the nearest hospital. Farraday, Moser, and the noon aides herded the student spectators away from the area. Farraday called his secretary. "Ring the passing bell. Let's get these kids to class now," he shouted.

Despite word of the confrontation on campus, which spread like wildfire, most students marched dutifully back to class. When some of the Goth kids hesitated, Moser sent them to his office, his voice steady, calm and the kids obeyed.

William Farraday spoke on the school's public address system when the grounds cleared. "A tragic event happened on campus during lunch" he said, his voice low, sad. "Some injured students were taken to the hospital by Paramedics. We hope and pray they will be all right."

The statement was false but he intended to calm everyone, not enflame emotions. "We don't have all of the information yet as to why the incident occurred," he continued. Another white lie, but one he felt necessary. "I will share that with everyone when it becomes available. Thank you for your understanding. Any of you need who may need to talk with someone about your feelings, can meet with designated staff later this afternoon."

Farraday placed the hand held microphone back on its hook and turned to see Styles and Segal standing in the small room. He leaned against the wall and sobbed.

Chapter 72

Wild Bill McClusky scanned the bar area at O'Hara's.

A man seated at a round table in a secluded corner caught his eye. McClusky threaded his way through empty tables and sat next to him. Neither spoke before a waitress in a short black skirt and multicolored blouse stood before them. "May I get you something to drink," she asked cheerfully. She was young, in her early twenties, blond and perky—a typical California poster girl. *"A health club fanatic,"* McClusky thought as he appraised her. *"I'd like to give her a private workout."* He said, "Bud light, please."

"You got it," the girl said and walked away smiling.

"We got a problem," McClusky said, leaning forward, keeping his voice low.

"Yeah!"

"Yeah! Log on records show someone accessed the entire department data base a few days ago, something only Captains and above are permitted."

"So."

"The code used is not one assigned to the appropriate officers."

"You know this how?"

"I have my ways," McLusky said.

"Goody told me he ran across two detectives working late. Both acted strange. One is OK. The other I wonder about."

The waitress returned and put a beer down in front of him. "May I get you an appetizer or anything else?" she asked.

"You can haul my ashes," McClusky thought. He said, "No thanks, perhaps later."

The girl smiled, turned and walked toward a couple that had taken seats two tables away. McClusky, never one to miss an opportunity to ogle a pretty woman, once again admired the waitress from the rear. She had a great ass and tight thighs.

Wouldn't mind having those legs wrapped around me, he thought.

The girl reminded him of his current secretary, a blond bimbo he used as a punchboard. The dumb broad couldn't type or even file worth crap, but she sucked a dick like a pro. He got hard thinking about it.

"Hey Bill," McClusky's companion said, breaking into his reverie. "She's too young for you. If not jail bait, she'd give you a heart attack."

"Yeah," said McClusky, "but what a way to go." He laughed at this witticism, and turned his attention from the waitress to the issue at hand.

"I've got a bad feeling. Why is someone's snooping around now and who's behind it? MALDEF and the ACLU are fucking us over. The whole community is jumpy over the murder of the two high school kids. Some of the guys begged off poker for a while. If the shit hits the fan, they'll jump ship faster than many of the passengers on the Titanic."

"Relax Bill. Everyone will keep quiet. They have as much to lose as we do. Are you losing faith in the cause?"

"Fuck no," McClusky said, too loudly. The couple two tables away peered over their menus. The woman frowned. The man dropped his eyes to the table.

McClusky smiled self-consciously and lowered his voice. He believed in the cause more than ever. He wanted to impress this on his companion. "This country has been going to hell in a hand basket since those commie, faggot, chicken-shit Vietnam protesters undermined all respect for authority. Now, the fucking illegals are streaming across the border from Mexico, no one is doing a damn thing about it. They're having babies like rabbits; overcrowding the schools; running down neighborhoods; packing five families into apartments barely large enough for one; refusing to speak English.

"Metzger had the right idea. Citizen patrols should pounce on the wetbacks at the border. Fucking liberal judges should never have stopped that. California's a damn Third World country---so's this fuckin city. No one speaks English anymore. Make no mistake; we're the thin blue line between order and chaos. Damn right I still believe."

McClusky's face was flushed, his breathing labored. "Ok, OK, maybe I'm overreacting," he said, looking at his companion. "But that doesn't mean I'm not going to keep an eye out—snoop around a little, see what I can turn up. I, we, have got too much to lose. I'm gonna retire soon."

"Are you going to tell me who the guys snooping around were?" Cunningham asked.

McClusky whispered the names in the man's ear as he got up, threw a five-dollar bill on the table and walked out of the bar.

His companion, Officer Randy Cunningham, finished his beer. He sat back in thought for a moment, flashed back to the last meeting at McClusky's when he thought he recognized the driver of a passing car but couldn't remember a name.

It came to him now---one of the detectives at the Ramos shoot. He smiled to himself and signaled for the check. He knew what he had to do.

Chapter 73

The city was still shaken by the tragic deaths of Raven and Spyder and by the potential massacre averted by the swift action of police and school administrators. Most Goth students had not returned to school for fear of reprisals. Some teachers and support staff angry with principal Farraday for not alerting them to the danger tempered the general feeling of relief.

Typical, thought Styles as she prepared to question student Nancy Holmes. You can't please everyone, ever.

She would try to break the girl; catch her in a lie. Reaper and his pals had not killed Alex Lyon or Kitty Richmond; their bigger plan thankfully foiled. A murderer still lurked out there.

Styles sat a rectangular table in the office of the Activities Director at East High School, Jonathon Moser, who sat behind his desk as an observer representing the school but would take no active role in the questioning.

Nancy Holmes faced detective Styles. She wore her orange and black cheerleader uniform; a white carnation pinned to the uniform above and to the left of the "T" in East, which was written across the front in script. Her oval face was devoid of make-up; her jet-black hair, parted just to the left of center, cascaded to her shoulders. She had that freshly scrubbed look, conveying innocence but hinting at mischief. Her lips were fleshy, sensuous, inviting, a girl on the verge of womanhood, someone who would drive adolescent boys crazy.

Holmes sat in a padded straight back chair hands folded in her lap, her back erect, head bowed, eyes darting from Styles to Moser

Styles spoke to the teenager in a soft, reassuring voice. "Thank you for meeting with me again, Nancy, I know this is difficult for you but I need to clarify some things. You want to help us catch whoever killed your friend, don't you?"

"I do," Holmes said, "I do," the corners of her mouth turned upward in a strained effort to smile.

"Good! Good!" Styles said, taking out her Palm Pilot. She scrolled through her notes until she found what she wanted. Holmes tensed.

"You said Alex was at the party after the game, right?"

"Yeah, uh Yes".

"But you didn't see her leave?"

"No!"

"Are you sure? This is important Nancy."

"I, um, can't be positive, you know! There were, um, lots of kids there, you know."

Styles, annoyed, pressed the point. "You're not sure or you don't know? Because some of the kids reported that you and Alex left together," she lied.

"Not true." Holmes stammered, her voice cracking.

"Nancy," Styles said patting the girl's knee. "Two of your friends are dead. The same person who killed Alex may have killed Kitty. We need to find out who did this so it doesn't happen again. We're not trying to get you in trouble. Please help us!"

Holmes' eyes welled up. Tears cascaded down her cheeks. Moser got up and placed a box of tissues in front of the sobbing girl, patted her shoulder and returned to his seat.

Holmes took several tissues and dabbed at her eyes, now red and swollen. "Shouldn't my parents be here," she asked, her voice quivering. "Isn't that the rule?" She looked toward Moser.

"Do you want your parents here, Nancy?" Styles asked.

The girl turned back away from Moser and shook her head. "I, I guess not!"

Styles remained seated but patted the girl's leg. She waited for Nancy to compose herself.

"Nancy! Tell me what happened that night----please!"

Several crumpled tissues now lay on the table in front of the distraught cheerleader. She reached out with her right hand and took two more from the box.

"We didn't kill her. We didn't kill her. It wasn't our fault," she blurted, burying her face in her hands. Her shoulders shook and liquid ran from her eyes and nose.

"We didn't kill her!"

Chapter 74

Cara Styles coaxed the story from the frightened girl.

"I believe you, Nancy," Styles assured her, "but you must tell me what happened."

Style's scooted her chair closer to the girl and placed her arm around her shoulders. Moser leaned forward.

Nancy Holmes, sniffing and dabbing her eyes, slumped in her chair, resigned. Her voice trembled when she spoke, words coming through choked sobs.

"Before the game some of the girls took a few bumps of crank. We, like, planned to leave the party early and have our own fun, you know."

Bumps of Crank? This kid is no innocent, thought Styles. She asked, "What girls?"

Nancy hesitated. Still unwilling to name names.

"Nancy," Styles said, her voice calm, but firm. "We aren't concerned about the drugs. Nobody's going to get in trouble."

"A couple of the cheerleaders, Alex, Anna, Kitty and me," the girl said.

"OK! Go on, please."

"After the game we went to the party but, like, to wait for the guys. Alex didn't come to the party right away. She was, like, supposed to meet someone first. She wouldn't tell us who. I don't know if she ever met him. She, like, was pissed off when she finally got to the house."

Realizing she said "pissed off" Holmes looked sheepish but didn't apologize. "I, like, really don't know how long we stayed," she continued. "We partied hardy, you know. We left when the guys showed."

"What guys, Nancy?"

This time the girl didn't hesitate. "Guys on the team. Derek, Michael and Floyd."

"Where did you go?"

"To the park. We, like, had beer and chips and stuff. Some crank, too."

"Why didn't Tommy, Alex's boyfriend, go?"

"He, like, got hurt in the game and had to go get some x-rays, you know. His parents took him to the emergency room."

"What did you do when you got to the Park?"

"We sat in the cars and, like, drank beer, ate and," she paused, "finished the crank. We fooled around a little."

"What do you mean?" Styles pressed, knowing the answer.

Nancy's face reddened. She glanced over her shoulder at Moser, who turned away.

Nancy sniffed and dabbed her eyes again. "You know. We made out, fooled around."

"You weren't all in one car?"

"No. Derek, Michael, Kitty and me were, like, in my car. Floyd and Anna went with Alex."

"What kind of car do you have, Nancy?"

"A Honda Civic."

Styles made a note in her Palm Pilot. The lab had indicated the tire tread found at the scene came from a compact car like a Civic.

"Go on, Nancy," Styles directed.

"It was kinda warm, you know. So, like, we went into the woods to a spot we knew of."

"All of you?"

"Yeah. We were wasted. We found the clearing on the trail and kinda flopped down. Somebody had a blanket. After a while, Derek belched and said he had to pee. I, like, thought he was gross. Somebody shouted to do it away from us."

Styles remained silent but continued to rub the girl's back.

"When Derek came back, the front of his pants were open and his, his, thing hung out. He made sure everybody noticed. He, like, had a stupid expression on his face, you know. One of the guys told him to put that hose away. Derek is, like, big."

Nancy kept her head down as she spoke. She leaned on the table and rested her head in her hands. Jonathon Moser strained to hear although he tried to appear disinterested.

"Can we get you some water or a soft drink, Nancy," Styles asked.

Nancy shook her head. "I'm okay. I just want to get this over with."

"Take your time."

"Derek like, stood there with his thing hanging out and Alex, she, she."

"She what, Nancy?"

"She crawled over to Derek on her hands and knees. Floyd jumped up and went over and dropped his pants in front of Alex too. She, like, did both of them."

Chapter 75

Styles blanched as Nancy Holmes described the teenage bacchanal.

Holmes face reddened, she lowered her eyes, slouched down in her chair when she finished.

"Alex gave oral sex to both guys?" Styles asked, avoiding the crude term for what the girl had done.

"Alex was wild but, like, I had never seen her do two guys," Holmes said.

"What happened next?"

"We were all wasted. So watching them kinda got the rest of us hot. Meth and alcohol can do that to you, you know. Anna and I did Michael.

Holmes dropped her eyes to the table. Her face flushed.

"Go on, Nancy," Styles said.

"After fooling around, like, we sat around, talking and drinking.

"Did anyone have intercourse with Alex?"

Holmes shook her head, as if fending off a fly annoying her. "No, don't think so. We started drinking again, you know. We had a lot of beer."

"What about Alex?"

"She passed out."

"With all of her clothes on?"

"Yeah! But, like, then her stupid brother ran out of the bushes screaming at Derek to leave his sister alone. He must have, like, been watching us. He tried to hit Derek but Derek is, like, really strong. He threw Brent to the ground and held him until he, like, stopped screaming and struggling. Brent ran off when Derek let him up.

Styles wanted to scream if Holmes kept saying "like." Instead, she asked, "So Brent was there?"

"Yeah. Yes."

"Did he come back later?"

Holmes shook her head.

"OK. Go on Nancy, please."

"We, like, let Alex sleep and partied some more. After a while, I don't, like, remember how long, you know, we decided to leave."

Nancy put her hand to her mouth, near tears. She wanted them to understand.

"We...we...we couldn't wake her up. Like, everybody tried, but she wouldn't budge. Like, you gotta understand. We were wasted, not thinking straight."

Her eyes pleaded for understanding, but Styles expression remained non-committal. Moser sat on the edge of his seat.

"We, uh, left her. We left her to get killed. I'm so ashamed. It was our fault."

She sobbed and put her head on her arms, which she rested on the table. Her shoulders undulated with each sob.

Styles struggled to understand how a bunch of kids, even those wrung out on drugs and alcohol, could leave their friend alone in the woods late at night. *The little bastards*, she thought, glad she didn't have children.

The girl showed remorse, but kept silent for days, a silence that impeded the investigation. Her story might have focused more attention on Brent, saved his life.

The other kids still had not come forward even though their behavior contributed to the death of a classmate. None of them planned it. None of them expected it to happen. But it did. They kept quiet--remorseful, maybe, but not enough to come forward.

Bastards.

Styles spoke to Jonathon Moser. "Nancy may need to go to the nurses office. We'll want to talk to her again later. Better call her parents."

Moser came around his desk and grasped Holmes gently by the shoulders, coaxed her to her feet and led her out the door, her head resting against him.

Styles reflected on her conversation with Nancy Holmes as she left the school administration building and returned to her unmarked car. She unlocked the vehicle, slipped behind the wheel and put the key in the ignition but did not turn the engine over. Instead, she sat back, shook her head, eyes moist.

If I were Alex Lyon's mother or father, I'd want to beat the crap out of every one of her so-called friends. How could they be so stupid?

She had seen a lot over the years, but this was tough to deal with. *I don't get it*, she said to herself. *I hope this sticks with these kids for the rest of their lives but I doubt it. They'll all be at a party this weekend.*

She put the car in reverse, backed out of the parking space and angled toward the nearest exit, her eyes still moist, her body shaking with rage.

Chapter 76

Lieutenant Deluca stood in the doorway to his office reading the California section of the L.A. Times when a telephone rang on the unoccupied desk of Cara Styles. He walked over and picked up the phone. "Lt. Deluca," he said.

"Oh, Lieutenant. This is Jonathon Moser, Activities Director at East High School. Is detective Styles available?"

"She's away from her desk at the moment, Sir, can I help you."

Moser hesitated, then continued. "You're in charge of the Alex Lyon investigation aren't you?"

"Yes, I am, sir."

"We found something here at school you should see." Moser paused and a long silence followed.

Deluca waited. Experience with witnesses had shown the longer you remained quiet the more they talked.

"Well, after Alex and Brent's death, our SRO searched their lockers with two of your detectives but, as I understand, they apparently didn't find anything helpful."

"Yes sir," Deluca said, encouraging Moser, by the brevity of his response, to get to the point.

"Well, today, Victoria Salazar, a cheerleader who has been away visiting her grandmother in Mexico, came back to school. Unbeknown to us, she shared a locker with Alex near the gym."

"Yes, Sir," Deluca said, now more interested in what the man had to say.

"Victoria brought me a purse that Alex had left in that locker. It contained an unlabeled videotape. I took it to a library viewing room, thought it might belong to the media center."

Moser paused until Deluca urged him to continue.

"The tape, and I didn't watch the whole thing mind you," Moser pointed out, "was shocking and might have some bearing on the investigation."

"Can you bring the tape to the department, Sir?"

"Yes, I, uh, could run it over right now."

"Good. Ask for me at the front desk. I'll meet you."

Moser hung up without further comment.

Fifty minutes later, Deluca rolled a VCR and TV on a metal stand into the conference room adjacent to his office where Styles waited. Segal had gone to check on his daughter, home with the flu.

Deluca inserted the tape into the VCR and explained its origin. "Jonathon Moser found this in a locker Alex Lyon shared with another student. He briefed me on its contents."

He located the power buttons on both the VCR and TV, turned them on and pressed play. After a few seconds of white static lines, a color picture appeared; Alex Lyon, lying on her bed, clad only in a pink bra and see-through pink panties. She smiled at a naked young man who moved into the picture and stood at the foot of the bed. He grabbed Alex's arm pulling her into a sitting position, her face inches from his crotch.

Deluca stole a sideways glance at Styles sitting next to him at the rectangular conference table. Her breathing seemed labored but she kept her attention riveted to the TV.

Deluca returned his gaze to the screen. Alex rocked back and forth as her head bobbed between the young man's thighs. This went on until the boy reached behind Alex releasing the clasp on her bra. He stroked her breasts for a minute or two then pushed her flat on her back, slipped both hands under her hips and pulled off her panties. The camera angle captured her lower body.

Alex and her partner switched places. He lay on his back while Alex, facing the camera, placed both feet on his thighs. With her hands on either side of him, she smiled and lowered herself so he slipped inside her.

Cara Styles gasped at the site of this intimate sexual coupling and grimaced as if personally impaled like the girl. Alex and the boy were not joined as God intended but in the way man invented.

Styles shifted in her chair, uncomfortable watching this with Deluca.

On the screen, Alex Lyon moved up and down piston-like, increasing her tempo until she and the young man shouted in unison and Alex collapsed backward across his chest.

When their show was over, Alex and her partner, brother Brent Lyon, sat smiling into the camera.

Just like a normal home movie, Deluca thought. *Right!*

Chapter 77

The screen became light blue. Deluca stopped the tape. He sat down in his chair, massaged his forehead with the fingers of his right hand and broke the awkward silence. "Guess that removes any doubt Alex and Brent were intimate."

Styles turned away, frowning. "True," she said "but it doesn't prove he had anything to do with her murder. Nancy Holmes put him at the scene though I doubt he killed her. He loved her, as horrible as that is."

Deluca grunted. He would not have used the term "love" to describe the relationship between Brent and Alex. "Maybe he returned after they ran him off," he countered. "Those kids were so wrapped up in each other and wasted, he could have been sitting beside them and they might not remember. We need to analyze Brent's DNA to see if any semen on Alex's body matches his."

"Still won't prove anything," Styles protested. "They may have had sex at home before the game or before the party."

"True," Deluca said. "But let's at least determine if they had sex that day."

Shaking his head, he leaned over and pressed the play button again on the VCR.

The blue screen gave way to another homemade sex scene in Alex's room. This time she sat astride a man lying on his back, her back to the camera. The man's face was hidden but his muscular, hairy legs indicated someone other than Brent.

The man reached around her buttocks and grasped Alex in his large, strong hands as she raised and lowered her hips. He had a silver wedding band on his left hand and a class ring with a blue stone on his right.

Soon, amid cries of pleasure, Alex collapsed forward onto the man's chest; the screen reverted to blue without revealing his face.

Deluca stopped the tape. "OK. Alex didn't make up those things in her diary," he conceded in understatement. "This guy was older and married. We need to get the lab to isolate one of the frames with his hands on her butt. We may be able to identify the college or high school the class ring represents."

"I'll take it to the lab as soon as we're finished here," Styles volunteered as she lapsed into stunned silence. She had seen her share of depravity undercover in vice but most involved adults. The plethora of porn on the Web did not interest her. Not her thing. This amateur version had appalled and aroused her. She was surprised and embarrassed to discover the physical effect on her and more than a little self-conscious though she knew Deluca could not know.

Deluca interrupted her thoughts when he announced they would view the rest of the tape. Styles focused on the screen as new images appeared.

Once again Alex starred. She lie on her bed, face down, with only a pair of white stockings and garter belt visible. Her legs were pressed together with the tops of her stockings reaching to the crease marking the juncture of her thighs and buttocks. A man, older, but not the same build as the one in the previous clip, straddled her. The camera angle caught only his lower body.

The scene ended prematurely in a blur of black and white lines as if the tape had been erased. Before Deluca could react, the screen filled with other images more disconcerting to the detectives.

Chapter 78

The camera zoomed in on the bed capturing two teen-aged girls, both naked, both now dead, legs entwined, arms wrapped around each other---Alex Lyon and Kitty Richmond.

It was difficult to say which shocked Styles and Deluca more, the intimate embrace or the fact they were now both gone---murdered. Neither detective spoke. The sterile conference room with its bare walls and scuffed, wooden furniture provided a tawdry backdrop for the lurid homemade sex tape.

On the screen, the girls touched and stroked each other, their lips and fingertips teasing, urging until Kitty's body convulsed and her hips fluttered, as if out of control. She dropped flat on her back on the bed emitting a soft cry. Alex leaned over and kissed her as the tape clanked to a stop, rewound and stopped with a thud.

Deluca reached over to push the off buttons on both the VCR and TV. He folded his hands on the table and took a deep breath ready to speak.

Styles cut him off with a look. She tapped the screen on her Palm Pilot a few times. "Alex kept Kitty's identity secret by using her real initials in her diary, not her nickname," she said.

"Alex made several references to an SR. Kitty's given name is Stephanie. Stephanie Richmond. Her parents told me she got the nickname Kitty as a child and everyone's called her by that name ever since, didn't register until now."

"That helps to identify one other person in the diary" Deluca said, "but that knowledge and this tape, only increases our possible suspects---older men, a jealous girlfriend or a boyfriend who found out she swings both ways. Maybe this relationship got both girls killed."

"Why would Alex tape this stuff?" Styles asked. "Very dangerous, especially for the men."

"Dr. Palmer would say it's part of the sexual addiction thing. A sex addict takes risks, adds to the thrill."

"For Alex," Styles said, "not the men having intercourse with an underage schoolgirl. What if they didn't know they were being taped?"

"Possible. If she left her closet door slightly ajar and placed the camera on a shelf, the men wouldn't notice. I found the camera during my room search, no tapes."

"This kid had sex with everyone and anyone in her own home, young or old, boy or girl," Styles added. "What if she threatened to expose a married him with the tape, guy panic's, ends the relationship permanently."

"Yeah," Deluca said. "But if he knew about a tape, wouldn't he have gotten it before killing her? And why would she tell him?"

"The guy wanted out and she didn't," Styles theorized. "She tells him to force him to stay. He meets her in the park to get the tape. She doesn't bring it. They argue. He kills her."

Styles shook her head to dismiss her own theory. "Doesn't fit with what Nancy Holmes told me about the party, though; nor the fact we found the panties of both girls on Eduardo Ramos."

Both detectives remained quiet mulling over their thoughts when Big Tony Segal burst into the room waving several sheets of paper.

Chapter 79

Segal's excitement was palpable. His chest heaved, his face flushed, droplets of sweat dotted his forehead. "My daughter was sent home with a touch of the flu," he said, sucking in air. "When I checked on her, my daughter, the Internet freak, had downloaded this stuff. Not sick enough to stay off the damn computer." He rolled his eyes. "She thought I might find this interesting."

"So!" Deluca said, opening his arms urging him to continue.

"An article from the Houston Chronicle about high school coaches having sex with their players."

Deluca stared at Segal, silent, not catching the relevance.

"A News-hound snooping around Texas high schools dug up dirt," Segal explained. "Over sixty coaches got the ax for diddling kids; not only players but student managers, cheerleaders.

"The article listed a couple reasons for this stuff goin' on in Texas. Coaches and kids spend long hours together, sometimes into the night and on weekends. And, the power and influence coaches wield in the community."

That made sense to Deluca. Kids revered successful coaches, sought to emulate and please them. Adults ignored or downplayed questionable behavior the same way they dismissed the peccadilloes of famous professional athletes.

"So?" Segal asked, "what coach is the big kahuna in this town right now?"

"Jimmy Phelan," Styles and Deluca echoed.

"JP" Styles said, referring to the initials in Alex Lyon's diary. "She was trying to seduce the coach, not Jeremy Peters."

After a few seconds of shocked silence, Deluca shook his head, frowned. "Get this tape to the lab and have them blow up the frame showing the rings on the man's hands," he directed Styles "And call that guy at East High, Jonathon Moser, the AD, find out where Phelan went to high school and college."

"What tape?" Segal asked but a clerk knocked on the open door of the conference room leaving his question unanswered. Deluca waved her in. She handed the head of homicide a manila folder containing the lab results on Alex Lyon's panties, the ones found in Eduardo Ramos' backpack.

"Another new twist," he said, shaking his head, after scanning the folder's contents. "Two different people left semen stains on Lyons panties but neither matches anyone in the database, including Ramos. And here's a kicker. A partial print did match someone, officer Mike Walker."

"What?" Segal asked in disbelief.

Styles' blanched, blinking her eyes several times.

"Did Walker handle the panties once you pulled them out of Ramos' backpack?" he asked Styles.

Styles did not take offense, the question had to be asked. "No, Boss. I held them up for everyone to see but then immediately placed them in a sealed bag, which I personally delivered to the lab. They were not out of my sight for even a brief period of time. The chain of custody is good."

"Then how does Walker's print get on them?" Deluca asked.

"Gotta be a mistake," Segal offered, "Gotta be."

Mistake or not, no one wanted to address the elephant in the room---the possibility that a police officer was involved in the murder of Alex Lyon. The room fell silent as each detective wrestled with that unthinkable possibility.

"We don't have much choice," Deluca said, resigned. "Let's get a DNA sample from Walker. His prints didn't turn up on those panties by magic."

"How do we do that without alerting him that he's a suspect?" Segal asked. "He could refuse."

"All officers are required to take an annual physical," Deluca said. "We use a couple of doctor's who contract with the department. Find out who did Walker's exam, get a urine specimen or blood sample from him or her."

The meeting broke up each detective left to ponder the unthinkable.

Chapter 80

Two federal agents sat at a rear table at a Starbucks located at the intersection of Ocean Avenue and Pacific Coast Highway in downtown Pacific City. Across the highway from the Starbucks was a concrete pier similar to others dotting the California coastline. It was a local landmark and tourist attraction. The agents were not trying to be secretive but they could not be seen from the street and the other two patrons in the coffee shop were engrossed in their laptops and lattes. One agent was dressed in a grey sport jacket, blue shirt and maroon tie, his companion a black blazer, white shirt, grey slacks. Each had a coffee of the day, tall, on the table in front of them.

Grey sport jacket, in his late forties, spoke first. He had an athletic build with wide shoulders tapered at the waist, blue eyes, strong jaw. He might have been mistaken for a typical middle-aged surfer, except for his conservative dress and closely cropped blond hair. He had, in fact, grown up in Manhattan Beach, several miles to the North and surfed during his youth. Now, he was the FBI Special Agent in Charge (SAC) for the Los Angeles Office. He kept his voice low as he leaned toward his companion. "What have you got so far?"

The special agent working undercover in the PCPD also spoke softly. "A mess, a probable conspiracy, some rogue cops acting as a hit squad to cleanse the city of undesirables. For several years the department has maintained a file on individuals and groups labeled extremists. At least three of the men in the file died in the last fourteen months, all of them during an arrest or in police custody. I haven't had time to check others on the list."

"Are the Officers involved in these deaths part of the Aryan group we're looking at?"

"Yeah. One guy in particular, a Randy Cunningham, participated in all three of the recent incidents. He's a regular at the meetings at McClusky's. Cunningham's also the officer who shot Eduardo Ramos, an escaped rapist who was a prime suspect in the high school cheerleader case. Ramos was a scumbag but he was unarmed when Cunningham took him out."

The SAC nodded, said nothing.

"In a new twist in the cheerleader's murder an officer is now a suspect. One of his prints turned up on the girl's underwear. The lab is running a DNA check now to determine if semen present also belongs to him."

"I thought I read the girl's panties were found on Ramos?"

"You did. We can't figure out how the officer's print got on them. I found the panties on Ramos. The cop never touched them."

"At least not while you were there."

"Correct."

"Am I to assume this guy is also part of the WAR group?"

"Yup," the undercover agent said, took a sip of coffee then

bent over, opened a black briefcase resting by a table leg, extracted a manila folder and pushed it toward the SAC.

"That's the PCPD file I printed. Some interesting groups like the Knights of Columbus and ACLU are listed as Extremists."

The SAC scanned the file. "Wonder what the Cardinal would think," he said, emitting a small grunt.

"I need you to follow up on a couple of things related to the file," the agent said. "Cunningham worked for the LAPD before coming to Pacific City. It would be helpful to get a look at his personnel file from that period, see if he had any serious discipline issues. Also, run down the other names on that list. Find out if any of them met their demise at the hands of the PCPD. I don't think I've drawn any attention to myself but I can't risk being discovered looking through the files."

"Ok," the SAC said, pushing his chair back and standing up. "This might be what we need to move on these assholes." He turned and left.

The undercover agent waited five minutes, finished the coffee and also exited. Once on the sidewalk, the agent mingled with several other people until the light changed, then crossed the street. Invigorated by a cool ocean breeze, the salt air and the smell of the sea, the agent walked halfway out onto the pier and leaned on the metal railing, face uplifted. Deceiving people was part of the job but it hurt to lie to those you had come to like and respect. Yet you couldn't let maniacs use the law for their own purposes and destroy public confidence in those sworn to protect them. In this case, the end did justify the means. The agent doubted everyone would agree.

Chapter81

Wild Bill McClusky stormed through the detective pen, burst into Deluca's office and slammed the door. Several detectives and clerks looked up from their desks distracted by the noise.

"What the fuck is going on JD," McClusky fumed leaning over Deluca's desk, neck muscles bulging.

"What do you mean, Sir?"

"Don't fuck with me JD. I know what goes on in my Division. Why are your guy's looking to hurt one of our own?"

"We're trying to be careful, Bill. Nobody wants to hurt anyone."

"Bullshit," McClusky shouted. He took his hands off the desk and paced back and forth. He pulled at his collar to suck in more air, his teeth clenched, his face red. He stopped in the middle of the room and glared at his subordinate.

"JD. If word leeks you're looking at Walker for the kid's murder, there'll be hell to pay. The bloodsuckers in the press will crucify this department. So will those turds in MALDEF and the ACLU."

"We're not ready to go public with this, Bill, we're only following up on some leads."

"What leads?"

"Right now a fingerprint on the girl's panties and a DNA search on some semen."

McClusky took a deep breath, put his hands in his pockets. Stared at the wall, then spoke, more subdued. "What does Walker say about the print?"

"We haven't talked with him yet," Deluca said, and quickly added, "We're waiting for the DNA results."

McClusky considered that for a moment as he turned and walked toward the door. With his hand on the doorknob, he stopped, looked back. "When and if you find something, you tell me first, understand?"

"Yes sir."

McClusky pulled the door open, let it slam as he walked past several detectives working at their desks, heads down.

Later that day, Cara Styles, walking by the captain's office on her way to a break room, saw Walker, Cunningham and "Pops" Parker leave McClusky's office. None of the officers were in uniform. None smiled.

Chapter 82

Cara Styles knocked on the open door.

Deluca motioned her in. Styles sat down in a chair against a wall to the left of his desk, a position affording him an unobstructed view of Styles, dressed conservatively in grey slacks, white blouse and black blazer. She kept her legs together, hands folded in her lap looking like a demure young woman applying for a job.

An attractive applicant, Deluca thought. He caught himself staring and shuffled some papers to stifle amorous thoughts of her.

She worked for him; she was beautiful, the ingredients for trouble. Many females in law enforcement fended off unwanted advances from colleagues or their supervisors. He did not want to embarrass either of them by saying or doing anything that might be misconstrued. He determined, once again, to keep their relationship on a professional level at all times. He had to admit, though, his daily contact with her weakened his resolve. She often took his breath away.

For her part, Styles was not unaware of the comments made about her nor the effect she had on many of her male counterparts. She often dressed provocatively to deflect other thoughts her colleagues might entertain about her.

Nevertheless, she found Deluca attractive and knew that, after his wife's death, he had not dated much. Under the circumstances, though, she doubted a relationship with him would be wise. His ardor would no doubt cool when he discovered her real purpose in the PCPD. In the meantime, she made it difficult for him to ignore her and suspected, by his uncomfortable manner, she was being successful. She found his behavior refreshing and once again felt guilty.

She had to keep their relationship professional. If he made a move toward a more personal intimacy, she would decide then what to do. For now, she took two pictures from a manila folder she held in her hand, reached over, and gave them to Deluca. "I got these from Segal a few minutes ago," she said. "They're the lab blow ups of the guy's hands from the video of Alex; a clear view of the class ring, from UCLA."

"And?" He asked, in anticipation of what was to follow.

"And, Coach Phelan graduated from UCLA."

"Ok! Let's get the son-of-a-bitch in here pronto."

Styles acknowledged his directive, got up from her chair and started to leave the office. She stopped, turned to face him, when Deluca cleared his throat.

"Cara, uh, I hope I'm not out of line," he stammered. "Would, uh, would you like to have a glass of wine sometime? I'll understand if you don't," he said, his face a deep crimson.

"Great," Styles said, catching him by surprise. "Tonight works for me. We both could use a drink."

"Tonight. Ok! The Olive Garden, around six?"

Styles agreed and left the office.

What the hell did I just do? Deluca thought. All that self-talk about keeping things professional, of doing nothing to send the wrong message was so much bull.

Jesus!

Chapter 83

Coach Jimmy Phelan, dressed in an orange and black sweat suit, sat in the small interrogation room. He folded and unfolded his hands, rotated his head around in circles as if loosening up for a workout and shifted his position in his chair every few minutes.

Phelan had dreaded this moment ever since the murder of Alex Lyon. He debated with himself whether to be honest with the detectives or to try to stonewall it. He was still unsure of his response when detective Cara Styles entered the room and took a seat opposite him.

"Thank you for coming, Coach Phelan," Styles said. She placed a manila folder on the table in front of her but did not open it. Phelan's jaw tensed.

"I wanted to ask you a few questions about Alex Lyon," Styles said, looking into his blue eyes.

Phelan held her stare briefly before looking down, idly twisting the class ring on the finger of his right hand. "I'll help in any way I can," he said, a slight tremor evident in his voice.

"Good. How well did you know Alex?"

Phelan clasped his hands together. "Better than most students, I guess. Her boyfriend, Tommy, is our quarterback. She hung around practice a lot with other cheerleaders and she was in my senior government class."

Styles next question rocked Phelan backward. "Did you know her outside of school?"

The blood drained from his face. He shifted in his chair, rolling his shoulders. He licked his parched lips, gulped for air. "May I have some water?" he asked, smiling, voice barely above a whisper.

"Sure," Styles said. She got up from her chair, took the file folder and left the room, closing the door behind her. She motioned for Tony Segal to stand guard.

Styles returned and put a large Styrofoam cup of water in front of Phelan. He grasped it, took a deep swallow and put it down. "I'm not sure I understand your last question," he said after a brief pause.

The response annoyed Styles. She would not play games. "What I mean coach is did you have a personal relationship with Alex Lyon outside of school beyond teacher/student?"

Not ready to concede, Phelan said. "Again, I'm confused about what you mean by personal. I often see my students and players in the community. I'm invited to their homes. I'm on a first name basis with many of their parents. If that's personal, then yes, I had a personal relationship with her."

Styles gave him one more opportunity to be truthful before she played her trump card. "By personal, coach, I mean more than knowing the first names of her parents. I mean an intimate physical relationship?"

Phelan attempted to put off the inevitable. "That's crazy, I." Styles held up her hand. She'd had enough of the verbal sparring. She opened the manila folder and placed two photos on the table in front of Phelan. The pictures showed a naked Alex Lyon straddling a man, her buttocks toward the camera, the man's rings visible as he held her.

Phelan stared in disbelief; clearly not aware Alex had filmed their encounter. He buried his head in his hands, didn't speak or move.

Styles let him stay like that for several minutes. She regarded him with both pity and loathing. His career was trashed. He had violated a child; his sacred trust and deserved to pay the price. *Had he also killed her?*

Suppressing her anger, she pressed on. "We have semen samples from Alex's panties. You're in deep Bandini coach if they match your DNA. Be upfront with me. You can't save your career but you might save your life."

Phelan couldn't control his emotion any longer. He sobbed, kept his head buried in his hands, managed to blubber: "I didn't kill her, I swear. I had sex with her. God knows that was wrong. We had sex in my car during lunch on the day she was murdered. My semen could have gotten on her panties then."

"Can you account for your time between ten and two on that night?"

"Uh, that might be kinda awkward."

"As awkward as spending the rest of your life in prison, or worse?"

"No, of course not. I, uh, to be honest, I, uh, I'm not sure what happened. Alex and I were supposed to meet in the park, I think, but we never got together. I was so drunk I don't remember. When I, uh, woke up the next day, I was with, uh, this woman, not my wife."

Styles shook her head. "Jesus Christ, Coach, can't you ever keep it in your pants?"

Embarrassed, Phelan clasped and unclasped his hands and kept his eyes focused on the tabletop.

"Whose the woman?" Styles asked.

"Can we keep her name out of this?" Phelan pleaded, almost whined.

"I can't promise anything at this point, coach. You'd better be more concerned about saving your ass than the reputation of some slut."

Phelan flinched at the use of the term 'slut.' He slumped back in his chair and hung his head. "Her name's Peggy. Peggy Deerfield. She's the mother of one of my players."

"I'll need her address and phone number?"

Phelan gave it to her, quickly this time, all of his resistance gone.

"What happens now?" he asked. "Am I under arrest?"

"Yes. For murder or something else depends on whether your story checks out. Will you submit to a DNA test?"

"Yes. I did not do this."

"OK. Sit tight. I'll get back to you," Styles said, getting up from her chair and walking out of the room.

Under other circumstances, Phelan would have eyed her as she left. This time he had more pressing concerns, sat with his head down, hands folded on the table.

Another detective, a large man entered the room and sat a few chairs from Phelan. He didn't speak. Phelan's eyes darted to the detective for a moment then returned to the tabletop.

He had been right to fear the worst.

Chapter 84

The Olive Garden staff greeted customers at the front door.

Deluca nodded his thanks to the young waitress in white blouse and black skirt, returned her smile with one of his own and proceeded straight ahead to the small café/bar. Cara Styles had settled at one of the round tables along the wall.

"Hey," he said as he slipped into a padded wrought iron chair opposite Styles.

"Hey back," she said, flashing a smile that caused him to catch his breath.

"Thanks for meeting here," he said, "too many badges at O'Hara's."

"I agree. Is this a secret meeting, then?"

"No, not at all, I don't want to be under a magnifying glass, is all. Don't want rumors flying around the office tomorrow."

She smiled but didn't speak.

Deluca changed the subject. "Let's have some wine to start," he said, signaling the waiter with his arm raised.

"Sounds good," Styles said clasping her hands together on the table. With her bright eyes and clear skin she looked like a college student listening to a professor she admired.

Deluca's hand shook and he tapped his foot under the table, at a loss for words until the arrival of a young waiter in black slacks and white shirt rescued him.

"Glass of Chardonnay," Styles said before the young man asked the inevitable question. "Merlot for me," Deluca said. "We'll just have drinks for now."

He could not take his eyes off Styles but he was uncomfortable here with her. Years of training and self-discipline made it difficult. He was attracted to Styles both for her physical attributes and her quick mind. Bright energetic and competent, she had earned his trust and admiration. Yet, a personal relationship with her would change their professional one. He could lose the respect of his squad?

This is only a drink with a colleague, he told himself and turned the conversation to business. "We've certainly got a mess with this Lyon thing," he said aloud.

"Yeah! The cheerleader, Nancy Holmes spilled her guts to me. Alex partied the night she died, had oral sex with at least two guys. They were all so wasted, they left her there alone as easy prey for some sicko."

"Jesus."

"Yeah! With friends like that." She didn't finish the well-worn cliché.

Deluca said. "Maybe she died during the fun and games, already gone when they left."

"No. Holmes is sure she was alive. Just passed out. She's feeling guilty, claims Alex had her clothes on and didn't have intercourse with anyone."

The waiter appeared and placed their wine on the table. They both stopped talking and sipped their drinks. Deluca looked over the top of his glass at Styles, again struck by the freshness of her appearance, perfect skin, sensuous eyes.

Not sure why, he broached a sensitive subject. His face reddened. "You know this oral and anal sex thing," he said.

"What about it?" she asked, a slight smile creasing the corners of her mouth, her eyes glued to his.

"The current teen attitudes are disturbing. These kids do anal and oral sex because they don't consider it sex--safe if you don't consider contracting an STD. The girl can't get pregnant and technically she's still a virgin. You know, the Bill Clinton Philosophy of "non sex, sex."

"Yeah! I've heard this line of thinking before," Styles said. "My niece subscribes to a similar view. We've had some talks that kind of skirt the issue, no pun intended." Styles had no niece but she thought the comment would relax Deluca.

He smiled. "If you remember the tapes, no vaginal intercourse occurred—only oral and anal stuff."

Styles face flushed.

"I don't mean to embarrass you," Deluca added. "This stuff amazes me. I don't want to think about what my daughter may be doing, or might have done. I can't even fathom the girl on girl thing."

Styles smiled. "I'm not embarrassed. But I wouldn't have imagined having this conversation with a man unless we were in bed together. And—that hasn't happened in quite a while."

Deluca was surprised. Not only because he couldn't imagine someone so beautiful not having been in bed with someone recently, but also because she would tell him.

Might be the wine, although *she really hadn't had that much. Was she giving me that information for a reason?*

He drained his drink, and signaled the waiter for two more when Styles finished hers.

"Now whose uncomfortable," Styles asked. "I'm not complaining just telling the truth. Shouldn't be so forthright with my boss."

"We're off duty, I don't want to be your boss right now." He impulsively reached across the table and placed his hand over hers. She made no effort to remove it.

They had two more drinks and spent the rest of the evening discussing many different topics, some business, some personal. Driving home, Deluca thought about the softness of her hand and the warmth of her smile. He couldn't remember much about what they said.

Later, Styles sat on the second floor patio of her ocean side condo sipping a bottle of water. The condo had been a college graduation present from her father, the president and CEO of his own pharmaceutical company. Her parents had divorced when she was a child but they remained cordial and visited Styles often, although separately. Her father thought lavishing his only daughter with presents, like the condo, would win her affection. It didn't, but Styles never rejected the gifts.

She was invigorated sitting outside with the cool ocean breeze in her face. The patio was an ideal spot to think, quiet, secluded, idyllic. She thought of Deluca. He was attractive in the way that an outdoorsman conveys strength, energy and vitality. Professional in his relationship with her at work, shy in his attempt to establish a more personal, intimate connection. Their difference in age didn't matter. His maturity and experience, even the fact he had been married before, attracted her. But she also wondered if the attraction was grounded in her desire for a father figure, one who was present. One who didn't substitute things for affection?

So what if it was. I like him.

Chapter 85

At 6:00 AM, the PCPD detective, Special Agent, stepped out of the shower and was startled when a cell phone, kept nearby always, sounded off with its distinctive ring. The phone rested on the counter by the bathroom sink

"Yeah," the agent said, figuring it must be someone from the department, not the time for a social call. Hell, since joining the PCPD, any social calls were rare.

"Are you alone," The SAC for The Los Angeles Office of the FBI asked?

"You're joking, right? Who the heck would I be with now?"

"You never know, you never know," the SAC teased. "You might get lucky one of these days."

"Bite me. What's up?"

"Got the info you wanted on officer Cunningham. Not easy though; had to call in a number of chips and I don't have many with the LAPD."

"No kidding. I'm surprised you have any. You Fibees aren't too popular with local PD's, especially LA."

"Do you want the info, or not?" he asked.

"Of course," the agent said, keeping the cell phone pressed to an ear while opening the bathroom door and padding toward a bedroom closet to begin dressing.

"Your boy has quite a checkered past," the SAC began. "In fifteen years on the force, he was involved in four shootings, all African-American males. Six years ago, he shot and killed a burglary suspect. Three years before that he killed an alleged shoplifter. He was put on leave, by policy, after each incident but cleared of any wrongdoing by internal affairs."

The SAC paused before finishing his summary of Cunningham's record.

"You said four shootings," the agent prompted when tired of the silence.

"Yeah! Just before going to Pacific City, he wounded two black men during a traffic stop. Cunningham claimed the driver pulled a gun and the passenger brandished a tire iron."

"Apparently they objected to being stopped."

"Apparently. They took him off the streets after another review, made him a firing range instructor at the Police Academy."

"Pacific City hired him with that background?"

"Cunningham had his file sealed in return for his agreement to leave the department.

"Great, they should cut the balls off whoever struck that deal."

"There's more."

"Can't wait to hear," the agent said, still cradling the cell phone while pulling on some underwear.

"This guy's a gem," the SAC continued. "He was the leader of a small band of officers calling themselves the White Hats. They harassed black community groups formed to protest excessive force by the police."

"Why didn't they run the guy up on charges—throw his ass in jail?"

"You're obviously not familiar with LAPD history," the SAC said, with not a little sarcasm. "The Department did not want any more negative publicity. The Rodney King debacle reverberates to this day. The brass sat on the information and forced Cunningham and his buddies out."

"Super! A cover up so he could bring his brand of justice to Pacific City."

"You got it."

"WAR might be doing here what the White Hats did in L.A," the agent said after a brief silence. "The so-called list of extremists I gave you the other day is basically anyone the department didn't like. A couple of guys on the list turned up dead. Some skinheads savagely beat another one; of course, no suspects as yet on that one.

"You think those deaths were deliberate, planned?"

"You go to the head of the class. We've got a conspiracy to commit murder here, condoned at the highest levels."

"How high?"

"Division Captain, at least. Chief's a question mark."

"Better not be. He's the only one aware you're there."

"You want out?" the SAC asked. "Should we move on this now?"

"No! Not yet. Got to tie up some things first."

"Watch your back," the SAC warned, then broke the connection.

Chapter 86

Styles and Segal sat on chairs in front of Deluca's desk.

"O.K. What have we got on Phelan?" Deluca asked.

"At the very least," Styles said, "a teacher who molested one of his students. A semen stain on Alex's underwear matched Phelan. He admitted having sex with her around noon on the day she was murdered but swears he didn't kill her. Says he was with another woman that night although he's vague on the details. Claims he was wasted. Stankovich is checking with the woman. For now, he's under arrest for unlawful intercourse with a minor. His coaching and teaching days are over."

"Did he kill Alex?" Deluca pressed.

"My gut says no," she said. "He's a pervert and a lady's man but not a murderer. His story will probably check out."

"Who does that leave us with?"

"Officer Mike Walker. One semen stain on the panties still hasn't been matched. The others found on Alex's body belong to the two kids who partied with her. They rolled over after Nancy Holmes spilled her guts. The little bastards used Alex and abandoned her but didn't kill her, at least not directly."

Styles' voice was venomous, unlike her usual demeanor. She seldom showed emotion.

"O.K.," Deluca said. "Any suggestions on how we proceed with Walker? He knows we're looking at him. He may ask for union representation and refuse to tell us a damn thing. We're gonna need more than a fingerprint on a pair of panties."

"What if we also match his semen?" Styles said.

"We might have to arrest him to get it. Any luck on finding a blood sample from his physical, Tony? Or anything else we can obtain DNA from?"

Segal shook his head. "Nothing yet. Still working on it."

"All right. Let's confront Walker."

Chapter 87

Officer Mike Walker braced himself.

He sat at a rectangular table in a conference room opposite Big Tony Segal when Deluca and Styles walked in.

"Mike!" Deluca said, nodding toward Walker.

“Lieutenant," Walker said his hands clasped together on the table. "What's this all about?"

"I think you know, Mike."

"No! No, I don't," Walker blurted, eyes darting from one detective to the other. They each remained impassive and silent.

Walker sensed trouble. He asked, in an almost pleading tone, "Do I need representation?"

"Up to you, Mike," Deluca said. "We just want to ask you a few questions--clear up some things dealing with the Lyon murder."

Walker brought the fingers of his right hand up to his mouth pinching his lower lip. He stared straight ahead, avoiding the looks of any of the detectives. In a barely audible voice he said, "I'll answer some questions."

"Good," said Deluca, “I'll get right to it. We lifted a fingerprint off of Alex Lyon's panties. The one's found on Ramos. The print belongs to you, Mike." He punctuated the sentence by spreading his arms wide. "How come?"

Walker considered his response for several moments. "I'm at a loss. Maybe I handled them before Styles and Segal got there. I don't remember."

Styles leaned forward to speak. Deluca gestured for her to do so.

“First, Mike, that would have been a violation of procedure. You're smarter than that. Second, the pockets in Ramos' backpack were zippered shut. I had to open each one before I found the panties. You didn't handle them in my presence."

"Mike," Segal added. "The panties was still in the backpack when we got there.”

Walker blinked several times, shifted in his chair. He rubbed his hands together and pursed his lips. He made a mistake agreeing to be interviewed. "You really believe I had something to do with the girl's death?" he stammered, raising his voice. "That I would rape and kill a kid?"

Walker's questions echoed in the room as each of the detectives kept still, their eyes riveted on the young officer, "One of their own," in the words of Wild Bill McClusky.

"I want a union rep, now," Walker said, breaking the silence.

"Are you sure, Mike?" Deluca asked.

At that moment, the door of the conference room flew open and detective Ed Stankovich thrust his head inside. "We got a problem Lieutenant," he said, concern evident in his tone of voice. "Can I see you outside?"

"Everyone sit tight until I get back," Deluca said as he walked out of the room.

Once outside he leaned into Stankovich, forcing the big man to step backward. "What the hell is so important, Ed?" he asked, his face red, the veins in his neck bulging like dancing ropes.

Stankovich was over six feet tall but carried too many pounds even for his large frame. His face was round, fleshy, dark hair molded into a 1960's flattop. His sport coat pinched at the armpits, giving him a pear shaped appearance.

Composing himself, he gave Deluca the news. "Coach Phelan hanged himself in the holding tank. They rushed him to community hospital. He's alive but they're not sure he'll make it."

Deluca was stunned. He hadn't considered the coach a suicide risk. He should have, but hadn't. "Jesus H. Christ," he said. "Get over there, Ed. Keep me informed. The stupid bastard."

Chapter 88

Everyone eyed Deluca as he returned to the conference room.

He sat down but did not tell them why he had been called out. Before anyone could ask, Walker spoke up. "I'd like to talk with you alone Lieutenant before I talk to my union rep."

Deluca dipped his head indicating to the other detectives he wanted them to leave. He noted the concern on each person's face as they left.

"Go ahead, Mike," Deluca said when the door was closed.

"I'm innocent, I swear. The semen isn't mine. No friggin way."

"What about the print?"

"I won't deny that. I handled the panties before Styles and Segal arrived, stuck them in Ramos' backpack. The greaser is a scumbag. He's guilty of more stuff than we could ever nail him for."

"Not your call, Mike. You're sworn to uphold the law not twist or bend it to fit your whim or prejudices." He let that accusation hang in the air, then continued. "By throwing suspicion to Ramos, you let a guilty man continue to walk free and fucked up our investigation. In fact, the guilty party might be you."

Walker ignored the reference to prejudice. "No guilty man is running around loose," he said. "I know. He won't be committing more crimes any time soon, at least not in this world."

"How can you be so sure, Mike?"

"Because of where I found the panties!"

"OK. I'm listening."

Walker fidgeted in his chair, ran his hand over his closely cropped hair, sighed. "I'm not sure you'll believe it."

"Try me."

"I got them from the kid brother when he went airborne at the beach. He had them in the pockets of his jacket."

Deluca kept silent as Walker continued. "Can't say why I took them. Maybe so the parents wouldn't find out their son was the prick who killed their daughter and her friend. I wasn't thinking."

Deluca rubbed his chin, eyebrows furrowed. "Quite a story, Mike. Sounds like something the scumbags we deal with every day would come up with. Somebody else is guilty. Convenient blaming a dead kid."

"Sounds lame, Lieutenant, I realize, but Cunningham and Pops will back me up."

"So what. All that proves is you planted the evidence on Ramos. Doesn't tell us where you got the panties. You're in deep shit, Mike."

"I didn't do it, Lieutenant," Walker said, his voice rising with each word. "I'll submit to a DNA test; not my stuff on her panties."

"May be a start," Deluca said, pushing his chair back and standing up. "In the meantime you're on administrative leave. I need your badge and gun."

Shaken and forcing back tears, Walker placed his badge and gun on the table and sat staring at them. Deluca allowed him a few moments before he picked up the items and left the room.

Chapter 89

He sat in his car at the beach watching the sun slip below the horizon; the sky streaked a bright red and orange. Joggers chugged by on the paved walkway, a couple of mothers pushed strollers in the opposite direction, an idyllic setting. He should have been calm and relaxed enjoying the time and place. Instead his stomach churned, his head throbbed. Night terrors left him with little sleep.

None of this was planned, everything turned to crap. His first mistake was becoming involved with Alex. He was weak and stupid, a fool, to think she was only doing him, rumors to the contrary.

The goings on in the park enraged him; he acted on impulse. He'd read somewhere once you made a bad decision or did something wrong, other bad decisions followed. How true.

Alex had been a mistake, a fit of passion, but not the others. Covering up his first misdeed plunged him deeper into depravity; too late now, no turning back. One person remained to be silenced. He didn't understand why the man hadn't notified the police, hadn't done his job, his duty.

He leaned back in his seat, took a sip from the Starbuck's coffee cup. The hot coffee lifted his spirits but nothing could change his predicament.

He must act now.

Chapter 90

Dr. Jeffrey Palmer sat at his oak desk in his home office, a large room with floor to ceiling bookcases on two walls. The wall opposite his desk held his many degrees and awards won for work with various psychological groups. A large picture window overlooked his expansive and well-maintained lawn and gardens. He had drawn the blinds and locked his door although his wife was not at home. Beads of sweat formed on his forehead; his shirt damp with perspiration.

From a briefcase beside his desk, he extracted a disk containing a video downloaded from his office computer. Foolish to keep it, but he was not rational about his work with sexual addiction. The video highlighted his conversations with Alex Lyon. She had been forthright with him, told him things Palmer had not revealed despite his obligation to report them to the authorities.

He inserted the disk into his I Mac computer, checking over his shoulder. His concern was unfounded. His wife, even if home, would not venture into his domain. She made the mistake of walking in on him one night as he viewed a similar file. His tirade reduced her to tears.

Palmer opened the file, clicked on the appropriate icon and leaned back to watch. The first image showed Alex entering the office wearing her short skirt and low cut blouse. She and the doctor exchanged pleasantries and she immediately asked to use his private restroom. When she returned, she sat on the couch opposite Palmer crossing her legs in an exaggerated manner to show him she had removed her underwear.

Palmer ignored her obvious attempt at seduction. Alex looked puzzled as she realized Palmer did not intend to maul her like the other men in her life. She slumped back onto the couch, embarrassed, tears cascading down her cheeks. "I'm sorry," she mumbled. "I thought…"

"OK, Alex, I understand."

Yet, he was still shaken. Female patients tested him often but never a teenager and never one so pretty. His restraint, though, proved to be a turning point in their relationship. Alex opened up, told him her secrets; secrets that explained her behavior; secrets Palmer legally should have reported; secrets that could send some men to jail.

"Men, boys," she said, "want only one thing from me. All my life, ever since I can remember."

"Tell me about it," Palmer said.

And she did. She named names. People she should have trusted. No wonder sex obsessed her. Adults and boys her age used her for their own pleasure.

"How do you feel about this?" he asked.

"I like sex. It can be fun; it gets me things I want."

"Are you sure?"

She shrugged. "What choice do I have?"

Her response saddened Palmer but he understood. Understood how a teenager exhibiting the symptoms of a sex addict could actually be one. Publishing his findings would enhance his professional standing but he should have reported Alex's allegations to the police as soon as she uttered them. He faced jail if this tape surfaced. Yet, he was convinced none of the adults she identified had anything to do with her death. He knew some of them.

Palmer paused the video, got up and went to a cabinet located below his degrees and awards. He took out a bottle of Jim Beam and poured himself a full glass. He went back to the desk, sat in his high backed leather chair and took a deep swallow of his drink. He'd spend the next few hours watching and listening to everything Alex said. He would write up their conversation and destroy the tape.

Palmer resisted Alex's advances but he, too, lusted in his heart, a la Jimmy Carter. He watched the tape for another reason. Often he stopped it at the moment Alex crossed her legs. He was at that point in the video now and so engrossed he did not realize he was being watched through the opening between the drawn blinds and the window.

Chapter 91

The house was engulfed in flames arching upward from the windows and the roof; black smoke choked the air. Firefighters poured water into the burning structure creating more foul air. Fire rigs and emergency vehicles parked on the street in front of the conflagration while groups of police held the usual looky-loos at bay on the streets and sidewalks to the east and west.

An hysterical woman screamed and struggled to break through the line of officers. "That's my house," she yelled. "My husband's in there. Oh my god."

A female officer restrained the hysterical woman and eased her toward a nearby patrol car; another officer opened the door and both officers pushed, guided, the women inside.

The officer put her arm around the woman and asked in a calm, modulated tone, "What's your name ma'am?"

"Alice. Alice Palmer," she said, sobbing and choking.

"Are you sure your husband was at home?"

"Yes. Yes. I'm sure. His car is in the driveway."

"OK. Ma'am," the officer said, patting the woman's back. "We'll do our best to see if he's alright."

"He's in there. I know it," the woman bellowed.

The female officer enlisted a colleague to sit by Mrs. Palmer while she sought out the battalion fire chief to ask if they had pulled anyone out of the house.

She found the chief directing firefighters around to the back of the house. "Get those hoses in place," he yelled as his men struggled to follow his commands.

The female officer dodged lengths of hose and other fire equipment to get near the chief. She shouted, "Anyone get pulled out of the house, Chief?"

His face was black with grime, wet with sweat, tired. He shook his head and turned back toward the action.

"Chief. Chief," the officer yelled, trying to get his attention again. "A woman says her husband's inside."

The chief shrugged: "Nobody got out," he said. "Nobody."

Chapter 92

Deluca heard the news on the car radio on his way to the department.

A body, burned beyond recognition, was found in the gutted house of psychotherapist Jeffrey Palmer, who worked with Alex Lyon. Deluca had no doubt it would be identified as the doctor.

Deluca now sat in his office alone reflecting on his conversation with Officer Mike Walker. If Walker took Alex's panties off Brent Lyon as he claimed, the kid might have killed his sister. He was at the park according to Nancy what's-her-name. Perhaps he became enraged watching the sexual gymnastics involving Alex, got his butt kicked trying to intervene. He hangs around till the others leave, confronts Alex in a jealous rage---winds up killing her. That explains Alex's murder but not Kitty Richmond's and not Dr. Palmer; killed in a house fire.

Deluca didn't believe in coincidences, especially those related to a homicide; Convenient murders of Brent and Kitty with notes of explanation. Palmer's demise in an accident stretched credulity. An intelligent killer was manipulating them sending the investigation around in circles.

Now he was without a team member. Walter Willis took a leave of absence to be with his wife and to repair the rift with his stepson. The kid needed psychological help and faced jail time for his murder plot. The loss of Willis handicapped the investigation.

Deluca leaned back in his chair, hands locked behind his head, as Segal and Styles entered his office. He got right to the point. "We need to rethink everything," he said. He stood and drew a large box on the white board behind his desk, divided it in half and labeled the left side **Suspects** and the right **Deaths**.

Suspects	Deaths
Reaper	Alex Lyon
Brent Lyon	Kitty Richmond
Coach Phelan	Bent
Mike Walker	Ramos
Ramos	Jeffrey Palmer

"We have, we had, a long list of suspects; the killer led us to some of them. Somehow he found out about Reaper and implicated him by killing Kitty and leaving the note. He planted the panties on Brent but Walker intervened to throw suspicion on Ramos instead. Phelan whored around with a minor, didn't know she videotaped him. He's a sleazebag but not a killer.

"I'm convinced the same guy killed Alex, then Kitty and Brent as collateral damage to throw suspicion elsewhere. Ramos was on someone else's agenda, as I'm sure you know by now."

"What's Jeffrey Palmer doing on the board?" Styles asked.

"He was Alex Lyon's therapist. She told him things. Maybe more than he revealed to us. If the killer found out, Palmer would be a threat to him."

Both Styles and Segal nodded.

"We need to revisit Alex's diary and look at the videotape again," Deluca said. "We still haven't identified the third man or put names to two of the initials prominent in the diary."

Deluca drew a line on the whiteboard under the list of suspects and wrote two initials: SD and D. He then wrote Videotape: Third man.

"Tony, anything turn up on the dad?"

Segal shook his head. "He's not in the system, squeaky clean. Not even a parking ticket. Friends and neighbors say he's a great guy."

Deluca wasn't convinced. "D for dad," he said. "D's the only one in the diary she didn't like. She did it with him, she wrote, because he 'made it worth her while.' Who would do that if not him?

"Another teacher, like Phelan," Segal offered. "Willing to pay for his jollies."

Deluca crossed his arms, head down, thinking. "Possible. Let's review the teacher roster. And that reminds me, Cara. We didn't ID Kitty because Alex used the girl's real initials, not her nickname. What if the reverse is true for SD and D? What if they represent nicknames, not given names?

"Could be," Styles said.

"Who would know that?" Deluca asked.

"Jonathon Moser, the activities director at East High."

"Good. Get to him fast before some other body falls into our laps."

He didn't wait for Styles to respond. "Tony, Get out the tape. Let's see if we missed anything about the third guy."

When Styles and Segal had gone, Deluca turned to what he had written on the whiteboard: the suspects, the deaths, the initials or nicknames, whatever the hell they were---D and SD.

D and SD. One of you bastards is our killer.

Chapter 93

Cara Styles stopped at the secretary's desk. She was young, bright-eyed, buxom, perky, eager to please. Styles held up her badge. "I'm detective Styles. I'd like a word with Mr. Moser please."

The young woman smiled, almost bounced in her chair. "Of course, yes," she said, in a high pitched voice. She picked up the phone. "Mr. Moser, a detective Styles is here."

The closed door opened quickly and Jonathon Moser stepped into the hall extending his hand. "Nice to see you again, detective," he said. "How can I help you?"

Moser's blond hair fell to his shoulders, the beginning of a moustache blossomed on his upper lip. He wore a short sleeve white shirt, red tie. His face was tanned and unlined.

"May we speak privately, sir?" Styles asked.

"Sir." Moser winked at his secretary and moved aside to let Styles go into the office first.

Styles took a seat in a chair just to the left front of Moser's desk. She wore an outfit similar to the one she had worn when they first met; a black skirt cut above the knee, a white blouse with a V-neck, black jacket to conceal a gun strapped to her waist. She sat down and crossed her legs and Moser, as before, let his eyes stray downward, something Styles counted on to help loosen his tongue.

"What can I do for you detective," Moser asked sitting down in his chair but angling so as not to obstruct his view.

"Do you remember the list of initials from Alex's diary I showed you?"

"Yes. Of course."

"We've identified all but two of the people---SD and D. Our thinking now is that the first letter of SD is a nickname. D might be one as well, like Bubba."

Moser's eyes narrowed, the color drained from his face. He sat back in his chair and raised his hand to his chin. A strange reaction, Styles thought. But before she could dwell on that, Moser recovered, smiled and leaned forward gaping at Styles' thighs.

"Possible," he said, nodding. "What do you want to do?"

"I'd like to review a list of students and faculty again with you. Perhaps you might recall any nicknames used by the kids or staff beginning or ending with a D. But I'm afraid I didn't bring my lists"

"No problem, Let me get them from my secretary." He got up, left the office and closed the door behind him.

Styles looked around in his absence. She had been in this office before while interviewing students, the walls covered with colorful plaques, banners and pictures of championship sport teams. On the wall behind his desk, Moser had hung his diplomas, certificates, family photos and assorted surfing paraphernalia like a miniature surfboard.

Two photos showed Moser, as surf coach, posing with his smiling co-ed team. A discoloration on the wall marked the spot of a missing photo, which Styles remembered showed Moser riding a wave. The caption at the bottom caught her eye then but she couldn't recall it now.

Moser interrupted her thoughts as he returned to the office. "Damn thing fell, glass broke," Moser said by way of acknowledging her stare at the wall. "I'm having it fixed."

Styles smiled.

"Let's use the conference table," Moser said moving to take a seat on one side of the rectangular table. Styles sat opposite him.

They quickly scanned the student list. Of 3800 students, twenty had last names beginning with the letter "D." No first names began with "S."

"I know many of these kids," Moser said. "None have nicknames starting with an "S." But he put a check by five students. "I don't recognize these names, I'll check with their teachers."

"Ok," Styles said and turned her attention to the teacher list. Five teachers out of one hundred and thirty had last names beginning with the letter "D." No first names began with an "S."

Moser laughed. "Uh, none of these teachers have, uh, an official nickname. But this lady," he pointed to a Janet Delaney, "is sometimes referred to by some, uh, male faculty as, uh, Big Boobs. Probably not what you wanted to hear."

"Probably not," Styles said, her voice flat, emotionless.

Moser dropped his head like a chastised little boy. "I'll uh, check with the teachers regarding any nicknames and call you."

"I'd appreciate it. We need to get on this fast."

She sensed Moser's eyes on her as she exited his office; no doubt checking out her legs and butt.

Styles walked down the hall and had her hands on the panic bar of the door leading outside when she stopped. Something about the missing photo on Moser's wall bugged her.

She turned and walked back to Moser's secretary; Joyce Beal her nameplate read.

"Joyce, Mr. Moser said he is having the photo missing from his wall repaired. I remember it showed him surfing. Does he still do that?"

"Oh yes," Joyce Beal replied, and sat up straight in her chair, her eyes wide. "Mr. Moser's very athletic. He surfs with the team every chance he gets. Why do you ask?"

"I was impressed with the photo but can't remember the caption. You know how those little things nag at you. I forgot to ask Mr. Moser. Do you remember what it said?"

Joyce Beal could have been a high school student herself. Her face flushed, she studied her hands. "The kids think it has a double meaning. It says: Surfer dude riding the big one."

She didn't elaborate and didn't need to. Styles understood how teenagers would interpret "the big one." She wasn't interested in that. "The caption said surfer dude?"

"Yes," Joyce Beal laughed. "Surfer dude. That's what many of the kids call him. He's like one of them."

Chapter 94

Like one of them, Styles thought.

It made sense now. She called Deluca as soon as she left the office.

"We caught the big one," she said when Deluca picked up.

"What?"

"I'll explain later but guess what many students call Jonathon Moser, the activities director at East?"

"Enlighten me."

"Surfer Dude."

Deluca made the connection after several seconds of silence. "SD. Surfer dude; buddy and confidant to a lot of kids. He knew what they were doing and where they were doing it."

Styles thought his voice sounded stronger, more energetic than when he had answered.

"The bastard," Deluca continued. "He jerked us around, gave me the tape, wanted us to ID Phelan and the other man. I'll bet he knows who that is too. But he's covered himself well. Initials in a diary aren't enough to nail his ass. SD could be anybody.

"I'll pursue a warrant for his home and office. See if I can convince a judge we have a serial killer doing kids," Deluca said. "Stay at the school and keep an eye on him. Follow him if he leaves."

Deluca paused, mentally assessing their next moves. "Even with a warrant nothing definitive may turn up at his home or office. Talking to more kids could be our best bet. If Moser had a thing with Alex, good chance she wasn't the only one."

Styles laughed. "No doubt," and thought about miss perky, the secretary, not much older than a student. Her eyes lit up when talking about Moser. Perhaps mention of the "the big one" embarrassed her for more intimate reasons.

Chapter 95

Styles sat slumped down in the front seat of her unmarked car.

Only a few cars remained in the parking lot at this hour. She pulled next to one to shield her from view from the administration building. She opened a bottle of water and brought it to her lips when Jonathon Moser and miss perky emerged from a side door.

She's like a little lap dog, Styles thought as she watched the young gal click her high heels on the cement walkway a pace or two behind her master.

Moser unlocked his blue mustang convertible with his remote and opened the passenger door for miss perky. As the woman slid in, her short dress rode up on her thighs flashing Moser a peek at her pink panties. She made no effort to pull her skirt down and Moser, smirking, admired the view.

"You little prick," Styles said. "We're going to get you."

Moser backed the mustang out of its space and drove out of the parking lot taking several speed bumps so fast the car bounced on its frame and the rear end shimmied as he pulled onto Pacific City Drive heading toward the beach.

Can't wait to get miss perky between the sheets.

Moser traveled three miles, then took a side street up a steep incline into a new housing development. Moser had apparently sold his home in an established part of the city to move here.

Huge signs at the entrance to the tract heralded the ocean views available to prospective buyers. Moser drove a few blocks and turned into the driveway of a home in need of landscaping, no plants or grass although two stone planters were complete. Moser got out of the car, made a show of looking over the yard, and he and his secretary disappeared inside.

Styles went down the street, executed a U-turn and parked diagonally across from Moser's house. She called Deluca with an update and gave him the address.

She waited perhaps an hour when Deluca called. "Got the warrant. We can always count on Judge Finley. Keep a close eye on Moser. Arrest him if he tries to leave. We're on our way and should be there shortly

"Roger that," Styles responded, a smile creasing her face.

Chapter 96

Police over-ran the quiet neighborhood. Three radio cars and two unmarked vehicles pulled in front of Moser's. Deluca directed the uniformed officers to watch the back of the house. He waited for Styles to join him and they strode up the newly paved walkway with Segal and Stankovich. Deluca rang the bell and punctuated the ring with a brass knocker on the door. The other detectives grinned.

Within minutes, a partially clothed Moser cracked open the door and peeked out keeping the security chain in place.

"We have a warrant to search the premises, Mr. Moser," Deluca said. "Let us in please."

Moser started to protest, but Deluca cut him off. "It would give me great pleasure to smash this door in, sir. Please stand aside."

Moser was frightened as Deluca's eyes bore into him. He unlatched the security chain and moved away. The detectives swept pass him and fanned out. Styles went to the bedroom, pushed open the door and startled miss perky who sat up in bed covering her upper torso with the sheets. "Oh," she muttered shocked to see Styles.

"Get dressed please," Styles directed but did not turn away or leave. Miss Perky soon realized Styles was not going to afford her any privacy so she slid off the bed with the sheet wrapped around her, grabbed her clothes from a chair and slipped into the bathroom.

"Don't close the door," Styles shouted after her.

The woman scowled but obeyed.

Styles began to search a large dresser in the room and was immediately rewarded. In the second drawer, she found several pairs of women's panties. "In here," she called to Deluca in the next room. "And bring Moser, please."

Deluca and Moser entered as Styles held up a pair of bikini briefs. "You want to explain these?" she asked Moser.

He shrugged. "I like women. I keep these to remind me of certain ones." He shot a glance toward the bathroom; miss perky glared at him.

"Not many women I know could fit into these," Styles countered. "More like a teenage girl."

"You can't prove that," Moser responded, his voice louder than necessary.

"The game's over pal," Deluca said, anger evident in his tone. "These young girls might have found it cool to play hide the salami with the surfer dude but when they find out you've been arrested for murder, they'll give you up in a heartbeat. Ask your secretary."

Miss perky came into the room, the color drained from her face, her eyes moist. "Murder. Oh my god. Oh my god."

Her reaction gave truth to Deluca's words. Moser knew protesting his innocence was futile. He'd had sexual encounters with three other schoolgirls. They all would turn on him. He walked over to the one chair in the room and slumped down into it. "I didn't mean for any of this to happen," he said, in a voice just above a whisper.

Chapter 97

Moser's reaction surprised the detectives.

Their evidence against him was weak. The initials in the diary, panties in the drawer, even testimony from underage girls that he had sex with them, did not prove murder. Not so a confession. One made in front of his secretary.

"Tell us what happened," Deluca said.

Moser wiped a hand across his mouth. "Alex came to my office on the day before the party in the park. She wore a short skirt, low cut blouse. We caressed, something we had been doing for several months. This time, I couldn't get aroused, despite her efforts. She gave up and taunted me. I'll never forget the look on her face. She told me about the party in the park on Friday where real men would satisfy her."

Moser paused but Deluca pressed him to continue.

Moser complied. "On Friday, for some reason I really can't explain, I went to the park upset and ashamed at my previous impotence. I guess I hoped I'd get aroused by watching."

He got no expression of understanding from the detectives so he dropped his head, ran his tongue over his lips and continued.

"The party had started by the time I got to the park, don't remember the exact time. I parked in the neighborhood across the street so my car wouldn't be seen and took a circuitous route to where the kids were drinking, smoking pot and snorting something; Coke maybe. They were in various stages of undress touching and groping each other."

Moser paused again He got a far away look on his face and remained silent. Then, he folded his hands, placed them in his lap and resumed his story.

"I don't know how long I watched but I got angry when Alex paired off with two boys. Yet, it aroused me and I fondled myself."

Embarrassed, Moser turned his head. "It was like being on the set of a porno movie. The kids were relaxed and carefree. I was jealous and pissed off."

He ignored the unspoken revulsion evident on the faces of the detectives, and the shocked look of his secretary. "After a while, Alex passed out but her friends kept drinking. They tried to wake Alex when they decided to leave, but couldn't budge her. To my amazement, they left, leaving her behind. I waited to be sure they had gone. Alex lay on her stomach with her skirt above her waist. I, I, lost it."

He paused again and gazed at a wall.

"Go on please," Deluca said.

The sound of Deluca's voice brought Moser back from his reverie. His head snapped back. He inhaled, clearing his mind. "As I pressed down on her from behind, Alex awakened, turned her head, recognized me, and laughed, like she had in my office. The harder I pounded into her, the louder she became. I couldn't stand it."

Moser's shrill voice echoed off the walls sounding like that of a deranged man. He balled his fists in his lap. "I had to stop her," he said, his face flushed, spittle forming at the corners of his mouth. "I ripped the cord from my sweat pants, wrapped it around her neck, got her to stop."

Neither Styles nor Deluca spoke. They waited for Moser to compose himself. After several minutes, he finished his tale uttering words that made both detectives shudder. "When she stopped laughing," Moser said, keeping his head bowed, "I finished.

"But just then, a car pulled into the parking lot and a spotlight came on, the police. I took off one of my socks and wiped my semen off her as best I could. I started to leave, remembered her panties, pulled them off, stuffed them in the pocket of my sweat suit, ran back into the woods. I stopped when the cop came down the path toward me shining his flashlight. I hid behind some bushes, afraid he would see me, amazed and relieved when he didn't."

"Why'd you take the panties?" Deluca asked.

Moser shrugged. "I'm not sure. I thought some of my semen might have gotten on them. I didn't want to take a chance. I wasn't thinking clearly."

Not thinking clearly, you asshole, Deluca thought, *when did you ever think clearly about any of this?*

"How'd the panties wind up on Edwardo Ramos?"

"I don't know," Moser said, shifting in his chair. "Alex's brother Brent called me after Alex died, distraught, feeling guilty. He told me he had been in the park and had fought with another boy over Alex. He got pummeled, left with his tail between his legs, without Alex. He blamed himself for her death.

"It dawned on me I could shift the blame to him, for both murders. We were in my car at Eagle Point. He got out, at my urging, to get some air. I retrieved the panties from a concealed space in my glove compartment, walked up behind the kid as he stood on the precipice, hit him over the head with a lug wrench, stuffed the panties into the pockets of his jacket, pinned the note on him and pushed him over the cliff."

"Oh my god," miss perky cried and bolted from the room. Moser's whole body shook and tears streamed down his face.

Neither Styles nor Deluca was moved by his show of remorse. "Go on," Deluca directed.

Moser wiped his forehead with the back of his hand. "I read in the paper the day after Brent died that the panties had been found on the rapist who was shot. I was confused and relieved. The police thought Ramos killed the girls; put me in the clear."

"Why kill Kitty?" Styles asked.

"To throw you off. I knew about the note from Reaper, of course and called the Chief to plant the seed. The kid took credit for killing Alex. I figured another murder and message would seal the deal."

"You killed an innocent girl just to confuse us," Styles shouted, starting toward Moser. Deluca restrained her, whispered something in her ear and let her go. She backed off but glared at the startled school administrator who flinched expecting a blow.

"And the fire at Palmer's?" Deluca asked, directing Moser's attention back to him.

"I couldn't take the chance Alex told him about us, feared he would report it."

Deluca dipped his head in understanding, the sequence of events now clear; Alex's death a fit of passion, Kitty, Brent and Palmer collateral damage, part of an attempted cover-up. Officer Walker unknowingly aided the scheme when he took the girl's underwear from Brent's body and placed them in Ramos's backpack in a misguided racist attempt to implicate the rapist and give the Latino community a black eye at the same time. Reaper was drawn into the mix by his own ill-advised note to the real killer.

A total mess Deluca thought as he placed Moser under arrest and watched Styles push him roughly out of the house.

At least Parents could breathe easier and the city could return to a semblance of normality.

Deluca was wrong and he would be shaken to the core.

Chapter 98

They stood on the balcony together.

Each wore the white terry cloth robe provided by the hotel. Their shoulders touched as they leaned on the wrought iron railing and looked down on the harbor below. Lights glowed from homes on the hillside across the water and from boats navigating through the channel.

Jonathon Moser was in custody, his murder spree halted. Time to focus on their relationship. Both held a glass of Merlot lost in thought. Deluca wondered if this was the right thing to do, and if not, how it would end. Styles thoughts were similar only she was more certain it could only end badly. Secrets will do that.

Despite his concern, Deluca wrapped his arm around her and pulled her to him. They remained like that for several minutes before he turned her toward him and raised his glass. "To friends," he said.

She clinked her glass with his. "To us."

They drained their glasses and he took them and placed them on a small white plastic table alongside the remnants of the cheese and crackers shared earlier. He cupped her face in his hands, bent down and brushed his lips against hers.

He marveled at her beauty. Her short black hair, not one strand out of place as if held together by some unseen magnet. Her cocoa brown skin, smooth and soft to the touch, bright eyes, intelligent and sensuous, smile radiant, white teeth perfect. He set aside his misgivings to cherish his time with her. He touched his lips against hers again, kissed her cheeks, her eyes, her forehead, the tip of her nose.

She smiled, stepped back and released the cord of her robe revealing only a bra and panties underneath. Deluca noted the high cut of the panties and the lace fringe. In the moonlight, he could see the dark circles of her nipples and the patch between her legs. He pulled her to him, her skin smooth and soft to the touch, the muscles in her back firm, taught. He held her like that for a long time, before scooping her up and carrying her through the opened sliding door placing her gently on the bed.

Impatient, he discarded his robe in one motion, dropped his boxers to the floor and straddled her, supporting himself on his elbows and knees. He freed her breasts from their restraint and pulled her panties down and off.

They made love with the urgency of two youngsters afraid time might pass leaving them with thoughts of what might have been. And when it was over, they clung to each other, bodies melded together as one. They fell asleep with many questions still unanswered.

In the morning, sunlight poured through the still opened drapes. They now lay side by side, his hand in hers, one of her legs draped over his. She slept but his eyes were open. He gazed at the ceiling wondering again if this would end well.

It wouldn't.

Chapter 99

How do you reveal a secret? Slowly with diplomacy or just get it out quickly and duck. Styles wrestled with the question as she prepared to meet Deluca. Last night had been marvelous but shouldn't have happened. Not for him, not for her.

She flipped open her cell phone and dialed his office.

He picked up on the third ring. "Deluca."

"JD. Cara. Can we meet for dinner?"

"A celebration?"

"Ah, something else."

Deluca was encouraged thinking this might be the first of many romantic evenings. "Sure," he said. "Where would you like to meet?"

"How about the Villa Nova in Newport around seven?

"Sounds good. See you then."

The Villa Nova, located just off Pacific Coast Highway, had faux Italian exterior and cozy tables inside with a view of Newport Harbor and the expensive sailboats and powerboats moored there. A nice setting for a romantic dinner Deluca thought as he spied Styles at a corner table, a glass of red wine in front of her.

He caught her eye and wended his way toward her through mostly empty tables. He resisted the urge to lean down and kiss her when he stood beside her.

"Thanks for meeting me," Styles.

"Why wouldn't I?" Deluca said, sitting down and reaching across to take her hands in his.

"JD, I need to tell you something."

"Good. Same here."

Styles face went pale and her eyes welled up. She gripped his hands. "You don't understand."

"I do, I…"

"No you don't JD. Please let me get this out before you say anything."

"OK. Sure," He said. He leaned back in his chair as a waitress in a short black skirt and flowered shirt came over to the table.

"Something to drink sir?" the girl asked as she pulled out a small pad to write on.

"A glass of your house Merlot please," Deluca said keeping his eyes on Styles.

The waitress nodded and left.

Styles forced a smile. "You won't like what I have to say."

Deluca, confused waved his arm in a signal for her to proceed.

Styles reached into her purse for a black wallet and flipped it open. She dug deeply into one of the slits and took out an identification card. Deluca examined it, his eyes narrowed, his jaw tightened. "You going to tell me what this is all about, Agent Styles of the F-B-I."

She had anticipated his anger. No one liked to be duped, personally or professionally. No local police department wanted to be infiltrated by any federal agency, especially one most viewed as unfriendly, antagonistic and condescending.

"I understand you're pissed," she said. "I was not comfortable doing this and my feelings for you complicated things. Let me explain, O.K.?"

Deluca remained silent but removed his hands from hers and sat back in his chair. The waitress returned with the Merlot before Styles could continue. "Can I get you anything else," the young girl asked with a smile.

Both Styles and Deluca shook their heads and the waitress left saying she would return shortly to take their order.

Styles began again. "I'm part of a Federal Task Force comprised of the Justice Department and the Bureau. We're investigating the infiltration of police departments by white supremacist groups. PCPD was selected because of past incidents."

Deluca listened, his face passive, blank, shaken by her confession and the thought she had shown an interest in him only to enhance her cover. He wasn't sure which bothered him more. He sat up straight, his hands clasped in front, resting on the table.

Styles wanted to reach out and touch him, to reassure him her feelings were genuine but she pressed on with her story. "A cell of the White Aryan Resistance is operating within the PCPD. Poker games at McClusky's serve as cover for meetings. McClusky is the brains of the group if we can say that with a straight face. Randy Cunningham's the heavy hitter, involved in all of the "suspicious" deaths of Hispanics in police custody. A sealed file at the LAPD documents his past racist acts. He executed Ramos hoping we'd pin him with the murder of Alex and Kittie. I'm sure of it."

Deluca said nothing.

"I've been monitoring the WAR group for several months," Styles continued, "but I'm not ready to move until I've identified all of them."

"So, then, how do you want to play this, Special Agent Styles?" Deluca asked, his voice low, sad. The woman he cared for, one of his detectives was a federal plant.

Styles heart sank, chest pounded. She knew from his pained look that he believed her feelings for him were a sham, a ruse to earn his trust; not true but she couldn't convince him of that now.

"I'd like to hold off revealing my identity," Styles explained. "Once I do we've got to move. That will take some coordination."

Deluca crossed his arms, waited. He needed to sort out many things not the least of which was his relationship to this women.

"This is a lot for me to think about," he said. "I came here to confess my feelings for you. Now I'm not sure what they are. I need some time."

"I understand," Styles said. She wanted to hug him, hold him close, tell him how she felt; couldn't do it under the circumstances. "I should go. I'll be at my place if you want to talk," she said.

Deluca remained seated, his head bowed. His eyes did not follow her as she got up and left.

Later, he regretted not making her stay and talk.

Chapter 100

Styles drove directly home from the restaurant. She lived in downtown Pacific City near the beach. As she neared her condo, she wrestled with mixed emotions. She felt good about putting Moser behind bars, yet apprehensive about the upcoming sweep through the PCPD to root out white supremacists. Many innocent officers would be shocked, Deluca devastated. He had been stunned when she revealed her identity and mission. She had little doubt their budding personal relationship was over. That saddened her.

Her two-story condo had a view of the Pacific Ocean but the main entrance was on a side street lined with thirty to forty foot tall Palm trees. Despite its proximity to the beach, the traffic on her street consisted mostly of residents or their guests. Styles enjoyed the quiet.

She pulled her car to the curb in front of her condo and turned off the ignition. She pushed open her door, slid off the front seat, her attention drawn to a blown out streetlight. It was the last thing she saw. A speeding vehicle, its own lights out, sideswiped her car, ripping the drivers' side door from its hinges. Styles was catapulted over the hood and onto the pavement where her mangled body lay splayed like a rag doll. The impact of the collision activated the car alarm, which blared loudly into the silence as if saluting the fallen agent.

Deluca was seated at the bar in O'Hara's when his cell phone rang. "Deluca," he answered.

"JD," a trembling voice said.

Big Tony Segal.

"Cara has been in an accident," he blurted. "Hit and run. Doesn't look good."

"Where are you?" Deluca asked.

"At College hospital. She's in surgery."

"Be right there," Deluca said. He reached for his wallet to pay for his drink. The bartender saw the concern on his face and walked over. "What's up?" he asked.

Deluca fumbled for his wallet unable to extract it from his back pocket.

"JD," the bartender said, raising his voice. "Forget the money. What's happening?"

Deluca's face drained of color.

"Styles is down, hit and run supposedly."

"What do you mean, supposedly?"

Deluca gave up wrestling with his wallet. "Never mind. I'll tell you later," he shouted over his shoulder as he all but ran for the door.

When Deluca arrived at College Hospital, an elderly, blue haired receptionist directed him to a second floor waiting room. Once there, he found Tony Segal seated on a couch, head bowed. Deluca walked over and stood before the big man who now appeared small, his face twisted in pain.

Segal looked up and spoke just above a whisper. "They don't think she's going to make it, JD. She's really messed up."

Deluca sat down beside his former partner, leaned forward, head in his hands. They remained like that for a long time until the door of the waiting room pushed open and detective Ed Stankovich, now helping with the investigation, walked in. Chief Dalton Phillips followed. He chose to stand and leaned against a wall. They all exchanged nods and nervous glances but no one spoke. The tension was palpable.

After about fifteen minutes, Stankovich broke the silence. "Anyone want coffee?"

"Why don't you bring everyone some," the Chief said.

Stankovich had been gone about five minutes when the waiting room door opened again. A young doctor dressed in green surgical garb entered and faced the group. The doctor was tall and slender, thirty-something, his boyish face grim as he riveted his bright blue eyes on Deluca whom he recognized. "I'm sorry, Lieutenant. We did all we could."

Chapter 101

The group of officers staggered out of the hospital rocked by Styles death. They huddled together on the sidewalk in front of the entrance, unsure of the next step. Deluca surveyed their faces, worried. Did any of them suspect, know, as he did, Styles death was not an accident. Surely the Chief did.

Were any of them part of this?

Styles did not name any of his team members when she revealed her undercover role. Didn't mean they weren't involved, just that she had chosen not to reveal that fact to him at the time. Now, he wished she had.

"Listen," he said, looking at Stankovich and Segal. "We're not doing any good moping around. The night guys will work with the techies at the accident scene. Go home. Get some rest."

"Good idea," the Chief broke in. "See you all tomorrow."

The group dispersed, each walking trance-like toward their vehicles. Deluca waited until they were out of sight then, unable to contain his grief any longer, he doubled over choking back the bile stuck in his throat. He fell to his knees on a strip of grass between the sidewalk and the street. A piercing scream penetrated the silent night startling Deluca until he realized it had come from deep inside him.

He remained crumpled over for several minutes, his face wet with tears, the knees of his pants soaked through by standing water remaining from an earlier irrigation of the area. Immobilized, distraught, only now did he realize the depth of his feelings for Styles. He had been stoic when his wife died, remaining strong for his daughter; strangely detached as he sought revenge for the deaths of his buddies in Vietnam. But now his façade crumbled as he felt the searing loss of the woman he loved—admitting it to himself—too late, too late.

Pushing himself to his feet, he stumbled back toward the hospital, anger supplanting anguish. Someone would pay for Styles murder. He smiled as he stepped into the shadow cast by the walkway overhang.

He re-entered the hospital lobby ignoring the astonished look of the receptionist as she surveyed his appearance. He asked to take charge of Styles personal affects hoping to retrieve the keys to her condo where he hoped she kept a list of the members of WAR

Yellow crime tape cordoned off the area when Deluca arrived at the scene. The techies were still processing Styles car and street for clues. He parked on a nearby street and walked the short distance back. He nodded to the leader of the CSU but did not stop to talk. He walked up the sidewalk to the condo and climbed the stairs. On his second try, he found the key to the front door. He slipped on a pair of plastic gloves and stepped inside flipping on the wall light-switch to his left.

The two-story condo was compact; a sparsely furnished family room on the right, kitchen and corridor to an outside patio on the left. Stairs in front of him lead upstairs to bedrooms, no doubt.

Deluca walked upstairs where one of the bedrooms had been converted to an office. He started there. The room contained a desk, a two-drawer metal filing cabinet and a stuffed chair with a floor lamp beside it. The desk was cluttered with the stubs from utility bills, advertisements for credit card deals, fliers from a house cleaning service and a brochure from the Chamber of Commerce extolling the virtues of the crime free city. Deluca smiled ruefully.

The search of the office proved futile so Deluca moved to the other room. The bed, pushed against a wall with a large picture window, was neatly made with hospital corners no less. He searched the bed, another stuffed chair, a dresser and a small nightstand without result.

He turned his attention to the closet. A dress uniform hung beside blouses, skirts, two blazers and some slacks. Shoes were stacked in a hanging rack. The single shelf held several books on law enforcement alongside three paperback novels, all Ed McBain 87th Precinct mysteries. *Wonder if Styles tried to pick up some tips from Detective Carrela,* Deluca mused. He leafed through the books on the off chance she had stuffed something between the pages. Nothing! The rest of the condo also proved clean.

Discouraged, Deluca descended the steps toward the front door when he stopped, turned around and returned to the second bedroom. Opening the closet door, he found, as expected, a removable ceiling tile used to gain access to an attic crawl space.

He retrieved a chair from the other room, stood on it, pushed the tile to one side. Reaching through the opening, he felt around until his hand touched something solid but moveable. He grasped it with both hands, pulled down a small black briefcase and placed it flat on the bed.

The case was not locked. He opened it and discovered copies of files from the department computer system with a paper-clipped list of names attached. But before he had a chance to examine the list, he turned, distracted by a noise behind him. The blow caught him above the right ear. The papers fell from his hand as he ricocheted off the bed and fell hard to the floor—unconscious.

Chapter 102

Deluca didn't know how long he'd been out; the condo was silent, dark. He pushed himself off the floor, tried to stand, fell back on the bed. The inside of his head felt like someone trying to punch his way out. He cupped his head in his hands and rested his elbows on his thighs. He remained like that for several moments trying to wait out the pain, clear his mind. Finally able to focus, his gaze fell on the digital clock on the nightstand beside the bed. The illuminated readout indicated he had been unconscious for several hours.

He stood up, weaved toward the doorway and flipped a wall switch on. The bright light flooded the room like a flashbulb exploding in his face. He staggered back against the wall snapping his eyes shut. He remained motionless for several minutes until he could blink his eyes open. He stood upright although the pounding in his head remained constant, thundering. He scanned the room to confirm what he instinctively knew; the briefcase and documents were gone.

Leaving the room, he stumbled down the stairs to the front door and stepped outside. Nothing, no one remained except the crime scene tape.

Chapter 103

Deluca was stunned; the euphoria of having solved the Alex Lyon murders replaced by the confirmation that a conspiracy existed within the police department; one more devastating and ruthless than even Styles suspected.

Thirty minutes after leaving Styles' condo, Deluca was back in his office. He had to clear his mind, determine his next move. Styles had been investigating the PCPD. She was dead, killed most likely by a cop, maybe one of his own detectives.

Deluca resented Styles when she revealed her identity and her reason for being undercover. But he'd heard the rumor about "cowboys" within the department dispensing street "justice." He couldn't ignore the ACLU protests and the now apparent validity of their civil rights claims. He thought some officers should have been disciplined in a couple of the cases, but it wasn't his call.

The former chief had been indiscreet in private conversation regarding his bigoted views. Deluca dismissed that as cop talk; a reflection of the mentality many developed after years of dealing with the dregs of society. He put a stop to any "racist" griping he overheard and came down on anyone within his unit who stretched the law or used it as an instrument of intimidation. But had he done enough? Had he been too naïve, too preoccupied with doing his job to see flagrant miscarriages of justice right before his eyes.

Styles couldn't be saved but her work could be salvaged. They could rid the department of the vermin who executed her; might be able to save the department's reputation, though he doubted it. Heads would roll on this, one way or the other, even his own.

A big reason he resented Styles was personal. He had developed feelings for her and wondered now if she had been playing him. He hoped not. At any rate it was clear what had to be done. He would start by making three calls, the first to the Los Angeles FBI office.

He found the number in his Rolodex and dialed. After several rings, an agent Twitchell answered the phone. "How may I help you sir?" He asked after Deluca identified himself and his organization.

"I need to speak to the SAC right away."

"I'm sorry sir," Twitchell said, protecting the privacy of his boss. "He's unavailable. May I take a message?"

"No," Deluca persisted, "I've got to talk to him now!"

Twitchell hung tough. "I'm sorry, sir," he repeated, "but…"

Deluca cut him off. "Agent Twitchell. Patch me through to the SAC now or I can assure you when he finds out you blew me off, your ass will be in a chair tomorrow in the FBI's northernmost field office. *Capisce?*"

Deluca's outburst was met with a few moments of silence, and then the agent conceded. "One moment sir."

After several more minutes, the SAC came on the line. "What's so important, Lieutenant?"

"I'm calling about Agent Cara Styles."

"Yes!"

"She's dead!"

The SAC exhaled. "How?"

"Supposed to be a hit and run."

"And you don't think so?"

"Do you?"

Another silence, then the SAC confirmed Deluca's thinking, "No!"

Chapter 104

"What's going on?" The SAC asked.

Deluca updated him on events since Styles murder; told him about finding the documents, then having them taken from him. "Any chance Cara gave you a copy of the list of WAR members?" he asked.

"No such luck," the SAC responded. She mentioned a few names but not the entire group."

"I was afraid of that," Deluca admitted. "Cara gave me some names too; McClusky's running the show. Maybe we start with him."

Deluca changed his mind before the SAC could respond. "But if we move now we're sure to lose some, many."

"Don't know we have a choice," the SAC said. "They may be getting ready to run after killing Styles. We take what we've got."

Deluca considered that. Any delay might screw things up royally. On the other hand, he doubted McClusky would run. These guys think they're untouchable. They have the fucking briefcase and a department captain watching their backs.

"Let me try something first," Deluca asked. "Give me twenty-four hours."

"Ok," the SAC said after a few moments of thought. "We'll move day after tomorrow unless I hear otherwise. I'll set it up tonight."

Deluca thanked him and moved to click off when the man spoke again: "What about Styles' body?

"What do you suggest?"

"She's not married. Her parents live in Massachusetts. I'd like to take custody of her remains, fly her back there. She'll be accorded full honors."

"All right" Deluca said, resigned, sad.

"Good," the SAC said. He was about to cut the connection when Deluca's voice stopped him

"Agent…"

"Yeah!"

"Cara was good people."

"Yeah!"

Chapter 105

Deluca reflected on his conversation with the FBI SAC before making his next calls. He had twenty-four hours to get the list or put together one of his own. He now had a good idea who whacked him on the head but without knowing his pals, he was reluctant to roll him up. The throbbing in his temple intensified as he struggled with his thoughts. Finally, he made calls to the two people he still trusted---Segal and Walter Willis.

He hoped Willis could put aside his personal difficulty and focus back on the case. Now that Reaper was no longer a suspect in the murders, no conflict of interest existed for Willis although his stepson would still face legal difficulties and a psychological evaluation. Willis and his wife had work to do on their relationship too, but don't we all, Deluca thought.

He made the calls and, to his surprise, Willis agreed to come back.

The two detectives arrived within five minutes of each other thirty minutes after Deluca's call. Both dressed in jeans and tennis shoes, Segal a pull over sweatshirt with PCPD emblazoned on the front, Willis a light cotton jacket.

When they took seats, Deluca walked to the door, looked out, then closed and locked the door surprising Willis and Segal though neither commented.

Deluca sat down hard in his chair, a worried expression on his face. "Styles was murdered," he said, without preamble.

Both detectives rocked backward as if slapped.

"Why? Who?" Willis stammered. He'd heard the news of her death, of course, through the cop grapevine.

Segal's face was ashen; he shifted in his chair fearing he might know the answers to Willis' questions.

Deluca then revealed Styles identity as an undercover FBI agent and the reason she had been inserted into the department. He told them of his immediate suspicion when Styles had been run down, his search of her condo, the attack on him when he discovered the hidden documents.

Segal exploded. "I can't believe some asshole had the balls to attack one of us. We're not going to tolerate this. No way. We've got to get these turds."

"That's our immediate problem, Tony" Deluca said. "We need the list of WAR Styles put together or develop a new one. The Federal Task Force can't move without knowing who all these guys are."

"Did she give you any names?" Segal queried, a deep frown creasing his brow.

Deluca hesitated. He wasn't sure why but he decided not to reveal all of his information. The fewer people dialed in right now the better. He remembered an old axiom told to him by one of his early mentors; a *secret is only a secret if you tell no one.*

Segal and Willis realized he held back information.

"Did Cara have a laptop at home?" Willis asked, breaking the silence.

"Didn't find one," Deluca said.

"What about her computer here?" Segal offered.

"Long shot," Deluca said. "I doubt Cara would feel safe keeping confidential info here. We can check but I'm not going to hold my breath."

"I agree," Willis said, "but…maybe…." His voice drifted off and he didn't finish the sentence.

"What?" Segal demanded.

"Back off Tony," Deluca directed, staring at Segal.

"What are you thinking, Walt?"

"Cara used a Palm pilot."

"So!" Segal grunted.

"So! Maybe she stored the list on her Pilot. You can download that to a computer and print it, which she obviously did to produce the hard copy JD found.

Deluca considered that for a moment. "There was a Palm Pilot in her effects at the hospital. I didn't grab it because I was only interested in her house keys at the time. Could be our best bet to get our hands on the names."

Segal jumped up and headed for the door. "I'll get it."

Deluca stopped him. "Sit down, Tony, for Christ sakes. You wouldn't know a Palm Pilot from a TV remote."

"But," Segal protested.

"Tony! Sit down will ya. Walt can scan the device there. I need you to follow up on something else."

Segal, ready to continue his objection, stopped, riveted by the look in Deluca's eyes. Willis left the room to go to the hospital.

When the door closed again, Deluca spoke. "I know who whacked me tonight."

Segal's jaw tensed. "Who?"

"Goodman."

"Goody? Come on JD!"

"Who then? Who gets into the condo but a cop? The techies would have stopped a civilian. The place was empty when I searched it. I observed Goody get to the scene as I entered. Why doesn't he check on me if he didn't see me leave?

My car was at the corner. When I came out, everyone was gone even Pete Gillon, the CSU lead. No way he leaves without checking with me unless someone in authority gives him the OK."

Segal slouched back in his chair, disbelief on his face.

"Got to be him, Tony."

Segal's shoulders drooped; his chin fell forward onto his massive chest. "What do you want me to do?" he asked.

"Goody trusts you. He's at his desk now. Get his take on the hit and run, report back to me. Don't let on you are aware of any of this. Then, get a hold of Pete Gillon. Ask him, diplomatically of course, why he left the scene without contacting me."

Segal pushed himself out of his chair like a man twenty years older, and shuffled toward the door. "Amazing" he said as he pulled it open and stepped out into the detective pen.

Chapter 106

Walter Willis, driving his personal vehicle, was a mile from College Hospital when a blue and white police cruiser eased in behind him its emergency lights signaling him to pull over. Why? Had Deluca sent a car to escort him? Or had the supremacist bastards been tipped off? They killed an FBI agent. They wouldn't hesitate to add him to the list. His first instinct was to flee but he dismissed that idea, running would play into their hands, give them an excuse to accidentally kill him during a chase.

His heart raced and his body tensed as he pulled to the curb. *How did they find out about his mission so soon?*

The blue and white stopped several feet from his rear bumper. Willis waited. He saw no movement from the other car, got no instructions to exit his vehicle. He slipped his gun from its holster. Would he use it against another officer?

Suddenly the spotlight from the cruiser blinded Willis as it reflected off his rearview mirrors. He sat bolt upright and closed his eyes to rid the spots dancing on his retina. When he opened them, he caught the silhouette of a police officer walking toward him. He could not determine who it was or if he had his weapon drawn.

Willis' gun rested by his right thigh, safety off, finger on the trigger. The officer tapped on the window with his left hand, right hand hanging by his side. Willis tensed. Should he roll down the window? Could he fire on a fellow officer?

The question went unanswered. At the moment of decision, another blue and white cruiser came around the corner in front of them. The officer, seeing the stop, crossed the street and placed his car in position to block Willis' exit. The detective reacted. He rolled down his window and thrust his badge outside as the officer exited his vehicle and walked toward them.

"Detective Walter Willis, officers," he shouted. "What's the trouble?"

Chapter 107

Deluca was unaware of the standoff between Willis and the two patrol cops. He dialed the number for College Hospital, explained to a receptionist what he wanted and was transferred to the administrator on duty. After a brief conversation, he determined that Willis had not yet arrived. He should have been there by now. His back stiffened and he shivered.

He asked the administrator to have Styles personal effects ready. The man assured him he would cooperate in every way possible.

Deluca replaced the phone in its cradle and leaned back in his chair. He felt a familiar churning in his gut. Did something happen to Willis?

Trying to shake the feeling, he got up from his chair, walked to the door and opened it. The squad room was empty, both Segal and Goodman gone.

The bad feeling returned.

Chapter 108

Walter Willis also had a bad feeling.

If these were rogue cops, he was in deep guano. He breathed deeply, exhaled. The officer standing by his car window took a step back as Willis thrust his badge at him. He moved his hand away from his hip and smiled as the other patrolman approached.

"Hey, Randy, what's going on," asked Kip Kearney. "I didn't get a warning you pulled somebody over. I'd have been here sooner."

"No problem, Kip," said Randy Cunningham, still smiling. "Thought the vehicle was reported stolen, misread the plate, I guess."

He turned to Willis. "Sorry for the inconvenience, detective, can I escort you somewhere?"

Willis fought to regain his composure. The arrival of officer Kearney saved him from a deadly confrontation; Cunningham had not stopped him by mistake. He was supposed to be on administrative leave pending the investigation of the Ramos shooting, probably one of the bad guys. Willis couldn't deal with that now. He had to get to the hospital and retrieve Styles Palm Pilot.

"No problem officer," Willis said, forcing a smile. "I'll be on my way."

Kearney waved as he backed his car up so Willis could pull out. In his rearview mirror, Willis saw Cunningham open the door of his cruiser and put a cell phone to his ear.

*****

Wild Bill McClusky was in bed when the phone rang.

"Yeah," he said.

"We're in deep trouble, boss," the caller said.

"What the fuck time is it?" McClusky asked as he forced himself to be alert.

"Real late, boss. Real late," the caller said explaining why he called.

McClusky got up from his bed taking the mobile phone into his family room. He plunked down in an overstuffed chair, took a couple of deep breaths and pursed his lips, thinking. "Willis is at the hospital by now, right?"

"Yeah."

"He may find nothing. We've been careful. We've kept no records. Even if Styles developed a list of our names, doesn't prove anything, a bunch of guys playing poker at my house, common knowledge. Everybody needs to keep calm.

We're OK. Pass the word. Sit tight. We can ride this out fucking FBI or no FBI."

"I can still head him off," the caller insisted.

"Jesus Christ man. Smarten up. Doing something now would lend credence to any allegations. Styles died in an accident. Nobody can prove otherwise. We sit tight. I'm counting on you, Randy!"

Cunningham sighed but understood. He missed his opportunity to act. He had to wait, something he hated.

"OK! Boss," he said and broke the connection.

Wild Bill McClusky slumped back in his chair and shook his head. He'd sounded more confident than he felt. He could run, pull out right now. But where would he go, to fuckin Mexico? The thought revolted him. To Canada! He'd never make the border and it would prove his guilt. Like he'd told Cunningham. They had no choice but to wait. He thought about Deluca and Styles.

A fuckin boy scout and a fuckin skirt!

Chapter 109

Walter Willis called Deluca on his cell phone.

Deluca answered and Willis said simply, "Got it."

"The Palm Pilot?"

"Yeah!"

"Find anything?

"Checking as we speak."

Deluca was tired and his head hurt. He sat on the edge of his chair, hunched over, elbows on his desk. He resisted telling Willis to hurry. He waited. The only thing he could do.

"Eureka," were the next words he heard. The words he hoped for, or not. This was going to wreck the department. Bring a lot of people down. The idea of burying this flashed through his mind but he dismissed the thought. Those responsible had to pay for Styles murder, even that of Eduardo Ramos and the others.

"Can you make a copy?" he asked.

"Sure! I'll do it at home. I live only a few miles from here."

"Be careful. These guys have eyes everywhere"

"Tell me about it."

"What do you mean?" Deluca asked.

"I'll fill you in later."

"OK. Bring the copy to me ASAP. The FBI is waiting on me to move."

"No problem," Willis said and broke the connection.

Deluca realized he had been up all night and would get no sleep today. As soon as Willis returned, he'd alert the Los Angeles FBI SAC and give him a list of the WAR group.

The task force intended to descend on the PCPD tomorrow rocking the department to its core. Every scumbag who had ever been arrested would claim police brutality. They'd want money and many would get it.

Deluca laughed. This morning, they would announce an arrest in the murders of three high school kids. Later, they'd reveal the existence of a racist cabal within the department. No need to guess which message the press would be pounce upon with glee.

Chapter 110

They held the news conference on the steps of police headquarters.

The High School detective team, including Captain "Wild Bill" McClusky, flanked Chief Dalton Phillips who proudly announced they had apprehended the murderer of schoolgirls Alex Lyon and Kitty Richmond and Alex's brother Brent Lyon. He gave a brief overview of the facts but made no mention of officer Mike Walker, Eduardo Ramos or Cara Styles and no one asked about them. The reporters concentrated on the sensational revelation that a respected school administrator had engaged in sex with a teenager, had killed her in a lustful rage and murdered two other youngsters to shift the blame to someone else. The Chief and McClusky both beamed for the cameras while the detective team stood behind them their faces emotionless.

The Chief's elation was short lived. Deluca followed him to his office after the press conference and delivered the bad news about the WAR group, the murder of Cara Styles and the impending FBI task force roundup of the culprits within the next twenty-four hours. He left the Chief sitting behind his desk, too stunned to respond.

Deluca returned to his own office to take a quick power nap and decide his next move. He remembered the minister's words at Alex Lyon's memorial service, his assertion death here on earth was not the final word, that people of faith believed more was to come, that death did not end one's spiritual existence.

Deluca wasn't convinced of eternal salvation. But he knew for certain the murder of Cara Styles, would not be the final word here on earth.

He would speak for her!

Chapter 111

Wild Bill McClusky slammed the phone down. The caller had informed him that a special federal task force planned to sweep through the department tomorrow and round up all known members of WAR.

How fast things turned to shit. He had been ecstatic at the morning news conference making sure he got credit for Moser's arrest. Now, his face ashen, his legs unsteady, he leaned against a wall for support. He brought his right hand to his eyes and closed them for a moment to think. But reason failed him. He saw no way out of this mess.

He could kiss his pension goodbye. His pension, hell! He might go to prison for a long time, face the death penalty if they proved he'd ordered the murder of the FBI undercover agent. Cunningham would throw him under the bus to save himself.

Fuck waiting. He'd run. He grabbed an overnight bag from a hall closet and carried it back to his bedroom, one he had not shared with his wife for many years. He stuffed some underwear in the bag along with a few polo shirts and a pair of Chino's. He dressed in similar attire, snatched his travel toiletry kit from the bathroom, put it in the bag and zipped it. He took his wallet and car keys from a dresser drawer but left his weapon. No use giving the feds an excuse to take him out.

McClusky took two steps toward his wife's room, changed his mind, turned, walked to the front door and peered out through a small window. Close to midnight only a yellowish glow from a few streetlights pierced the darkness; a large tree on the sidewalk cast a shadow on his front yard blocking the glare of the streetlight. The shadow shimmered as strong winds buffeted the tree. The eerie scene further unnerved McClusky.

His car was in the driveway, had been since he'd converted the garage to a meeting room. He exited the house, stepped off the paved walkway, cut across the grass and slipped his key into the door lock. He feared unlocking the car electronically would be too noisy. He looked around, his shoulders hunched, eyes narrowed, spooked by the shadows and the night sounds.

A gloved hand covered his mouth as he turned the door handle. His eyes widened as he caught a glimpse of steel from a knife drawn across his neck. He crumpled to the ground making no sound. Blood spurted from the gash in his neck, his lifeless body lying where it fell.

A black clad figure stood over the fallen lawman for a few seconds before bending to wipe the blade of his knife on his victim's shirt. He felt no compassion for the man lying at his feet and would have none for the next man he would visit tonight.

Chapter 112

Randy Cunningham, the PCPD officer, and member of WAR, was at home but not alone. He scored big time with one of the cop groupies who trolled O'Hara's bar. A few years older than Cunningham she had a good body, a great rack. He plied her with several drinks to get her in the mood and he had been rewarded for his patience.

She laid spread eagled and naked on the carpet in the living room of his rented condo. Cunningham perched on his knees above her, ready for an encore of their earlier sexual gymnastics when the ringing doorbell startled both of them.

"Who the hell can that be at this hour?" he said, annoyed and not a little pissed-off.

The woman shrugged her shoulders and giggled.

Cunningham pulled himself away, snatched his briefs from the floor and lurched toward the door banging his knee on the couch. The scotch he consumed dimmed his senses.

He peered through the peephole in the door but saw no one. He reached for his service revolver on a nearby table, turned the deadbolt and pushed the door open a crack. He still couldn't see anyone so he stepped outside, grabbing a decorative railing for support.

"If this is a prank, I'm gonna kick someone's ass," he shouted; sure the neighborhood kids were playing ding-dong-ditch. "You better haul ass out of here," he bellowed slurring his words.

A rustle in the plants lining the side of his street level condo caught his ear. The plants lay in shadows cast by moonlight.

"This is your last chance," he yelled as he moved off the concrete step and staggered toward the noise.

In his drunken stupor, he didn't hear the stealth figure behind him. He took one more step before a hand clamped over his mouth and a sharp knife raked his throat. He tumbled face first into the shrubs where he thought the mystery doorbell ringer hid. His gun fell from his grasp.

The figure in black stood over the fallen white supremacist, bent down and wiped the blade of his knife on the man's shorts. He then slipped it back into the military sheath on his belt.

"Randy honey, what's going on?" A female voice called from inside the condo.

She got no response.

Chapter 113

The Federal Task moved the next morning.

Using the list provided by Deluca, agents rounded up all known members of the PCPD Chapter of the White Aryan Resistance throughout the city and neighboring communities. Three officers were taken into custody while on duty, their shocked buddies watching in silence. Agents themselves were stunned at the discovery of the bodies of Wild Bill McClusky and Officer Randy Cunningham when they swooped down on their residences to arrest them.

For the second day in a row, the chief held a news conference. This time, Chief Phillips, his face blank, eyes downturned, stood by as Special Agent Todd Harris, commander of the Los Angeles Federal Task Force, announced the arrest of fifteen officers of the PCPD on charges of conspiracy and violations of the federal Civil Rights Act. When Harris completed his brief comments, Chief Phillips stepped forward and, in a monotone, read a prepared statement. He refused to take questions, turned and entered the headquarters building through the front double doors. Two large uniformed officers moved in after the Chief passed blocking the entrance.

Phillips went to his office, closed the door and wept.

Chapter 114

Big Tony Segal choked back tears. He had expected to be arrested earlier in the day by the task force. He wasn't and suspected why. He stood in the open doorway of Deluca's office and rapped on the doorframe.

Deluca waved him in. Segal closed the door behind him and sat in a straight-backed chair in front of Deluca's desk.

"How come?" Segal asked, his voice cracking.

"How come, what?

"How come I didn't go down with the others?"

"You kill anybody?

"Nope."

"Rough anybody up?"

"Nope. I was stupid is all," Segal said, his mouth upturned in a weak attempt at a smile.

"Stupid isn't a crime, last I checked," Deluca said. "But you better get your head on straight."

Segal nodded and placed both hands in his lap, dejected, relieved until reality hit. "Some of the guys arrested will make deals, rat out anyone they can to save themselves," he said. "The Feds are going to come for me."

Deluca shook his head in agreement. "Better prepare yourself then. Get out in front of things. Go to them first. Might save your badge."

Segal slipped further down in his chair, holding back tears.

After several minutes of awkward silence, Deluca changed the subject. "We still have one piece of the puzzle missing in the Lyon case. Do you remember what Moser said when we arrested him?"

"Nah," said Segal, shaking off his funk, happy to be moving on to something else. "Some psycho-babble about us not knowing everything and looking closer to home."

"That's right. We identified everyone in Alex's diary except the person she referred to as "D."

Segal shrugged. "Do we care? He didn't kill anybody."

"Hell yes we care," Deluca said. "D's got to be the other man on the tape screwing a teenager. We can't ignore that.

And it can really only be one person."

Chapter 115

They missed it even though Drs. Westin and Palmer spelled it out. Sexual addiction was often the result of abuse at an early age, a friend, a relative, a neighbor. But Deluca dismissed the addiction theory believing Alex's behavior mirrored that of her peers.

Yet, they should have dug deeper. He suspected the guy from the first but all the psychobabble about today's "enlightened" attitudes toward teen sex sidetracked him.

He pulled up to the house with the manicured lawn and the white Ford Taurus in the driveway. He got out of his car and strode up the walkway to the front door, stabbing the bell several times with his right index finger.

Mr. Lyon opened the door, the same fragile figure that once enlisted sympathy from Deluca. Now, the rage and hatred within the detective threatened to overwhelm him. Only years of suppressing such feelings prevented him from punching the man.

Lyon stood with his arms folded, surprised. He didn't speak or invite Deluca in.

"I'd like to talk with you for a few minutes about the case, Mr. Lyon," Deluca said.

Lyon stepped aside as Deluca entered the foyer and walked into the family room. He didn't sit down. He stood and turned toward Lyon who followed him into the room.

"What about the case?" Lyon asked. "The murderer is in custody, right?"

Deluca fixed Lyon with a penetrating glare locking eyes and forcing him to turn away.

"We know, Mr. Lyon," he said, letting the statement hang in the air, which now felt stifling to both men. Beads of sweat formed on Lyon's brow and his upper lip. He slumped down in a stuffed chair; held his feet together, put his folded hands into his lap. He made no effort to wipe the perspiration from his face.

"What do you mean?" he asked.

"I mean," said Deluca, "you sexually abused your daughter. You used her, took away her innocence. She struck back by being promiscuous, so out of control you forced her to see Dr. Palmer."

"Ridiculous," Lyon shouted, launching himself from the chair. "I want you out of this house now."

His outraged parent act didn't sway Deluca.

"Sit down, Mr. Lyon," Deluca said. His tone and glare convinced the man to comply.

Deluca, who remained standing during this verbal exchange, sat on the couch opposite Lyon and held up a videocassette.

"Alex caught you on tape?" Deluca said, spitting out the words.

Lyon rubbed his hands together, turned his head from side to side.

"Alex filmed several encounters in her room with a camera concealed in her closet. You're in one."

Deluca leaned into Lyon, his body coiled to strike. "How long had you been sexually abusing your daughter?" he asked, and added, "Don't lie to me you son of a bitch or I might take you apart right now."

Lyon flinched at the venomous diatribe, kept his eyes averted. "Your wrong detective, I never abused my daughter."

Deluca fought to restrain himself. "How can you deny it, you're on tape, in her diary."

"Not me, detective. I swear."

"The person Alex identified by the letter D in her diary is the only one she detested," Deluca stressed. "The only one she succumbed to because 'he made it worth my while' she wrote. Who else but you? D for dad."

Lyon dipped his head, swiped his sleeve across his forehead. "I don't know what Alex wrote, but D does not stand for dad."

"Who then?" Deluca pressed, not convinced but now unsure.

Lyon squirmed in his chair, stared off into space considering his answer.

"Mr. Lyon, if you're harboring a child molester, you will go to jail. I promise you," Deluca threatened.

"This will push my wife over the edge. She's very fragile now."

"I can appreciate your concern but we can't let this individual prey on other children,"

Lyon exhaled, resigned. "I'm ashamed to say I think the D stands for David, my wife's brother, Alex's uncle."

The response deflated Deluca though he still believed the dad guilty. "Why do you think that?" he asked.

"David and his wife baby-sat for us for years because we feared exposing our children to strangers," Lyon said, emitting a strained laugh.

"Some time ago," he continued, "Alex began acting out, walking around the house half naked, teasing her brother, sitting on my lap, letting her hand graze my groin."

He stopped briefly to wipe the sweat from his forehead, then resumed. "Her sexual acting-out always escalated after David and Judith baby-sat or after they spent time with us for family get-togethers. My wife caught her brother in Alex's room at bedtime on one occasion rubbing her back. Alex was naked lying on the bed. David had an erection and was, uh, touching himself."

Lyon paused, put both hands behind his head, closed his eyes. Deluca watched sensing the man's pain.

"My wife confronted her brother, they almost came to blows; we banned him and his wife from our house permanently. When Alex's behavior continued and we caught her having sex with Brent, we made the appointment with Dr. Palmer.

"David was the man you saw me arguing with at the school memorial for Alex. The son-of-a-bitch wanted to attend the funeral and come to our house afterward. If my wife hadn't restrained me, I would have killed him."

Deluca now understood. He'd jumped to a conclusion and put the father of two murdered teens through unnecessary anguish. "I'll need the full name and address of David," he said in a tone far less confrontational than his opening salvos. "He won't terrorize any other kids."

Lyon nodded. "If an older man is on the video in your possession, I suspect you will discover it's him. The bastard apparently didn't stay away from Alex as we demanded. He went far beyond touching, ruined my daughter," Lyon said, tears running down his face.

Deluca let himself out of the house leaving Lyon alone with his pain.

Epilogue

Three weeks later

The headlines blared: COPS AS WHITE SUPREMACISTS.

Editorials called for the Chief to resign. MALDEF and the ACLU pushed for a civilian oversight committee to serve as a department "watchdog." Everyone had an opinion of what went wrong and how to avoid it in the future. The murders of Alex and Brent Lyon, Kitty Richmond and Jeffrey Palmer became old news. Conspiracy trumped murder, even the multiple murder of youngsters.

Tucked on the inside pages of the LA Times, a brief report on the slayings of Captain William McClusky and Officer Randy Cunningham, identified them as members of the White Aryan Resistance in the Pacific City Police Department. Speculation was that associates of the supremacists killed the men to silence them about the group's activities or to keep them from identifying more conspirators. Some thought it might be Mexican gangsters, payback for the killing of Eduardo Ramos.

The article went on to say that although the murders occurred within the jurisdiction of the PCPD, the Federal Task Force responsible for uncovering infiltration of law enforcement agencies nationwide would investigate their deaths.

James Deluca, recently appointed Captain of the Investigation Division of the PCPD, sat behind the desk in his new office assessing his new digs. The office, twice the size of his old one, contained a large, glass topped desk, a couch, two armchairs and a conference table capable of seating eight. The floor to ceiling windows gave a panoramic view of downtown Pacific City and the ocean beyond.

The walls of the office were bare, as the transition between the present and former occupant had not yet been completed. Three cardboard boxes containing Deluca's personal items were stacked against one wall. The desktop was barren except for a white telephone on the left side, an in/out box on the right and a manila envelope in front of Deluca

The office might remain as stark for quite some time. Deluca accepted the promotion to help Chief Phillips restore normality to the department. But his stay could be brief. Style's secret had undermined their personal relationship; his could deal a knockout blow to the department.

Deluca fiddled with the envelope on his desk, tapping his fingers as he thought about its contents, the federal task force report. Twelve patrol officers, and two detectives had been arrested on conspiracy charges ranging from murder to civil rights violations. Three faced manslaughter in the deaths of four men, including escaped rapist Eduardo Ramos. Five resigned who had not been charged, including Big Tony Segal. No suspects had been identified in the slayings of McClusky and Cunningham.

Deluca remained seated, his attention riveted toward the window. His thoughts drifted back to Cara Styles. He realized the depth of his feelings for her only after her murder. His wife died needlessly in an accident, Styles doing her job.

His reverie was interrupted by the presence of someone standing in the open doorway to his office. Detective Walter Willis smiled. Deluca returned his smile and waved him in.

Willis plunked down on the couch. Deluca got up from behind his desk and sat in one of the armchairs opposite him. He did not take the envelope with him.

"You doing OK?" Deluca inquired.

"Yeah, I think so, Stephanie and I are in counseling with Jared. We're working on things."

Neither man spoke for several minutes until Willis broke the silence, "Ugly mess, huh." He crossed his legs, right ankle resting on his left knee, left hand holding the leg in place.

"Devastating," Deluca said. "The Chief may be another casualty. Doesn't matter he had no clue to what was going on. Happened on his watch. Other heads may roll."

Willis remained silent sensing his boss wanted to talk.

"Damn shame," Deluca continued. "It will take years for the department to overcome this. Everything we do from now on will be under the microscope. Everyone's going to hunker down afraid to make a wrong move or a move someone will interpret is wrong. Some good officers will bail out; others won't come here."

"We did solve all the murders," Willis offered trying to put a positive spin on an otherwise bleak scenario. "Well, not McClusky and Cunningham. But they're not our problem."

"Phelan botched his suicide attempt and will spend time in jail," Deluca continued, ignoring Willis' comments. "Moser won't prey on any more kids; neither will Alex's uncle. Ramos is no loss although how he was taken down adds to the black marks against the department." He didn't mention McClusky and Cunningham.

When he didn't, Willis jumped in. "Strange about Wild Bill and Randy though. Who killed them?"

Deluca didn't respond. His eyes fixed on something outside the windows.

To break the silence, Willis offered his own theory. "Probably some gang-bangers. Pay back for Ramos and the others."

"Probably," Deluca said.

The End

CPSIA information can be obtained at www.ICGtesting.com
Printed in the USA
BVOW06s1428100116

432399BV00007B/49/P